Dear Reader,

Do you ever wish that you [...] wonder at the approach of t[...] that you used to feel as a child? We certain[...]. In *One Starry Christmas*, three women who've endured more than their share of life's trials feel some of that joy and wonder when they receive a second chance at love during the holidays.

From *USA TODAY* bestselling author Carolyn Davidson comes "Stormwalker's Woman." An emotionally and physically scarred young widow must learn to listen to what her heart is telling her—and not what people say—when she falls in love with a half-breed in this poignant romance.

In "Home for Christmas," popular author Carol Finch brings us a moving tale about the power of forgiveness and family ties. Estranged from his daughter, who is too proud to admit that he was right about the man she loved, a conniving rancher masterminds a brilliant plan to bring her home— and into the arms of the man who is *right* for her.

And to complete the collection, we have a charming romance from Lynna Banning set in the early twentieth century. In "Hark the Harried Angels," a man who was imprisoned for a crime he didn't commit falls in love with his beautiful neighbor. Sensing the woman's sadness, he sets out to woo her by giving her a Christmas gift from the heart!

We hope you enjoy this wonderful collection celebrating Christmas in the Old West as much as we did! And in November look for our Regency Christmas collection, *The Christmas Visit,* with three scintillating romances from Margaret Moore, Terri Brisbin and Gail Ranstrom.

From our family to yours, have a very happy holiday season!

Sincerely,
The Editors
Harlequin Historicals

Acclaim for the authors of
ONE STARRY CHRISTMAS

One Starry Christmas

CAROLYN DAVIDSON
CAROL FINCH
LYNNA BANNING

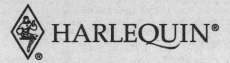

HARLEQUIN®

TORONTO • NEW YORK • LONDON
AMSTERDAM • PARIS • SYDNEY • HAMBURG
STOCKHOLM • ATHENS • TOKYO • MILAN • MADRID
PRAGUE • WARSAW • BUDAPEST • AUCKLAND

ISBN 0-373-29323-2

ONE STARRY CHRISTMAS

Copyright © 2004 by Harlequin Books S.A.

The publisher acknowledges the copyright holders
of the individual works as follows:

STORMWALKER'S WOMAN
Copyright © 2004 by Carolyn Davidson

HOME FOR CHRISTMAS
Copyright © 2004 by Connie Feddersen

HARK THE HARRIED ANGELS
Copyright © 2004 by The Woolston Family Trust

This edition published by arrangement with Harlequin Books S.A.

® and TM are trademarks of the publisher. Trademarks indicated with
® are registered in the United States Patent and Trademark Office, the
Canadian Trade Marks Office and in other countries.

www.eHarlequin.com

Printed in U.S.A.

CONTENTS

STORMWALKER'S WOMAN   9
Carolyn Davidson

HOME FOR CHRISTMAS   133
Carol Finch

HARK THE HARRIED ANGELS   227
Lynna Banning

Available from Harlequin Historicals and
CAROLYN DAVIDSON

Gerrity's Bride #298
Loving Katherine #325
The Forever Man #385
Runaway #416
The Wedding Promise #431
The Tender Stranger #456
The Midwife #475
The Bachelor Tax #496
Tanner Stakes His Claim #513
One Christmas Wish #531
"Wish Upon a Star"
Maggie's Beau #543
The Seduction of Shay Devereaux #556
A Convenient Wife #585
A Marriage by Chance #600
The Texan #615
Tempting a Texan #647
Texas Gold #663
†*Colorado Courtship* #691
The Marriage Agreement #699
One Starry Christmas #723
"Stormwalker's Woman"

*Edgewood, Texas
†Colorado Confidential

Please address questions and book requests to:
Harlequin Reader Service
U.S.: 3010 Walden Ave., P.O. Box 1325, Buffalo, NY 14269
Canadian: P.O. Box 609, Fort Erie, Ont. L2A 5X3

STORMWALKER'S WOMAN

Carolyn Davidson

To those men who have been blessed
with the gift of seeing and looking beyond a woman's
physical imperfections, I dedicate this book. Although
they are few and far between, such men are keepers.
I am fortunate to be married to such a guy and thank
heaven each day for my good sense in accepting his
proposal. So to the man who sees my faults and accepts
them—warts and all. I offer my everlasting love
and devotion. To Mr. Ed, who loves me.

Chapter One

⟨⟨⟨∘∘∘⟩⟩⟩

Comstock, Wyoming
November 1889

She was a vision to behold—though certainly not a woman he would ever dare to dream of. Golden waves cascaded to her waist and her profile was classic, reminding him of a Greek goddess whose picture he'd once seen in a book. For a moment she turned her back to him, bending to lift something from the back of the farm wagon she'd driven into his yard, and his eyes were drawn to the slender form, almost hidden beneath the heavy coat she wore. As she reached within the wagon bed, her skirt lifted, revealing slim ankles and his gaze snagged, then rested there.

It was enough to make him pinch himself, enough to cause his heart to beat at a faster pace. Any man who'd been without female companionship for as long as he had was entitled to dream once in a while. The only problem was that he was standing on his back porch and his eyes were wide open.

She was no dream, but a flesh-and-blood female. A woman he, with his dark skin and native heritage, could not afford to admire, even from afar. He was a breed apart, neither Indian nor white, scorned by both races. The woman who tempted him from just fifty feet away was not for him. Even if she was in his own backyard.

And then she turned from the wagon, a burden lovingly cradled in her arms, and faced him. The shock of his first glimpse of her face, the side he'd not seen until this moment, might have shown in a tightening of his mouth, a frown of disbelief or even an unbelieving gasp.

But Jesse Stormwalker had learned long since to hide his feelings, to cover his reactions with a mask of indifference and a veiled look of disinterest. The woman glanced up at him, hesitating as she took one step, then a faltering second step in his direction. A look of fear touched her features, perhaps triggered by his dark features and unsmiling countenance, but was erased as quickly as it had appeared.

"I know I'm trespassing, sir, but I found this litter of puppies by the side of the road, back about a mile or so. This was the first place I came to, and I…" Her voice trailed off, her eyes lowering to the bundle she held against her breasts.

"Let me see." His voice was gruff, unused to speaking words aloud, and she looked up at him quickly. "My dog has been missing since yesterday," he said. "I couldn't find hide nor hair of her. She was ready to drop a litter, and I've been worried." And then he made his way to where the woman waited, careful not to move too quickly or come to a halt too close to where she stood, as if poised for a fast retreat.

"Did you see the mother?" he asked, his hand resting

on the side of the wagon as he bent to look inside the bed. No soft brown eyes met his gaze. No wagging tail greeted him, and he looked questioningly at the woman. "She was a shepherd mix."

"Brown and gray, with white markings?" As if she knew she carried a message of gloom with her, she spoke the words softly, and at his brusque nod, she nodded and murmured another phrase.

"She was dead, curled up around them." Her eyes were blue, shimmering with moisture, and once more she looked away from him to peer into the piece of quilt in her arms.

"I thought perhaps they might live if they can be fed some way. I couldn't just leave them there for the critters to find."

He reached for the tiny mites and took them from her, his big hands brushing against her bare fingers as the slight weight was transferred into his keeping. The skin he touched was warm and smooth, and he caught her scent, that of woman and fresh air—an enticing aroma.

The pups were wiggling, a good sign, he decided. Probably not all of them could be salvaged, but even one would be a victory over the death that had claimed his female shepherd.

With tender care, he unwrapped them, counting pink noses, noting the round little bodies. Four of them, two of a size, one larger and a runt whose head lifted as if he scented a new human. *I don't smell as good as she did.* The words were unspoken, but a half smile touched his lips as they passed through his mind.

He looked up at the woman. "Thank you. I'll see what I can do." Reluctant to leave her standing there, but aware of the impropriety of spending more time than was necessary in her company, he turned toward the house.

"Can I help?"

His eyes closed at her words, and he halted before the two steps that led to his porch. Not for the world could he refuse the soft plea he heard. She'd found them. The least he could do was allow her to have a hand in their first feeding.

His instincts prodded him to deny her, but something in the tone of her voice melted his resistance. "Sure. Come along. I'll take care of your horse in a minute."

"He'll be all right. He won't go anywhere," the woman said, breathless now as she scurried behind him and hastened to open the screened door that led into his kitchen. "I won't be here long. And it isn't too cold out."

"We're due for snow," Jesse said bluntly. "You don't want to be out in the weather."

"I'll be fine. I don't have much farther to go anyway." She stood in the kitchen doorway, hesitating as he placed the pups on the seat of his rocking chair. His mother's chair actually, the last of her possessions.

"I'm Jesse Stormwalker," he said, feeling obliged to at least be civil.

She looked a bit uncomfortable, as if she recognized that courtesy required a reply but seemed to think otherwise. Instead, she merely asked, "What can I do?"

"There's a jar of milk on the shelf in the pantry. I just brought in the pail from the barn and set some aside for drinking. Should still be warm." It was the longest speech he'd indulged in for weeks, he realized. Except for his words of encouragement when he milked his black-and-white Holstein, or worked with the horses he trained, and the muffled curses he spoke when he was pecked by his bad-natured hens, he had little opportunity to use his voice.

She removed her coat and tossed it on a chair, then

crossed the kitchen and disappeared inside the long, narrow room where his foodstuffs were stored. "There's a medicine bottle in there," he said, raising his voice a bit. "Bring it out with you. Bottom shelf."

She was at the table in moments, setting the milk down and peering through the medicine bottle. "It's empty. Shall I just rinse it out?"

He nodded, busy with adding a chunk of wood to the fire in his cookstove. If those pups were going to survive, they'd need to be kept behind the stove where the heat lingered. The lid clanged into place and he took a moment to wash his hands at the sink, reaching for a towel as he turned back to where she waited.

"If this doesn't work, we can use a reed to suck up the milk and then drip it into their mouths," he told her.

Her glance encompassed his kitchen. "A reed?" She met his gaze squarely, lifting her chin as if defying him to turn away from her ruined cheek. The scarred flesh drew his gaze and he made no attempt to ignore it, measuring the length that ran from beneath her eye to the curve of her jaw, the skin rough and reddened.

"There are some in that flat container," he told her, pointing to a carrier he used to gather a supply from the marsh. "I make baskets from them. They fetch a pretty penny in town at the general store."

"You do?" Surprise touched her words and she bent to pick up two short bits from the basket. "Did you make this one?"

His reply was an affirmative nod. "Fill that bottle and stretch a bit of towel over the opening. Fasten it with string. There's some on the cabinet over there."

She did as he asked, her fingers working quickly at the small task, her movements graceful. One pup was lifted from the warmth he'd shared with his littermates and she held the tiny creature on his back, in her hand.

"Wrap him in this," Jesse told her, reaching for another towel and offering it for her use. He watched as she deftly tucked the pup inside the towel, so that only his head was exposed. And then she touched the tiny mouth with the bit of fabric, watching as a drop of milk found its way into the seeking mouth. The pup wiggled even more and his mouth opened wider as the woman allowed a slow dribble of milk to touch his lips.

He swallowed, and she laughed, a soft, triumphant sound that sent a message Jesse could not mistake. "Look," she said softly. "He's taking to it, right off."

"I'll try one with the reed," Jesse told her. In moments he'd settled on a nearby chair with a second pup, and with his index finger stoppering the reed once it was filled with milk, he allowed it to drip into the creature's mouth. It was the runt, he realized, the one he'd thought might be the most difficult to save.

The kitchen was silent as they worked, the woman intent on her task, Jesse's gaze intent on the woman. Her identity was a mystery, he decided. He'd not heard of a lone female in the area, although he was not the recipient of neighborhood gossip as a rule. But it seemed likely that he'd have seen her in town, on one of the rare occasions he'd made his way there.

"You live nearby?" he asked. Her head came up quickly and her eyes widened in surprise, as though she'd almost forgotten his presence, so focused was she on the pup she held on her lap.

"Yes, just down the road."

"Down the road?" He frowned in her direction. "Toward town?"

She shook her head. "No, west of here."

"There's nothing west of here. At least not for three miles or so. Thompson's place is the next farm. And it's deserted now."

"I know." Her head bent again, her words abrupt, as if she dismissed his interest.

"Then who are you? You don't look like a squatter." His voice sounded darker, just a bit menacing, he thought. A ploy he'd used more than once to get the answers he wanted.

"Molly Thompson." Her mouth, which he'd thought was soft and plush, drew into a hard line as if she would say no more. Apparently, her name was all he was entitled to.

"Mrs. Thompson?" he asked. "I didn't know there was a wife on the premises."

"Not a wife," she said flatly. "I'm a widow."

"I understood that Thompson was gored by his bull a few months ago."

Blue eyes met his and she nodded briefly. "You heard right."

His attention focused once more on the pup he held, and even to his own ears, his curiosity bordered on rudeness. "I didn't know he had a wife."

"Well, he did," she answered. Then bending her head lower over the pup she held, she continued grudgingly. "Now I run the place on my own."

He glanced again at the line of her profile. "I'm surprised you haven't had men from hereabouts calling on you already. That's a prime piece of property."

He thought her brief laugh was a mockery of his assumption. "You can't be serious. I'm not a very good candidate for courtship."

"You think not?" he asked, ashamed of himself for a moment as he recognized the pressure he was exerting on her. Curiosity was no excuse for rudeness. And why should it matter to him?

Her words were harsh, denying the suggestion he'd put forth. "I have a mirror, sir, and though I try not to look into it more often than necessary, I'm well aware of how I look."

"So am I. I looked you over real well before you ever walked into my house." If he was trying to scare her off, he was doing a good job of it, he thought, watching as she shifted in her chair.

She looked exceedingly uncomfortable, bending her head to concentrate on the pup she held. "I think this one's full. For now, at least. You do know they'll be wanting to be fed every couple of hours, don't you?" she asked.

"I know. This won't be the first time I've played wet nurse to animals."

Molly rose and replaced the pup, lifting another in its place. "I wondered if…maybe, you'd like me to take two of them home with me. I could take care of them for a few weeks, until they can drink out of a bowl anyway. Not that I'd expect to keep them or anything," she added hastily.

"You must be a glutton for punishment. You've got a farm to run, and if you're one of those folks who celebrate Christmas, you've got a busy time ahead of you, don't you think?"

She laughed, a sound without humor. "I have no plans for Christmas. I'd enjoy minding the pups."

"I'd think you might need to hire help," he said, watching as her face took on a wary look and her eyes glittered with an emotion he could not name.

She shook her head quickly. "No, I get along just fine by myself. And yes, I live there alone. Unless you want to count the horses and chickens and my cow."

"I won't need to send milk along with you then. Can I repay you somehow if this works out, if the pups survive?"

"No." The single word was abrupt. "I don't need anything from anyone." And then her voice softened, as if she realized that she'd spoken harshly. "I'm used to being on my own. I don't mind."

"You don't miss your husband?" The words seemed unnecessarily cruel, he thought, but somehow he doubted she was a grieving widow.

A shiver caused her shoulders to hunch as she bent over the tiny creature in her hands, and she shook it off, then bent to replace the pup with his littermates. Lifting another to her lap, she wrapped it carefully, then held up the bottle to the light. It was almost empty, and Jesse handed her one of the reeds.

"Use this. It seems to be working well with this one."

She did as he told her, and he watched her, aware that she would not answer his query without him applying pressure. "Were you alone there when he was gored?" he asked, pressing the issue.

She nodded, and lifted her face to meet his gaze. "I watched him bleed to death."

Her eyes closed for a moment, and then her mouth twitched as if she suppressed words that ached to be spoken. "I was a surprise to some of the townsfolk. Very few of them knew he was married, and when I drove the wagon into town with him in the back, I got a lot of attention."

"How long were you married?" Jesse asked. What he

yearned to ask was not any of his business, but the sight of beauty marred by a crimson scar made his heart ache within his breast. Had Thompson taken her as his bride while her beauty was unflawed? Or had he married her because she thought she was not worthy of anyone better?

Her laugh was bitter. "Too long. Almost three years."

That answered Jesse's speculation. The scarring was fresh, probably not much more than a year old. He'd seen wounds before, had watched the healing process many times in his life and recognized that Molly Thompson wore scars that were new enough for her to feel the lingering pain of whatever had brought about her injury.

"I'll stop by in a week or so and see if you've managed to keep either of these little fellows alive," he said quietly.

"I didn't realize you were planning on coming to call," she said haltingly, looking up at him. "I'm not sure that's a good idea."

"Because I'm a half breed?" His words were soft, but held a note of anger.

Her eyes widened and she shook her head. "No. That has nothing to do with it."

She had reasons of her own, he supposed, and that was her right. Shrugging, he leaned to deposit the little bundle he held back into the warmth of the quilt, then lifted the last of the quartet into his hands. He held the tiny thing up and examined it closely. "I think this one looks the most like his mother, don't you?"

She shook her head. "I didn't take a good look at her. I was more interested in bringing the pups into someplace warm."

"How did you know they belonged here?" he asked.

"It seemed like a good place to start." And then she pursed her lips. "To tell the truth, I've seen your dog down at the road when I came by a couple of times. I knew they were yours."

"And you wondered what the half breed looked like?" he asked.

"No," she said quickly, denying his theory. "I thought you'd want to have the pups. I know what a half breed looks like."

He reached to fill the reed from his milk jar again and began the slow process of feeding his charge. "I don't mind going along with your suggestion. If you want to take a couple of these animals home with you, you're welcome to the task. Since you have milk available, you'll be all set."

"I'll stop in when I go to town and let you know how they are."

"Just understand that if folks know you're neighboring with me, you'll be a subject of gossip," he warned her.

"I already am," she said simply. "Children run screaming when they see me, and most of the adults look the other way. They all wonder what happened to me, and they're afraid to ask."

"Do you go to town often?" He hadn't asked so many questions of another human being in his life. But there was an indefinable something about this golden creature that made him want to keep her here. She exuded an air of sorrow he could understand, a sense of loneliness that matched his own.

And then he listened, admiring the soft, even tones of her voice as she answered his question. "I trade at the general store. I swap out eggs and butter for lard and tea and whatever else I need." Her head down as she spoke, she turned her face so that the unscarred side was visible to him.

"Why did he keep you isolated?" He knew what the word meant, having lived alone by choice, seeking no other companionship but his own. But this woman must have needs that could only be fulfilled by others of her gender. Women were made differently than men.

And wasn't that the truth. He allowed his eyes to feast on her for a moment, noting the soft curves that even her ill-fitting dress could not hide. Her feet were small, her hands slender and graceful as she performed the task she'd taken on. And above all, she was a vision of beauty. At least from this angle, and he ached as he thought of the times she'd turned her head so as not to present the scarred side of her face to him.

For surely, the rejection of the townspeople brought distress to her heart. A woman like Molly must have been accustomed to admiring glances in earlier days. His own were appreciative of her, not because of golden hair or blue eyes, or even the single unblemished profile she owned, but because of the courage she displayed by allowing others to view the damage she lived with every day of her life.

His mother's people would have considered her scars to be a badge of honor. And perhaps they were right, Jesse thought. He looked beyond her then, out the kitchen window. The snow had begun to fall, the flakes large and fluffy against the pane of glass. He felt a reluctance to speak of it, knowing it would bring about her departure, but his good sense prevailed.

"You need to be getting on your way," he said. "I'd hate to think of you caught in the storm."

She looked up to where snowflakes stuck to the glass pane, her eyes widening at the sight. "I didn't think the weather would change until at least tomorrow," she said, and her mouth twisted in a parody of a smile. "You warned me, didn't you?"

"Do you want me to follow you home?" he asked. "I can saddle a horse and ride along."

Molly lifted the pup she held, smiling as a dribble of milk ran from his mouth, then placed him carefully with the others. "No, I can make it just fine." She stood and reached for her coat, sliding her arms into the sleeves and buttoning it quickly. "Which two shall I take?"

"Take your choice," he said. "Since you found them, I'll give you first pick."

She glanced up at him, as if surprised by his amiability. "They're your dogs."

"Once you picked them up, you became responsible for them," he said softly.

"Isn't that an old Chinese proverb or something?"

"My people take responsibility seriously. The Chinese aren't the only race who follow that precept."

"In that case I'll take the runt and one of the others. You can keep the other two."

"Don't feel bad if the runt doesn't make it," he warned her.

Her jaw clenched and her eyes narrowed. "He'll make it."

Jesse picked up the two he'd been assigned and carried them to the pantry where he found another towel to wrap them in. A basket from the bottom shelf held them nicely, and he felt satisfaction as they curled together for warmth and snuggled in sleep.

When he turned around, Molly was holding the bit of

quilt in her hands. "I think I'll carry them inside my coat," she said. "It'll be warmer there."

Jesse hesitated, suddenly unwilling to let her walk from his house. "Are you sure you can make it home? You can stay here if you'd feel better about it."

Molly shook her head. "And risk you being the subject of gossip if someone found out? I don't think that would be wise." She looked out the window again. "Anyway, I have supplies in my wagon. I need to go home."

Jesse put the basket he held behind the stove and reached for his own coat, donning it quickly. "Let me give you a hand up onto the wagon seat," he offered. She could no doubt clamber up herself. Had probably been doing just that for a long time. But the temptation of lifting her, of catching her scent once more, of perhaps brushing his face against her golden hair combined to seduce his senses.

"I can make it," she protested, casting him a look of doubt. Probably not willing to have a man's hands on her, he thought.

"Maybe so, but I'll feel better about those pups if I give you a hand." He followed her out the door, closing it behind himself, then walked to where her patient horse waited, his hindquarters to the wind.

Reaching the wagon, she leaned over into the back and snatched up a hat in her free hand. "My hair will be soaked," she murmured.

"Let me." He took it from her, and a guarded look appeared on her face, her eyes watching him closely. He ignored it, concentrating on settling the broad-brimmed hat atop her head. "That's better."

His hands gripped her waist, his muscles barely straining as he lifted her from the ground and settled her on the seat. "Can you get those little mites inside your coat?" he asked, then watched as she unbuttoned it and placed the small bundle of pups in her lap, snuggling them against her belly. The coat was buttoned again and she looked down at him soberly.

"I'll take good care of them."

"I know you will." He backed away from the wagon. "You'd better move out," he said gruffly. "That snow is settling in for the night."

Her nod was abrupt and she lifted the reins, turning the wagon in a half circle, her feet braced, her hands clutching the leather straps securely. The woman was no stranger to driving a wagon, Jesse decided. No stranger to hard work, either, he'd warrant. He'd give a lot to know what secrets she held securely within her, and realized he stood very little chance of being given entry to her thoughts.

He was an outcast, respected only by those few who bought their horses from him or gave him the job of training their own stock. Then, his native heritage came into play and he was afforded the looks of admiration of those who took advantage of his abilities and the inborn knowledge that allowed him to turn intractable animals into well-behaved mounts.

And that was all right with him. He didn't need the approval of the white community. He was a law unto himself.

Watching the wagon disappear into the falling snow, he folded his arms across his chest. He'd spoken more in the past hour or so than he had in the past month. The woman had touched a well of compassion within him, a fount he'd not known even existed. She was alone, her face damaged irreparably, and her spirit was almost broken by the pain of her isolation.

He thought of the words he'd spoken to her and her reply.

I have no plans for Christmas. She'd sounded as though her Christmases had long since brought her little joy. The white man's holiday was a happy occasion, he'd noticed over the years. But for Molly Thompson, there seemed to be a dearth of pleasure. Alone and lonely.

Jesse walked back into the house. He wasn't responsible for the woman. If he showed her any more attention than he'd already done today, and it was noticed by anyone in the community, she'd be shunned by the townspeople. A white woman could not associate with a half breed.

His mouth was grim as he hung his coat on the peg and brushed the snow from his hair. Her scent lingered in the kitchen and he ignored it, determined to put her from his mind. What had she worn that the faint aroma should linger behind? Some sort of soap, he supposed.

One of the pups whined and nosed against the side of the basket that held him, catching Jesse's attention, and he reached down, lifting him to his face. He smelled of newborn puppy, yet carried on his soft hair the faint scent of the woman. Molly had fed this one. Dark eyes closed as Jesse inhaled deeply.

For the first time in longer than he could remember, he felt a pang of loneliness, an emptiness within him that had not been a part of him for years.

He would set aside the pleasure he'd found in her company, relegate it to the back of his mind, where such indulgences belonged. Jesse Stormwalker was alone by choice. He walked alone. He needed no one.

He had nothing to offer a woman.

Chapter Two

There was a certain amount of comfort to be gained from holding the pup in her lap, Molly decided. Though the heat of its body was negligible, the satisfaction attained by feeding the tiny mite warmed her soul. Huddled on her chair beside the kitchen table, her shawl around her shoulders, her feet tucked almost beneath the cookstove, Molly concentrated on the open mouth of the runt she held. She'd heard its soft mewling a few minutes since and left her warm bed, as if the small sounds were a clarion call to action.

She smiled at the thought and wondered idly if Jesse Stormwalker was even now tending his own half of the litter in the middle of the night. She closed her eyes, recalling the dark hair that hung to his collar, the black eyes that offered her little insight into his thoughts and the hands that had been so gentle. Hands that could have crushed the life so easily from the four infant dogs, but instead lent themselves to the task of nurturing the wiggling bodies.

Jesse Stormwalker was an enigma. He'd not really

wanted her in his house, yet once she was in the door, he'd been all that was courteous. His size—the width of his shoulders almost filling the doorway—had seemed larger within the confined space of his kitchen. His profile was stern, his lips unsmiling, as if he'd found little in life to bring him joy.

She'd felt a moment of panic in that final moment as he'd lifted her onto the wagon seat. Held in midair for those short seconds, she'd looked down at him. And then he'd settled her neatly and stepped away, as though he sensed her reaction. Her waist had felt the warmth of his hands.

How foolish, she thought as she considered the layers of fabric that had separated those wide palms and long fingers from her flesh.

The pup she held became limp in her hand, a bit of milk running from the corner of his mouth, and she recognized his surrender to sleep. It was what young animals did best, she recalled, thinking of the host of pets she'd been indulged with during her childhood. Rising, she placed him back in the box where his littermate was blindly nosing the quilt. At her touch, the larger of the two sniffed at her fingers and lifted his head, as if he could sense her presence.

Molly picked him up and held him next to her face, inhaling the sweet scent of his coat, then wrapped him warmly and resumed her seat. His feeding went well, she thought, his tongue working to suckle the reed, and she allowed tiny amounts of the milk to flow into his eager mouth. Even the knowledge that she was facing broken sleep for the next week or so, until the pups could last for more than a few hours between feedings, was of little concern. She felt no impatience at the task she'd assumed.

Having companionship was a novel situation. There was something about a dog or cat that allowed one to speak as if they understood, and their response to humans was much more satisfactory than that of the chickens, who demanded their daily rations and then seemed reluctant to give up the eggs she gathered as her just due. The cow was always eager to be milked, but was ornery some days, lashing Molly with her tail or kicking the bucket on occasion, spilling the milk across the barn floor.

Were it not for the butter she churned and the milk she drank and used for cooking, she'd be tempted to sell the miserable creature. She'd never come across a temperamental cow before, and she wondered if the animal had been mistreated by George. Heaven knew he'd had the art of cruelty down pat.

Feeding the puppies offered her a time apart from her work, and she looked forward to the small span of pleasure as she regarded the plump body she held. It would not do to become too attached to them. Dogs were too valuable to be given away indiscriminately, and she had no extra cash to offer, should Jesse decide to sell one to her. She poured warm water on a cloth and wiped the puppies clean, placing a fresh bit of quilt in their box before placing them in it.

And then she went to bed, only to find that sleep eluded her. The strong features of Stormwalker filled her mind. He'd been gentle with the pups and with her. She hadn't known that a man could use his hands to bring comfort. Closing her eyes, she courted slumber, listing in her mind the tasks that lay ahead come morning. By the time she'd counted beyond the daily chores and settled on chopping wood as the big project for the afternoon, she dozed off. Only to be awaken again to the sound of hungry pups.

Morning brought about a change of plans, for the depth of the fallen snow presented an immediate chore. She shoveled a narrow path to the barn, did her chores, then swept her porch and found herself eating breakfast with the sun almost overhead, filtering watery rays through the clouds. The stack of wood next to the porch would keep her for today, but no longer, she decided.

Bread must be baked and butter churned. Feeding puppies was a time-consuming task, but she relished each moment she spent with them, taking satisfaction in their progress.

In midafternoon she heard a horse outside the house, and she rose from the churning to peer between the curtains into the yard. A man was tying reins to the hitching post near the watering trough and she watched as he turned toward the house, already aware of her visitor's identity.

"*Jesse Stormwalker.*" She spoke the words aloud, hastening to the door to open it as he stepped onto the porch and stomped his heavy boots. His eyes met hers, and she saw again the watchfulness that seemed to be his usual expression. No smile greeted her, only a mere nod as if he acknowledged her presence before him.

"Come in," she said, standing back as he stepped across her threshold. He ducked a bit, as if he'd banged his head on more than one lintel in his life. "Is something wrong?" she asked anxiously. Surely, the man was not prone to go calling without a good reason.

He shook his head, and she recognized that he was not given to speaking aloud his thoughts. Perhaps he'd thought her a magpie, giving him chapter and verse of her life, and her cheeks flushed as she remembered all she'd divulged in his hearing.

"Nothing's wrong," he said, standing before her, his hat hiding the expression in his eyes, his coat unbuttoned. One hand lifted to his hat and he swept it from his head, holding it against one thigh. "I wanted to be sure you'd gotten home all right, and that the pups weren't giving you too much trouble."

"No. Not at all," she said quickly. "I'm enjoying them. It's nice to have someone to talk to," she told him, and then flushed anew as she considered the foolishness of that statement. Her hand motioned in the direction of the box containing her charges. "Take a look if you like."

"That's all right. I won't bother you for long." And then he shifted, a bit uncomfortably, she thought. "I noticed you don't have much wood chopped. Can I give you a hand?"

"I couldn't ask you to do that." Her glance at the wood box was quick and he followed her gaze to where only a few short, squat bits of logs lay, mute evidence that it was past time for a trip to the woodpile.

"You didn't ask me. I offered."

His gaze moved slowly around her kitchen, his sharp eyes taking note of each small bit of comfort she'd put in place over the past few months. George had not allowed foolishness in his house, and that word encompassed any number of things, among them curtains and an oilcloth on the table. She'd resurrected her mother's bits and pieces of china, those George hadn't broken before she hid the remainder, and now they sat on a shelf above the dresser where her everyday dishes and cutlery were stored.

A rug to keep her feet from the cold floor sat before her chair and his gaze rested there. "Did you make it?" he asked and glanced up as she nodded.

"I used George's shirts." She smiled as she spoke, aware that her satisfaction was visible. She'd taken great pleasure in cutting his clothing into long strips and braiding them, hoping that wherever he was, he was fuming over her wastefulness at the expense of his wardrobe. Now she thought of him every time she stepped on the oval surface; and though it might be a childish reaction, she reaped a certain amount of enjoyment from those moments.

"George's shirts? Your husband?" he asked, though certainly he knew, she decided. "What did you do with the rest of his things?"

"Cut them up for rags." Her voice was low, but triumphant, and she made no attempt to hide the satisfaction she felt. She looked directly into Jesse's eyes. "I was married to a brute. I didn't mourn him for one single, solitary minute, Mr. Stormwalker."

"Jesse," he said quietly. "My name is Jesse." With a deliberate movement, he sat his hat back in place and then buttoned his coat. "Where is your ax?"

"In the barn," she told him, and then added quickly. "Please don't feel obligated. I'm used to chopping wood and toting it inside."

"I can see that. But, for today, you don't have to."

He was gone from the house, making his way to the barn and then returning in mere seconds to where a pile of logs lay beside the chicken coop. She watched as he sat one up on end, then lifted the ax over his head and brought it down with a solid whack. It broke in half, and he bent to place each half upright. Another two swings of the ax and a quick movement to stack them aside were coordinated as if he'd done this often, she decided. And then he repeated the ritual.

Within ten minutes he'd opened his coat, and in a half hour he'd stacked her porch more than a quarter full of short chunks of wood, the exact size she needed to replenish her cookstove. She'd started a pot of coffee when he began the chore, and as he came back in the house, his arms carrying a day's supply and more to deposit in her wood box, she was ready for him.

"I made you some coffee," she offered. "You must be cold."

"No. Chopping wood keeps the blood churning," he told her, removing his coat and placing it on the back of a chair. "But I'll take the coffee anyway."

"Have you eaten dinner?" She paused, a wrapped loaf of fresh bread in her hand, and noted for the first time a bit of lightening in his stoic features.

"I thought when I came in I smelled fresh bread." Not a request, but a gentle nudge in her direction, and she responded quickly.

"Sit down and I'll cut you some. I've just finished churning the butter while you chopped wood. I'd be pleased if you'd have a bite to eat."

He hesitated a moment. "Coffee is one thing. Eating a meal at your table another. If anyone even knew I was in your kitchen you'd be shunned, Mrs. Thompson." It seemed she was to call him Jesse while she bore the title of a married woman.

"I don't receive callers, sir. And it's highly unlikely that anyone would be out and about in this miserable weather."

He almost smiled then. She caught just a glimpse of

white teeth as his mouth twisted, and then his abrupt nod served as acceptance of her offer. He sat in the chair before the table. "I can't stay long. The pups at my house will be hungry within the hour."

"Did you have trouble getting here?" she asked, pouring coffee with a hand she forced to remain steady.

He shook his head. "No, my horse is used to plowing through the snow. The trees next to the road provided a good windbreak and it wasn't too hard to travel." He leaned back in his chair and watched her, and she fumbled with the towel she'd wrapped around her bread, opening the towel so that she could slice the loaf on her wooden board.

Her hands trembled as she drew the knife through the fresh bread, then placed two thick slices on a plate, reaching across the table to set it before him. "I'll get you a knife to spread your butter," she said, turning toward the dresser and sliding open a drawer. Placing the utensil on his plate, she reached for the butter dish and pushed it nearer to where he sat. "Would you like jam?"

He glanced up, as if surprised. "No, this is fine. I'm not used to being waited on."

The words were almost identical to those she'd tossed his way when he'd offered to chop wood for her and she smiled at the memory. "We're an independent pair, aren't we?" Sitting across from him, she lifted her own cup of coffee and viewed him over the rim. "I'd like you to take a loaf of bread home with you," she offered.

"You don't owe me anything," he said shortly, spreading butter on his bread with a light touch. "I appreciate your help with the dogs. Leave it at that."

Her reply was slow in coming and she spoke hesitantly, feeling keenly the rebuff in his words. "All right. I didn't mean to infringe."

He chewed his bite of bread slowly, then lifted his cup and swallowed a mouthful of the steaming brew. "You didn't. But I don't intend to offer you any insult by my presence here. I shouldn't have come by, and I'll just assume you have things under control from now on."

She shrank in her chair, aching from his gruff manner. She'd enjoyed this visit, more than she should have. The presence of this tall, dark man in her kitchen was not a threat, as she'd thought it might be upon his arrival. She didn't understand him, but had felt for just a few minutes that they might be friends. All to no avail. He offered on one hand a gesture of friendship, and then, just as quickly, withdrew in a forbidding manner.

Within minutes he'd finished his coffee, polished off both slices of bread and was rising from the table to don his heavy coat. His hat was placed low on his forehead and he drew gloves from his coat pockets, plunging his fingers into their depths as he walked to the door. There was a hesitancy in his steps she thought, and then he turned his head and his dark eyes touched her, a slow appraisal she could not mistake.

"If you need anything," he said, and then paused as if he searched for words.

"I'll be fine," she told him quickly. If the man was determined to remain distant with her, so be it. And yet, his piercing look of assessment, with just the slightest hesitation as his gaze had touched upon her bodice, made her shiver with a strange delight.

He was immune to her. Certainly he was. And yet.... She shook herself at the foolish thought that swirled through her head. As if she were attractive in any way to any man. Although George had admired her looks before the wedding. Only to change from the warm, thoughtful man she'd married into a possessive, jealous brute. All with no good reason.

Hadn't George told her bluntly, more than once after she'd been burned, that if he put a bag over her head he might be able to take what he needed from her? He hadn't put a bag over her head as he'd threatened, but his rough, rapid possession of her on occasion was enough to deliver the message. She was repulsive. Her scarring causing him to be even more cruel than he'd been in the first years of their marriage.

Ugly. He'd called her ugly, as if it were her name. And she'd cringed from the lash of his cruel tongue.

But no more. No man would ever treat her so again.

She watched from the window as Jesse Stormwalker lifted himself easily into the saddle, then glanced her way. Dark features unsmiling, he nevertheless tipped his hat brim just a bit, a silent salute in her direction before he turned his mount back to the road heading east.

Foolish. He'd been foolish to allow his need full sway. The woman was not available to him. Jesse hunched in the saddle, pulling his collar high to shield his neck from the wind. It came from the west and carried a hint of more snow on its wings.

His thoughts had run rampant from the first glimpse of her slender form in the doorway of her kitchen. Without the heavy coat she'd worn yesterday, she was slim, rounded but narrow in the waist. She filled the bodice of her dress nicely, he decided, though he'd had no right to allow his gaze to linger there several times as she worked around the kitchen.

And then she'd served him, as might a woman who cared for him, and he'd lapped it up, he thought angrily, like the pups sought the life-giving milk he'd offered them just hours ago. He'd allowed her to slice bread, eaten it and then denied his need for a loaf to carry with him. Damnable pride. She'd meant well, and he'd turned her offer aside, as if it were of little account.

Her look of hurt remained in his mind, and he cursed himself silently. The woman had been damaged enough by a man's careless use, and now he'd added to her pain. Yet, he could not allow himself to infringe on her again. The threat was very real. If word should ever get out that he'd visited her farm, she would suffer. He'd never caused harm to a woman in his life, except for the pain of his defection from his mother's people, with the resultant sorrow he'd brought upon her.

He would not begin with Molly Thompson. There was no future for him there. His days would be spent doing as he'd done for the past years, ever since he'd settled on his father's land and begun to build upon the foundation laid by the man who had been his sire. Whether the white men liked it or not, he owned the property and all it encompassed, and he'd made a nice livelihood there, gaining the respect of the men he dealt with. They bought the horses he bred and trained, paying a high dollar. His reputation was well-known among the ranchers and farmers of central Wyoming.

His yearning for a companion, a woman of his own, would go unfulfilled. There was no woman for Jesse Stormwalker.

It was past time for a trip to town, Molly thought, looking down at the pups in their box. Over two weeks old now, they'd begun exploring the confines of their space, and their eyes were beginning to open. It wouldn't be long before she'd have to find a larger container for them.

Perhaps today would be a good time to set off with her eggs and butter. Once the pups were well fed, she could leave them for four or five hours without danger of them starving. They might be crying pitifully when she returned, but their plump little bodies showed the evidence of being well fed, and her twinge of guilt at leaving them was quickly subdued.

The sun was shining, the snow having melted a bit, and she suspected that the road would be easily traveled into town. Settling herself in the chair, she lifted the pups to her lap, one at a time, and fed them until they could hold no more.

"Little piggies," she murmured, holding one against her cheek. She felt little sensation on the side where her burn still flared a bright crimson, and she turned her head to brush the pup's coat against the unflawed cheek. Perhaps, in time, the scars would fade.

And perhaps the flowers would bloom in December, she thought ruefully. She'd looked in the mirror this morning, something she seldom did, choosing instead to braid her hair by touch. Her fingers had touched the red, rough patch of skin and she'd thought perhaps it was some lighter, and then closed her eyes against the sight.

Going to town was an ordeal, but she'd make it a quick trip, she resolved.

The wagon was pulled from place and the horse hitched in moments; and then she drove it to the back door and carried out her eggs and butter, wrapping them in a quilt and placing them in the wagon bed, right behind the raised seat. A final peek in the box assured her that the tiny mites there would sleep for several hours, and she left the house.

The wagon bogged down twice and she slid from the seat and tugged at the horse's harness, lending her strength to help him pull the load. The snow on the road became more packed as she traveled closer to town, due to the traffic from nearby farms. The hitching rail before the general store was almost empty and she tied her horse there, then readied herself for the shopping expedition.

Pulling her scarf around her face a bit, she reached into the buggy and gathered up her goods, pushing the door open into the general store, careful not to drop her eggs. She'd stored them in a burlap bag, and now she placed it carefully on the counter. The butter was in rounds, wrapped in waxed paper, a luxury to be sure, but necessary if she were to sell it to Mr. Sheldon.

He approached her now, careful, as usual, not to look directly at her face, as if he would spare her embarrassment. "Hello, there," he said jovially. "I see you've been busy. I can use the butter. There's a number of ladies in town who have been asking. The weather kept some of the farmers at home, and I haven't had a delivery of butter this week." He hefted the burlap bag. "How many dozen?" he asked.

"Four. I'll put them in the crock if you like."

"Fine," he answered, and then reached out his hand. "Do you have a list?"

She paused in her counting as she transferred the eggs to a wide, shallow crock on the counter. "Eighteen," she said aloud to insure she would remember the figure. Then she dug into her pocket for a small scrap of paper. Mr. Sheldon preferred to work from a list, and she was willing to oblige. "Just a few things," she told him, and then resumed counting the eggs as she placed them with care, checking her count as was her usual practice.

Mr. Sheldon carried items to the counter and placed them before her. "You have any extra potatoes out at your place?" he asked. "I can always use a few for the folks that didn't plant a big enough garden here in town."

She shook her head. Her root cellar held an ample supply for herself, but she couldn't afford to spare any, in case she was stranded in bad weather and had to exist on potato soup. It had happened more than once over the years, when supplies ran low and the snow piled around the house.

Molly looked over the supplies he had assembled. Bacon, baking powder and soda, three pounds of sugar and a sack of coffee. "That looks like all of it," she said, reaching for her burlap bag. She tucked the wrapped bacon inside, adding the rest with care before she tied the top with a piece of string. "Are we square?" she asked, hoping that her account still remained in the black.

"Yup," Mr. Sheldon said, using a pencil stub to write tiny figures in his black account book. "You're still some to the good," he told her. His grin was flashed quickly. "Just keep that butter coming, ma'am."

He was almost her only contact in town, the ladies only casting measuring glances her way on the occasions when there were other customers in the store. Only one woman had smiled and approached her, a lady obviously pregnant, clearly reluctant to impose her presence.

"I'm Amanda Green," she'd said quietly. "I understand you're new in town."

Molly had shaken her head. "No, I was married to George Thompson, who owned a place about three miles west of here. I've lived there for several years."

Amanda's gaze had focused determinedly on Molly's

undamaged cheek, then met her gaze fully. "I didn't know Mr. Thompson was married," she'd said with surprise.

"He wasn't very proud of me," Molly had answered. "He liked me to stay on the farm and keep things running when he had to make a trip to town."

"How strange," Amanda had replied and then made small talk for a few moments before she turned away.

Since that day, Molly had been largely ignored in this place. Today, there were no other customers in the store, and Molly took her leave without incident. Mr. Sheldon waved a hand in farewell and she stepped out the door, pulling it shut behind her. Across the street, a man was mounted atop a large, dark horse. He watched her, almost idly as she placed her bag in the wagon and climbed onto the seat. Lifting the reins, she cast him a quick glance and then slapped the leathers on her gelding's back.

What on earth was Jesse Stormwalker doing, sitting over there and watching her?

He'd seen her go past the house, heading for town almost an hour ago and had saddled his horse quickly, following well behind her, in her wake. Why, he didn't know. Perhaps to make certain she ran into no trouble. Maybe, he admitted to himself, because he needed to lay eyes on her again.

Either way, Jesse had gone to the livery stable, picked up some nails and several spare horseshoes. His draft team was about due for shoeing, a task he had assumed years ago, unwilling to pay someone else to do a job he was more than capable of. Then he'd stopped at the newspaper office, picking up the weekly sheet, folding it and placing it inside his coat.

He'd spoken to the editor for a few minutes, gauging the length of time Molly would be in the store, and then had gone to his horse and settled the load of horseshoes behind the saddle. She came out of the store as he mounted, and he was hard put not to nod a greeting.

It would not do, he decided as he watched her drive from town. At the general store, he purchased three items he didn't need and left with no attempt at conversation. It was easier that way, he'd discovered. Mr. Sheldon would have spoken to him, the store being empty of customers, but above all Jesse despised duplicity.

The half breed was beneath the notice of most of the townspeople. And he liked it that way. It made his life more manageable. He depended on no one, needed only his own resourcefulness in order to survive.

The wagon tracks were not discernible, melding with others that had gone before: but he knew exactly where she was heading, and on horseback he could be close behind her within ten minutes. His gait was slow but steady as he made his way past the edge of town, and he looked neither right nor left, only straight ahead, his eyes peeled for the sight of a slow-moving wagon with a woman driving.

His mouth twisted as he recognized his folly. She'd made it to town just fine without his following behind. She'd no doubt make it home just the same way, and he was acting foolish by lagging behind her like a schoolboy following the prettiest girl in class.

But he owed her. Nothing tangible perhaps, but at least his protection. It was cold, the road was narrow in places, and she'd been stuck more than once on the way in. He'd noted the places where her wagon had slewed to the side of the road and she'd had to help the horse find its way.

Now, he rode on, catching sight of her a quarter mile ahead as he rounded a bend in the road, and he kept his horse at a steady pace, not wanting to frighten her by his approach. And yet, there was within him the need to speak with her.

When she passed by his farmhouse, he followed, and within a hundred yards she had looked over her shoulder to where he rode, and he nudged his mount into a trot. He'd just ask about the pups, he decided. See if she needed any help.

His heart pumped heavily in his chest as he neared the wagon, and she turned her head to watch him as he rode beside her. "Mr. Stormwalker," she said by way of greeting, tipping her head politely. A woven shawl covered her golden hair today, rather than the hat she'd worn before.

"Mrs. Thompson," he replied, lifting his hat just a bit. "I wanted to make sure you were all right," he told her, and knew a twinge of guilt at his own blatant lie.

I needed to see you up close. Needed to hear your voice. Words he could not speak aloud.

Ever.

Chapter Three

Jesse followed her home, put her horse and wagon into the shed, and then, with a tip of his hat, mounted his horse and rode away. Molly stood in the middle of her kitchen floor, her arms still laden with her supplies. She'd watched him from the porch as he tended to the chore he'd chosen to perform, waiting till he closed the shed door behind himself. His dark gaze had focused on her, the intensity of that long look piercing her to the core.

George had looked at her sometimes, back in the earliest days of their marriage, with just such intensity, and she'd learned that it was the prelude to his possession of her body. She'd come to hate those times and over the years had learned to withdraw from him into a world he could not enter. Even as he'd used her with harsh and sometimes cruel treatment, she'd escaped him, his death giving her freedom from his tyranny.

Jesse's eyes had delivered a similar message and yet, she felt no twinge of fear, no shiver of apprehension. He would not impose himself on her—of that she had no doubt. There was no comparison between the two men.

Unless Jesse hid himself from her, somehow concealed the man he was behind a smokescreen.

The sound of the pups squirming and whimpering in their box drew her attention. Experience had taught her that they'd soon be crying pitifully for a feeding, and she smiled at the thought. They were round and healthy-looking and she knew a moment of intense satisfaction that she'd been able to be of help to Jesse, even in this small way.

Her supplies were quickly put away and her coat hung on a peg. The morning's milking was in the pantry and she dipped a small pan into it, taking part of the cream that had risen to the top, along with the skim beneath. She swirled it in the pan and placed it on the stove, allowing it to heat a bit as she gathered up one of her charges.

The milk was nicely warmed, and with the pan transferred to the table beside her chair she began her task. "Are you starving?" she whispered, enjoying her role as wet nurse. Brown eyes blinked as the tiny creature choked a bit, his greedy mouth suckling hard, and Molly laughed aloud.

Her laughter filtered through the door, the notes of pleasure unhampered by the heavy wooden barrier; and on the porch Jesse halted, his hand lifted to knock, captured by the sound of her amusement. He'd made it several hundred feet down the road and then halted, looking back at the house where a golden-haired woman lured him to return as surely as if she'd flashed a teasing smile in his direction or offered an invitation into her presence.

She'd done neither, had only nodded her thanks and watched him ride away. And now he was about to make a fool of himself, simply because he ached to inhale her scent, hear her soft voice, perhaps allow his gaze to feast on the pure line of her profile.

His knuckles rapped sharply, and her laughter broke off with a suddenness that told him he'd frightened her. "Mrs. Thompson? This is Jesse. May I come in?"

"The door is open," she said, raising her voice to be heard.

Her blue eyes were fastened to his face as he entered the kitchen and closed the door behind himself. He leaned back against it, and spoke in a harsh voice. "Don't you know better than to be here alone with your door unlatched?"

A rare anger filtered through his words as his shuttered gaze took in the sight before him. She was holding one of his dogs, had been feeding it, and upon hearing his words she'd looked up at him. As he watched, the reed slipped from the pup's mouth and milk puddled on the dark coat.

He took a long step toward her, noting her instinctive movement as she shrank back against the chair. "You're spilling, Mrs. Thompson," he said softly, halting his forward motion as he recognized her automatic reaction to his gesture. She bit her lip, jerking her hand in quick response to his words, and the reed settled once more in the pup's open mouth.

"I came back to talk to you," he said quietly. "I didn't mean to startle you."

Her face turned to him and she shook her head, a minute movement. "I was surprised that you came back, that's all."

But it wasn't *all*, and he knew it, sensed the fear that had gripped her for that brief moment. He moved to the other side of the table. "May I sit down?"

She looked flustered, he thought, but her response was immediate. "Certainly. I didn't mean to be rude."

He slid his gloves off and tucked them in his pockets,

then unbuttoned his coat and placed his hat on the edge of the table. "I won't be here long. I just wanted to make an offer."

"An offer?" She sounded truly baffled by his words.

"I wondered if you'd like to keep one of the pups. I haven't any use for four dogs at my place, and I'd think you could use one here. It would be company for you and might come in handy as a watchdog."

A flush rose to color her cheeks. "I really can't afford to buy one of them," she said. "Dogs are in demand, and I know it. You could sell every one of them ten times over when they're old enough to eat on their own."

He nodded, enjoying the sight of her rosy face, the quick glances she delivered in his direction as she spoke. "I know that. But I don't know if I could have handled all four of them. Chances are they wouldn't have all made it this far if you hadn't pitched in to help." He watched her hands as she worked at her task, her fingers long and slender, graceful in their movements.

"I wouldn't want to take advantage of you that way," she said firmly.

"Maybe we can work something out." His mind scanned the options, and he leaned over the table. "I'm not much good at mending," he said, and noted the quick twist of her lips as if she repressed a smile. "Another thing," he said. "I was wishing I'd taken you up on your offer of a loaf of bread when I was here before. Maybe you'd agree to baking a little extra if I came by to pick it up a couple of times a week."

He thought her eyes glistened as she looked up at him. "Why are you being so nice to me? You told me before that we shouldn't neighbor, Mr. Stormwalker, and now you're making plans to be a regular visitor."

"Jesse," he said firmly.

"No." She shook her head. "If you can't use my name, then it would be rude of me to call you by your Christian name."

"I'm not sure there's anything *Christian* about me," he murmured.

"Your name is from the bible," she said insistently. "Jesse was the father of David, in the Old Testament."

"The giant killer?" At her look of surprise he offered another bit of his background. "My father sent me to the white man's school for a couple of years. They had Sunday school classes every time the circuit rider made his rounds."

"You told me you don't celebrate Christmas, though." She rose as she spoke and exchanged the sleeping pup she held for the waiting supplicant, whose mewling cries were becoming louder. Holding the plump little fellow against her cheek, she murmured soft words Jesse could not hear, and a powerful urge rose within him, a need to place his own cheek next to hers, that he might feel the silken texture of her skin against his face.

"I don't," he answered, forcing his mind back to the conversation. "My father had no use for foolishness, and any sort of celebration came under that heading."

"He must have been related to George," she murmured, almost beneath her breath. And then she looked at him apologetically. "That was rude. There isn't another man in this world—" She broke off, biting her lip again, and he frowned at the sight of her white teeth pressing against her flesh.

"Don't," he said softly. "You have a habit of doing that…biting your lip that way." He reflected for a moment on the words she'd spoken. "I think you'd be surprised to know how many men are very like George."

"You're not," she said, the words impetuous, as if she spoke them without forethought. Her eyes widened and she looked away from him, concentrating on the animal in her lap. "You're a kind man," she whispered. A soft laugh found its way past her lips. "You'll think I'm forward. And maybe I am."

Jesse was silent, his thoughts racing in circles. He had no business here. And yet, he felt a yearning to be with her, a woman he barely knew, a widow with enough problems without him adding to them. And so he plowed ahead, in a manner totally unlike his usual behavior.

"Can we come to an agreement...Molly?" It took courage to speak her name, to take that small step toward intimacy. "Will you bake for me and mend a few things once in a while?" He rose and walked to stand behind her, watching over her shoulder, smiling at the greedy dog she held.

"I'd feel guilty, taking your dog." Her hands were deft as she wiped the pup's mouth and lifted him before her face. She touched his mouth with her own, barely grazing him with a soft kiss and Jesse felt a knot of desire deep within him.

He'd been without a woman in his life, indeed he hadn't gone in search of female companionship in over three years. There were women who were drawn to the danger implicit in flirting with a half breed, and he'd learned to recognize their availability years ago. But the allure of such encounters had become tawdry and distasteful. He'd learned to exist without a woman's touch or the pleasure of soft curves against his muscular frame.

Until now. Until he'd caught the clean, sweet scent of Molly Thompson and felt the longing for her companionship.

Molly rose from her chair, returning the pup to its bed, and then turned to face Jesse, her expression guarded. "I wouldn't cause you trouble for the world," she said. "I'm not worried about myself. I don't have any friends in town, anyway, but I don't want to make any problems for you." She searched his face as if she sought to catch a glimpse of his thoughts.

Then her mouth curved into a half smile. "I'd dearly love to have a dog. If you think that my mending your things and baking bread for you will be payment enough, I can't afford to refuse your offer."

Jesse reached out a hand to her. "Should we shake hands on it?" he asked. He held his breath as she looked at his dark skin, at the width of his hand and the length of his fingers, and then she murmured a response and met his gesture. Her hand was warm, the skin as soft as he'd remembered and he held it immobile in his palm. Her eyes flashed surprise in his direction, but she made no attempt to withdraw from his touch.

"I'll bring you some of my shirts the next time I come," he said, unwilling to release her from his grasp. "I'm missing some buttons, and I've split a couple of seams."

Her nod was slow, and then she dropped her gaze to where their hands were joined between them. "Jesse?" She spoke but a single word, whispering his name in a wondering tone, and he relaxed his hold, releasing her from his grip. Her hand plunged into her apron pocket, and he wondered if it held the heat of his palm, if she'd felt the same awareness of him in that simple brush of flesh as had jolted through his body with a flare of heated desire.

Probably not. Yet, he was already torn between leaving the woman alone or staying here, searching for some inane reason to remain in her presence. She was watching him closely, her brow lifting a bit as if she sought to read his thoughts, and then she smiled, a quick flash of amusement that pleased him.

"I have an extra loaf of bread, Jesse. I'd be pleased if you'd take it with you." She looked up at him and smiled, and for the first time he recognized that she was smaller than he'd thought. So sturdy was her independent nature, so strong the depths of decency and courage she displayed, he'd gifted her in his mind with a stature like that of a taller, more stalwart female.

Her head was tilted upward, and for the first time in their short acquaintance she made no attempt to turn her head or hide the ruined side of her face from him. It touched him that she should offer her trust so unknowingly. His emotions had not been so exposed in years: his need for a woman's presence had been placed aside for longer than he wanted to recall.

And now this small, delicate woman stood before him and offered her friendship with a simple gesture. A gesture he could not refuse. "I'd be pleased to accept the bread," he said, his voice sounding a bit husky.

"Would you also be pleased to stay for a bowl of soup?" she asked, her expression sober, as if she expected him to refuse her offer.

"Against my better judgment," he answered.

"And why is that?" She'd turned half away from him, heading for the stove, and then halted at his words.

"I've been here too long already. I meant it when I told you that I fear you might be an object of scorn if it's known that you've been friendly with me."

"And I told you that I'm already a woman without

friends, that the attention I receive from people in town is revulsion at worst—and pity at best."

"How did you…" His hesitation was obvious and then he plowed ahead, determined not to allow her to retreat from him. "What happened to your face?"

Molly lifted her hand to touch the scarred flesh, her fingertips tracing the limits of the reddened, roughened patch of skin. "I was canning one day late in summer, over a year ago, putting up raspberries for the winter." She smiled as if the memory was bittersweet. "I thought to lift the first jar up to the light coming through the window, admiring the beauty of sunlight shining through the fruit."

Her smile vanished and her hand fell from her face to fold into a fist at her side. "The glass burst and the berries splashed against me. I only felt the burns on my shoulder and—" She looked down and her hand rose again to touch the gentle curve of her breast. "By the time I'd torn my clothes off my face had begun to feel scalded. The fruit stuck to my skin." Her hand moved in a helpless motion and her eyes closed.

"Molly." He could only speak her name, and then he reached for her, his hands gentle as he touched the rounding of her shoulder, the side of her face. He ached to encircle her within the shelter of his embrace, to give what comfort he could. And then he wondered how much consolation she'd received at the hands of her husband.

"Couldn't the doctor do anything?" he asked, aware of the anguish that touched his words.

She opened her eyes and he was struck by the bitterness that dwelt within the shimmering depths. "George refused to take me to see him. He said I'd been careless and I could just tend to the burns myself." Her shrug told the story as she related the end of the tale. "So I did."

"I'd thought the scar was fresher than that," he said softly, his fingers tracing the shape of her disfigurement much as her own had done but moments past. "Has it faded much?"

She shook her head, and then laughed, an uneasy sound. "Maybe, a little. I try not to look in the mirror."

"Scars are sometimes badges of honor, my mother used to say," he told her. "Yours is a reminder of a day of great pain, a time when the one who should have tended you left you without his support." He looked into her eyes, feeling a depth of anguish he could barely tolerate.

"You're a beautiful woman, Molly. This—" His palm fitted itself to her cheek as he spoke. "This is only a small part of the woman who lives inside your skin. It doesn't make you ugly."

Her eyes were awash with tears, and then she blinked and they fell to her cheeks. "He called me Ugly, used it as a name for me."

Jesse barely blinked before his reply hung in the air between them. "He lied. And it's my opinion he lied to hurt you. You're far from ugly, Molly. I should know." His hand was touched by the dampness of her tears, and he gathered the moisture onto his fingertips, then lifted his other hand to where salty drops trickled down her unblemished cheek. "Don't let his memory bow you down with grief," he told her. "Forget his words. Put him out of your mind, and accept that your life can only be better from now on."

It was too much. Her scent rose to him, the faint aroma of soap and freshness that was uniquely her own. He bent his head to her, his lips touching hers in a fleeting caress. And then he rested his forehead against hers. "I mean you no disrespect," he murmured.

She lifted her hands and clasped his wrists, as if she would hold his warmth against her face. He spread his fingers wide on her skin, capturing her with gentle care, gazing down into blue eyes, tear-washed and filled with an expression he could not decipher. Rising on her tiptoes, she kissed him in return, her lips barely brushing his.

"Thank you, Jesse."

Reluctantly, he lowered his hands, feeling bereft as her fingers released their hold on his wrists, yearning for that brief moment that he might clasp her to himself, might hold her softness against his long, lean body and soak up the warmth of her curves and hollows.

Her laugh was self-conscious, he thought, as she turned from him and picked up a ladle from the top of the warming oven. "I invited you for a bowl of soup, but you didn't answer," she said lightly.

"I'd be honored," he said. He backed away from her and circled the table, pulling the chair from the other side and easing himself onto the seat. His discomfort would be of short duration, but he needed to conceal it beneath the edge of the table. He would not insult her by such an obvious display of desire.

She brought him a bowl of soup, her eyes not meeting his, her hands trembling a bit as she found a spoon and knife for his use. A loaf of bread was sliced, and again she pushed the butter dish closer to him, then joined him with her own steaming bowl.

"Tastes like rabbit," he said, looking down into the thick, rich mixture.

"It is," she said agreeably. "I shot it yesterday."

"I suppose I hadn't thought about your meat supply. You can't eat your chickens or there wouldn't be any eggs."

She smiled as if his words amused her. "I always have chicks in the spring, and I can up the young roosters. Then, when the pullets begin to lay on a regular basis, I have one of the hens on the table once in a while. I can eat four meals from one chicken."

"How about deer?" he asked, quietly amazed at her resourcefulness.

"George used to shoot one once in a while, but I fear I'm not cut out to handle one. Too heavy to drag home for one thing, and I don't have the patience to sit in the woods half a day and wait for one to stroll by anyway."

"I had a notion you were a quiet sort. I almost had to pull every word out of you when you stopped by the day you found the pups."

"I learned a long time ago not to speak my mind," she said flatly.

"Not around me." There was a dark edge to his words, and she looked up at him quickly. "I'd like to know what you're thinking," he told her, moderating his tone. Anger filled him, fury he'd like to pour out on the man who'd been so cruel to her. George Thompson had been a fool.

He ate his soup slowly, and when the last scrap of vegetable was gone and the broth barely a memory in the bottom of the bowl, he sent a long glance at the stove. "I don't suppose you have enough left for me to—"

"Of course I do," she said quickly, rising to take his bowl from before him. "I should have offered." Her skirt swayed as she turned to the stove, and he watched her every movement, each step she took. In a moment, she'd brought the second helping to him and placed it before him carefully.

"Thank you. I haven't had this good a meal for a long time." He bent over the succulent offering and plunged his spoon into its depths. It was hot and he lifted a bite to his mouth, then blew on it, catching her eye, noting the glimmer of amusement she made no attempt to hide.

"I'm glad you're enjoying it," she said nicely. She folded her hands before her face, elbows on the table. "Have you begun to offer your pups milk out of a bowl yet?"

He shook his head, his mouth full, and then chewed and swallowed before he spoke. "I'm thinking it's about time though. Have you?"

"I thought I might in the next day or so. They're close to three weeks old. I'd think it wouldn't be long till they could lap it up themselves."

Jesse ate steadily, aware that time had passed rapidly since his arrival, and his departure from home was more than four hours ago. "I need to be getting back," he told her, rising from his chair. "Thanks for the soup. And the company." He slid his arms into his coat sleeves and pulled his gloves from the pockets, aware of Molly's eyes on him as he buttoned buttons and lifted his hat from the table.

"Oh, I almost forgot," she said quickly, turning to the kitchen dresser. "Your bread." She picked up a wrapped loaf and eyed him for a moment. "I don't know how you'll carry it."

"Inside my coat," he answered, smiling, aware that he'd smiled more since he'd met Molly Thompson than he had in several years before that time.

She followed him to the door, stepping out onto the porch in his wake. "Let me hold the bread while you get on your horse," she suggested, and reached for the wrapped bundle, taking it from his grasp.

He lifted himself into the saddle with an easy movement, then turned his horse, riding up to the edge of the porch. She watched as he undid his coat, then handed him the bread. "Is there room?" she asked. "Don't smush it."

"I won't." He left the coat partially undone, amused at her warning. His fingers touched the brim of his hat and he turned the horse in a half circle, nudging the gelding into a trot. A hundred yards from the house he looked back, unable to leave without another glimpse of the warm haven he'd inhabited for such a short time.

She was watching him, hugging herself against the cold, and her hand lifted, for just a moment, in a brief wave. "Bye," she called after him, and he raised his right hand into the air, answering her with the gesture. Another nudge of his heels against his horse's barrel prodded the animal into a rolling lope and Jesse looked ahead down the long, lonely road to the dark, empty house where he lived.

December 1889

The general store was redolent with the aroma of pine boughs. Mrs. Sheldon obviously thought that Christmas should be celebrated in fine style, and her grumbling husband was busily tacking up bundled arrangements in several places, while she stood behind him, hands on hips, directing his work.

"Hello there, Mrs. Thompson," she said politely as Molly came through the door, stomping her boots on the rug placed there for that purpose. "Are you all ready for Christmas?"

Molly attempted a smile and shrugged. "I don't do much for Christmas," she said quietly, approaching the counter with her bundles. "I have ten dozen eggs. I wasn't sure if you'd be able to use all of them or not, but the weather was too bad for the last couple of days for me to come to town."

"We can always use your eggs," Mr. Sheldon said, looking down from his stepladder. He peered at her over the top of his spectacles. "No butter today?"

Molly shook her head. "I did some baking. But I'll be churning tomorrow. Maybe I can come back and bring it with me."

"Either that, or I'll have Tom Green stop by on his way day after tomorrow. He always comes in on Wednesday afternoon to work at the livery stable. One of his boys will be by here later on today, and I'll give him the message."

Molly felt a moment's apprehension. "Does he live out beyond my place?" The thought of a man she didn't know riding up to her door was not to her liking. But at Mr. Sheldon's assurance of Tom's dependability she nodded her acquiescence.

"Now," Mrs. Sheldon said, looking at Molly's list, "let's see what we can do for you, Mrs. Thompson." Molly eyed the jars of assorted goodies on the counter. Brightly colored ribbons of hard candy caught her eye, next to peppermint sticks, some of them straight, some curved into shepherd's crooks.

"I believe I'll have a few of these," Molly said, pointing at the striped candy, "and a bit of the ribbon candy." Not since she'd left home to marry George had she had store-bought candy. He'd thought such things were a waste—frivolous, he'd said scornfully. Now, this first Christmas since he'd been buried six feet deep in the churchyard, she felt a sense of rebellion, an escalating satisfaction, as she broke the bonds he'd set in place during the past three years.

"You gonna have a Christmas tree?" Mrs. Sheldon asked, lifting a bag of flour to the counter.

Molly considered the idea for a moment. "I don't think so. I haven't anything to decorate it with."

"Everybody oughta have a tree. It wouldn't be Christmas without one," Mrs. Sheldon announced firmly.

"Maybe next year." Molly smiled brightly, remembering the tall, fragrant pine trees her father had always set up in their front parlor. "We always had one when I was a girl," she said.

"Where'd you come from?" Mrs. Sheldon asked, her bright eyes inquisitive.

"Denver," Molly said. "That's where I got married, and then Mr. Thompson brought me up here to a piece of land his family had."

"Strange we never saw you much till just lately." Mrs. Sheldon pried gently, her curiosity obvious.

"Mr. Thompson didn't take to me going to town with him," Molly told her. And sometimes she hadn't been fit to be seen, she thought, anger filling her as she remembered the bruises she'd borne more than once.

"Well, he wasn't ever a very kind man, I always told my mister," the woman said in a low tone. "Had a real rough and abrupt way about him."

You don't know the half of it. Molly swallowed the words and gathered her purchases, picking up the list to be certain she had everything. Her eggs deposited in the crock, she held the burlap bag open and filled it with the supplies she'd gathered. Mrs. Thompson wrote in the account book and looked up, smiling. "You're still in the black," she said cheerfully. Then, as Molly turned to leave, the woman spoke up quickly. "Don't forget your candy, now."

Three women came in the store, one of them shooting a glance in Molly's direction. "Hello, there," she said
quietly. "We've met before." She was heavily pregnant,
likely ready to have the baby any time, Molly thought.
"I'm Amanda Green."

"I remember you." It wasn't hard to recall the only
woman in town who'd made an effort to be polite, Molly
thought. "Are you feeling well?"

Amanda touched her rounded belly and spoke softly.
"I'll feel better when this baby comes. My Tom said I
could come in on Wednesday, but he works at the livery
stable all day and I've got too much to do to be gallivant-
ing all over the country for a full day waiting for him to
take me back home." She motioned to the other two
ladies she was with.

"I'm here with two of the ladies from church. Tom
will give them a lift, and then take me on home a little
later on."

Molly put the names together…Tom and Amanda.
"You live out beyond me, don't you?" At the other
woman's nod, she smiled and picked up her supplies. "I
need to be on my way. You be careful now, you hear?"
Her eyes rested with more than a trace of envy on
Amanda's swollen body.

To be so loved, so confident of a man's attention and
protection was more than she could imagine. And yet,
Jesses would treat her in such a way, should she carry his
child. She knew it, knew with certainty that he would
cherish her, treat her tenderly. Knew that his arms would
hold her close and keep her safe from all harm.

Jesse held a wealth of love within himself, and she'd
seen it spill forth to include her more than once. Not that
he would name it as such, but should she ever… She

closed her eyes, envisioning herself heavily pregnant, her body swollen with the evidence of a man's love, and her heart twisted within her.

Amanda Green was more fortunate than she knew, Molly decided, and yet she could not envy her, only admire her for her kindness. And so she turned to the woman who had befriended her and waved her hand in farewell as she went out the door.

Chapter Four

The pine tree traveled behind him, tied with a rope to his saddle horn. It rode atop the crusted snow, sliding with ease, and Jesse smiled as he turned his head to view its progress. Perhaps he was assuming too much. Bringing Molly a Christmas tree and planning to help her decorate it might not be a good idea after all.

Never in his life had Jesse done so many impetuous things in such a short length of time. And all because of one small woman. Inside his coat, two small, wiggling creatures vied for space, and he spoke to them softly in his own language, one hand reassuring them. They settled down for a moment, but he knew it would be but a short time before they needed to be released.

Ahead of him, smoke rose from her chimney and he felt his heart pick up its pace as he neared the back door of her farmhouse. Even now, she might be watching him from the kitchen window where a lamp glowed softly in the wintry afternoon light. Behind him, in two sacks draped over his gelding's hindquarters, was an assortment of items he'd thought might appeal to Molly. Candles and the holders to fit them on the ends of the pine branches, red holly berries together with the distinctive leaves that surrounded them that he'd gathered in the woods and a bag of popcorn.

One of his finest memories of childhood involved Christmas celebrations at the school where he'd been sent as a young boy. He thought he could still catch the scent of popcorn as each small kernel burst into a fluffy ball. They'd strung it on white thread, sitting on the floor, barely able to contain their excitement at the thought of decorating the huge pine tree that was awaiting its adorning of shimmering ornaments.

Maybe Molly had never done such a thing before, but then, he suspected she'd done several things lately that had been new to her. Kissing a man of her own choosing had apparently been one of them, he thought, recalling her flushed face as she'd placed her lips against his for that fleeting moment. Her breath had caught in her throat and her gaze had shifted from his, as though she feared he might read her thoughts.

He looked at Molly's kitchen window, hoping for a glimpse of her through the curtains, but to no avail. Only a few feet from the porch now, he drew his reins, halting his horse, then watched as the heavy door swung open and she appeared before him.

"What have you done?" she asked, her whole attention focused on the tree he'd cut and brought to her. And then she spoke words in a manner that pleased him, her tone soft and filled with anticipation. "You've brought me a Christmas tree." Her face lit with pleasure, and he could barely resist the urge to leave his horse, the tree and the assortment of odds and ends he'd gathered up for her to stride onto the porch and gather her to himself.

Instead, he stepped down from his saddle with a casual movement and scooped his hat from his head, holding it before him. "I take it you don't mind?" One big hand supported the pups he concealed beneath his coat, and it was toward that gesture her attention flew.

"You've brought the pups with you," she exclaimed. "Here, let me take them."

He transferred them to her hands and she deposited them inside the kitchen door, then turned back to where he waited.

"Oh, my." Her eyes shone as she stepped to the edge of the porch and looked eagerly at the tree. "Where did you find it?"

"Out on the far side of your property. It belongs to you, anyway, so I decided you might as well enjoy it for a few days. It'll be prettier in your parlor than it was in the woods." Reaching to his saddle horn, he released the rope and wound it up as he stepped to where the tree lay, then bent to stand the small pine upright.

"It's not very big," he said. "I wasn't sure how much we could come up with to decorate it, so I thought a little one would be better."

"Any size will do," she told him, her gaze intent on the full branches. "You don't know how I've yearned to do this over the past years."

"Well, here's your chance, ma'am." He held the tree in the air, then thumped it on the bottom step, watching as loose snow fell from its branches. Another thump pretty well cleared it off and he climbed the steps, holding it before him. Molly backed off, hugging herself against the cold, and he nodded at the back doorway.

"You're letting all the heat out. Get on in the house. I'll bring the tree in."

"Yes, all right." Her words were rapid, her movements swift as she turned and preceded him into the kitchen. He thought she moved like a deer in the forest, gracefully, with a light step. His mouth twisted as his thoughts dwelt on what he was doing. He had no right—no right at all to be here. He'd vowed to leave her alone, to protect her reputation, and what he'd done instead was to bring possible disaster upon her head with his recent behavior. But for now, he'd lay aside all his qualms and concentrate on pleasing Molly.

"This is going to drip on the floor. It's still a little wet."

"Pooh, I don't care," she said with a wave of her hand, leading the way into the parlor. "I know how to wipe up a floor. I've been doing it on a regular basis lately," she said with a glance at the two cavorting puppies in the corner.

Standing in the middle of the room, she turned in a slow circle. "I think in front of the window. Don't you?" she asked, ending her revolution with a swish of skirts as she faced him fully.

"Whatever you like. I'll need to make a stand for it. All it'll take is a couple of pieces of wood. I bet I'll find some in the shed."

"There's a stack in the last stall," she told him. And then her face sobered a bit and she gripped her hands before her. "Jesse...I don't know how to thank you. You've been so good to me."

I can think of a way. The words popped into his head and came close to being spoken aloud. Instead, he bent to place the tree on the floor and muttered beneath his breath.

"What did you say?"

He stood erect and shot her a glance that made her

blush. "I don't do anything I don't want to. If I enjoy getting you a tree, and if you like it, that's all that matters."

She inhaled visibly, obviously confused, maybe even a bit aware of his feelings, he thought. "Well, I appreciate it, Jesse. This will make it a real Christmas, won't it?"

He shrugged, unable to voice aloud the words he wanted to speak.

"Jesse? What's wrong?" she asked, moving a step closer, her skirts brushing his trouser legs.

He reached for her, his hands gripping her shoulders firmly, bringing her against his long body. He watched her closely, fearful of bringing panic into those blue eyes as he slid his arms down to enclose her in his embrace. She was silent, shivering once, but with a sigh that touched him to his depths, she relaxed against him. Her head dropped to rest on his chest, her arms circling his waist, and he closed his eyes.

In a voice that was guttural with emotion he murmured his plea. "Let me hold you, Molly. Just for a minute. I won't hurt you, I promise." Bending his head, he buried his nose in her hair, inhaling the clean scent of her, the sweet, almost intoxicating aroma that surrounded her.

She trembled, and he drew her closer, until the firm contours of her breasts were cushioned by his muscular frame and her hips were drawn to rest where his arousal made itself known.

"Jesse?" His name was a high-pitched sound, and he gritted his teeth. Damn the man who had made her dread the evidence of desire, whose touch had bequeathed her with memories that left fear behind.

"I won't hurt you," he said, repeating his vow, and uttered a silent word of thanksgiving as she nodded abruptly, her head nudging his chest.

"I think I knew that, Jesse, the first time I saw you."

"I shouldn't be here, Molly. I vowed I wouldn't do this. I meant to leave you alone, after that first time when you came to me with the dogs. I knew...I *knew* you had the power to bring me to my knees."

"I don't want you on your knees," she said quietly. "I want you right where you are." She tilted her head back. "Look at me, Jesse Stormwalker."

He opened his eyes, meeting her gaze. "I've already looked at you more than I should. And now, I've let you know my intent, bringing the pups with me. I'm here for more than an hour or two, Molly."

"Don't regret this," she whispered. "Please, Jesse."

He felt pain slice through him, the ache of knowing he could never own her as his woman, forbidden as she was to a man like him. "No regrets, Molly. Just know that this cannot be more than what we share in these few minutes." And then, as if he negated his words, he bent his head and covered her mouth with his own, tasting the honey of her kiss, relishing the soft sigh that passed her lips as she raised her arms to circle his neck, lifting herself against him.

He reined in the surge of desire that threatened to burst the bonds of his self-control, even as he shifted, widening his stance to draw her more firmly against himself. She was soft and precious, and if he but coaxed her into acquiescence she would offer herself to him. Of that he was almost certain.

Yet, he would not take her as a man might claim a woman whose only value was that she was available. Such a woman could be easily forgotten, simple to leave behind. Molly deserved more, more than he could offer. But for this moment, he assuaged his need against her welcoming warmth and took the sweetness she offered.

"Jesse." Her voice was soft, her breath shuddering against him. He felt an overwhelming urge to protect her, to gather her up and keep her to himself, to bring her to his home and complete the act that would make her his wife. But it could not be. With hands that trembled, he reached up and removed her arms from his neck, holding them at her sides, and then stepped back from her.

She looked up at him, her eyes wounded, her mouth quivering. "I'm sorry," she said. "I shouldn't have done that."

"Done what?" he asked, his voice rasping. "Kiss me?" His laugh was harsh. "I'm the one who started this, Molly. But I had no right to put my hands on you."

"I gave you the right," she said, denying his words. Her eyes filled with tears and she blinked to keep them at bay. "No one has ever touched me the way you do. If you want me, Jesse, I'm here for you." Her face was pale, but her eyes shimmered as if tears were not far from the surface. His gaze dropped to her mouth, trembling as she spoke, and he noted the ruddy hue of her scars standing out like glowing embers in the fire. She was exquisite, this woman who tempted him. Not even the flaws fate had dealt her could detract from the innate beauty she owned.

But his intelligent mind had already scanned the future and his path was set—a road that could not include Molly as more than a friend.

"You don't know what you're saying." He released her hands from his grasp and took another step back from her. "I'm going out to make a tree stand for you. I want you to forget these last few minutes ever happened, Molly. We're neighbors and we can be friends, but that's all it will ever be between us. We'll enjoy this time together as any two friends might. I think we both deserve this little oasis of Christmas cheer."

Turning on his heel, he left her behind. In the shed he found the wood she'd spoken of and in less than five minutes had put together a stand that would hold her tree in place. He carried it back into the house, his eyes seeking her as he walked through the back door. The kitchen was empty, and he walked on into the parlor.

Molly was curled in a corner of the sofa, looking up as he entered the room, one of the puppies on her lap, curled into a ball, its nose pushed against her palm. "I was afraid you'd gone home," she said.

"I told you I'd be back." He knelt by the tree and fit the trunk into place in the framework he'd put together. Removing nails from his pocket, he hammered them through the wooden stand and into the tree. "That should do it," he said, placing it upright before the window. Shooting a glance at her, he released the tree from his grip. "Is that where you want it?"

She nodded. "It's beautiful, Jesse."

"You'll like it better when it's decorated."

"Decorated?" She looked doubtful for a moment, and then a smile lit her face. "I bought some ribbon candy and some peppermint canes. Maybe we could hang them on it. I'll tie the ribbons with bits of yarn and drape them over the branches."

"I brought some other things," he said. And in minutes he'd retrieved his bags from the horse and carried in his offerings. Molly exclaimed over the candles, admired the holly berries and leaves and then looked askance at the bag of popcorn.

"What will we do with that?" she asked.

"We'll pop it and string it on thread. Surely you have thread."

"Yes, of course I do," she said, rising from the sofa. "I just never heard of such a thing before. My mother had boxes of ornaments we used to put on our tree at home. Back when my folks were alive." She picked up the bag of popcorn and smiled up at him. "This will be more fun than that."

He smiled, pleased by her enthusiasm. "It doesn't take much to make you happy, does it?"

"I haven't been really happy for so long a time, I hardly know how it feels anymore," she told him. "But now…you've brought joy into my life, Jesse."

The pups were deposited into the box with their siblings and they snuggled on the warm towel next to the stove, first investigating the limitations of their space, then settling down to sleep.

Jesse had brought clever little candleholders, designed to clip over the branches, holding a candle upright, she found. Two dozen candles would have better suited a larger tree, she thought, and said as much. But Jesse only laughed and shook his head.

"Watch and see. We'll need every one." He poked his needle through a bit of popcorn and added it to his string. "I'd forgotten how long this takes," he said, concentrating on his task.

Molly lifted several canes and approached the tree, deciding where they would show to the best advantage. "If I'd known you were going to do this, I'd have gotten a few more of these." The ribbon candy glistened in the light of the kerosene lamp on the table and she tilted her head a bit, the better to view the beauty.

"Tomorrow is Christmas," she murmured. "I hadn't planned on celebrating it, you know. I'd thought to ignore it, in fact."

"I wouldn't think a woman like you could do that." He shot her a quick glance, and she intercepted it.

"A woman like me?" She returned to her chair and picked up a second bowl of popcorn, preparing to join in his project.

"You were raised to believe in Christmas, and all it entails, I would imagine."

"My life in the past few years has not included a tremendous amount of celebration of any kind," she told him, bending her head, allowing her hair to fall forward to conceal her face.

"He's gone, Molly." His words were simple. "He can't hurt you any longer."

"Are all your memories good? Do any of them still have the power to cause pain?"

He hesitated, and his laugh was low and held a tinge of anger, she thought. "I have good and bad recollections of the past. I've learned to live with them. Now I concentrate on the future."

"And what does your future hold, Jesse?" Would he admit to a yearning for a wife and family? For surely such things were of utmost importance to any man. And Jesse Stormwalker could pick and choose if he so desired. Even with the stigma of his heritage, there were women who would welcome his courting.

"Breeding and training horses. Expanding my operation and making enough money to buy a second stud."

"What about Jesse, the man?" she asked softly.

"What about him?" The room was silent, and then he spoke her name. "Molly?"

She looked up, sensing his withdrawal. "You don't need anyone, do you?" she asked. And then added with haste, "I'm not suggesting that I'm the woman to fill the needs in your life. Please don't think me that forward."

He smiled, a singularly sweet expression that expressed tenderness without speaking a word. "Far from it. If there were such a possibility, you'd be exactly the woman I'd choose to fill the empty places. But I can't do that to you. Not to any white woman. You'd be cast out, spit upon by the community—if not literally, then at least figuratively."

She eyed him, considering his words. "Where did you learn to express yourself so well?" she asked. "At the white man's school?"

He nodded. "I suppose so. And at the university where I attended classes for over three years."

"Three years? Why not finish when you were that far along?"

"They found ways to make me leave. Giving a diploma to an Indian was not their first choice."

She shook her head sadly. "What a waste."

"No," he said, denying her pity. "I learned in spite of them, and what I learned there I've used. I don't regret those years."

"And then you came here, to your father's land."

He nodded. "I've made a place here for myself. But I've known all along that I would be alone. The women of the tribes are loyal to their people. I'm an outcast." His shrug made it a simple statement of fact.

He rose and held up the string of popcorn. It hung almost to the floor and he knotted the thread and tied it off, biting it with a quick nip of white teeth until it hung freely. With a sure hand, he looped it over the highest branches in front of the tree, allowing it to drape gracefully between several limbs.

"How does that look?" he asked, and then glanced toward the kitchen, his eyes narrowing as the sound of a voice was heard at the back door, and a horse neighed a greeting from the yard. He shot her a look of appraisal. "You have company. Were you expecting anyone?"

"No. I don't have callers."

"Well, you have one now. Shall I go into the other room and wait?"

"No." The single word was harsh. "I won't hide you behind the door, Jesse. You should know better than that."

He waved a hand toward the doorway. "Then go and see who your visitor is."

She rose and placed her fluffy string of popcorn before her before she brushed down her skirts and made her way into the kitchen. Through the window she caught sight of a horse and wagon near the porch and she reached for the latch, swinging the door open.

A man faced her, his hat in hand, brushing back dark hair with the other. His words were apologetic as he spoke swiftly. "Ma'am. My wife said I should come by and see if you might be of help."

"Your wife?" Molly asked, confusion alive in her voice. "I'm afraid I don't know your wife, sir. Why would she be asking for my help?"

"She said she'd met you in the general store a couple of times, and that you lived here on Thompson's place."

"I'm George Thompson's widow."

The man's hand rose in a gesture of impatience. "No matter. My woman is having her baby, and the weather looks bad. I doubt if the doctor would come all the way out here to her, but she thought just having another woman there might ease things." He met her gaze fully, his eyes careful not to touch the scars she wore.

"Amanda Green is your wife?" Molly asked. And, of course, it had to be Amanda. No other woman had given her the time of day. Only the kind-eyed, pregnant lady who had chosen to speak and smile at the outcast. For that woman, Molly would leave the warmth of her home and travel with this man to the neighboring farm, offering whatever comfort she could to another woman in need.

"I'll be ready in a moment," she said, turning quickly to find her heavy coat and snatch up her shawl.

"You'll need your hat, Mrs. Thompson. And we'll need to offer the pups some milk before we go." Jesse's voice spoke from the doorway, and Tom Green looked toward him with narrowed eyes.

"I didn't know that the lady had company," he said sharply.

"I'm her neighbor and I stopped by to lend a hand," Jesse told him, his voice controlled, his eyes focused with chill intent on the man who scanned him with measuring eyes. "Mrs. Thompson is tending to a pair of pups for me."

Tom Green nodded, a trace of respect visible in the look he offered. "I hate to drag her away, but my woman is in need of help."

"Mrs. Thompson is certainly able to lend a hand," Jesse said. "I think I'll ride along if you don't mind. Perhaps I can be of assistance. But first, I'll feed the dogs and then catch up with you."

There was no give in his voice, Molly thought, no question as to his intent. Jesse Stormwalker had made a decision and would not veer from his purpose. She felt a sharp sense of relief that he would be so willing to watch over her. For certainly that was the message given and received.

"All right. Whatever you say," Tom said agreeably. He turned back to Molly. "Can we leave?"

"As soon as I bank the fire," she told him.

"I'll tend to it," Jesse offered. "I'll be right along. Go ahead, the both of you." He opened the door, watched as Molly reached for her hat and jammed it on her head, then stood in the open doorway as they left the house and headed out into the darkening afternoon.

The ride went quickly, Tom hunkered down on the wagon seat, Molly beside him, holding her shawl over her face to shield it from the wind and blowing snow. "I didn't realize it was going to get bad again today," she remarked, turning her head to watch him as he guided his team with care.

"Me, neither," he said gloomily. "Didn't know the missus was about to have this baby, either. Thought we had another week or so to go." His smile was sheepish as he turned to look at Molly. "I guess we don't have a lot of control over these things though."

"Mr. Green?" Molly spoke impetuously. "I don't know how much help I can be to your wife. I've never had a child."

"She has. We got two little ones already. It's not something new to her. She just needs another woman there to keep things calm. I can look after the boys and tote water or whatever you'll need, but Amanda can pretty well call the shots when it comes to the actual birthing, I suspect. She didn't have a bad time with the others, so she don't seem worried about that part of it."

"Why did she think of me?" Molly asked, curious as to the woman's motives.

Tom cast her a look, a quick glance that nonetheless seemed to survey her fully, from top to bottom, leaving nothing out. There seemed to be no revulsion in his face as he looked for long seconds on her cheek, only a stirring of pity perhaps. "She said you might be sympathetic with her pain, even if you'd never suffered this sort of thing. For some reason or another, she took to you, just seeing you in the store."

"She was neighborly. I haven't received a lot of friendship from the folks hereabouts. Your wife broke the mold."

"She's a good woman. I'd made up my mind that if she wanted you to come, I'd get you there, one way or another."

"Well, it's a good thing for both of us that I was agreeable then, wasn't it?" Her humor shone through the words, her smile warm as she turned it in his direction.

"I appreciate it, ma'am."

The ride was long, in one sense. The road had drifted over since Tom's passing this way such a short time before, and the horses plodded carefully, Tom keeping them in the center of the tree-lined trail. For it was not much more than that, having lost the width of a genuine road once it passed beyond Molly's farm.

"How much longer?" she asked, after fifteen minutes of slow travel.

"Not far, now," he told her. One gloved hand lifted to point into the near distance. "If you look at the top of that little rise you might be able to make out the outline of the house. It's pretty hard to see with the snow."

Molly's eyes narrowed as she searched the horizon, and within a few minutes she saw the blurred image of a cabin ahead. Not large enough to be distinguished as a farmhouse, it was, nevertheless, a solid-appearing structure, snuggled against a stand of trees. The wagon approached the porch and Tom brought his team to a halt.

"Here we are, ma'am," he said, climbing down from the wagon seat and circling the wagon to lift Molly down. "I'll put up the team and you go on ahead inside. The young'uns might still be asleep. I put them down for a nap before I left."

She trudged through the fallen snow to the porch and stomped her feet before she opened the back door. The warmth of a well-kept kitchen greeted her and the scent of a meal cooking attracted her to the stove. Leaving her coat and hat on a peg by the door, she approached the simmering kettle and lifted the lid with a handy dish towel.

A rich aroma of meat and spices greeted her, and she inhaled deeply. The woman knew how to cook, and even with impending childbirth had thought of her family first before she went to her bed. Molly washed her hands thoroughly at the sink and headed out of the kitchen, seeking the bedroom.

"Amanda?" she called softly, and was rewarded by an answering voice.

"I'm in here," the woman said from behind a closed door just off a small sitting room. Molly pushed it open and squinted into the semidarkness.

"You need a candle lit," she said. "I can barely see you."

"I was waiting for Tom to come back," Amanda told her, her voice trembling. "I'd begun to worry." She struggled to sit up on the bed and Molly hastened to her side, supporting her shoulders.

"Don't try to get up. I'll take care of things."

Amanda smiled, a shaky effort to be sure, but Molly thought she saw relief in the woman's expression. "I'm counting on that. I told Tom I thought you'd come, and I was fearful of him going all the way into town to get someone else. I didn't want to be alone when the baby arrived."

Molly sat on the edge of the mattress. "I confess I know nothing about this sort of thing. But if you'll tell me what to do——"

Amanda nodded. "Just have Tom bring in some hot water so I can be washed again. My waters broke a while ago, and I'm kinda in a mess. I dropped everything on the floor behind the bed, but I couldn't make it up to get clean towels or sheets."

"Heavens, I can do that," Molly said quickly, relieved to be offered a chore she could handle. She rose and sought out a candle, lit it and placed it on the table beside the bed. The room was lit with a soft glow, suited to this occasion she thought, and her gaze touched the woman who watched her. Pale, but smiling, Amanda seemed more at ease now that she was no longer alone. And her words verified Molly's notion.

"I'll be all right now. I just didn't want Tom to be alone with this." Even as she spoke, her breath caught and her eyes closed as a grimace of pain tautened her features and drew the skin against her cheekbones. She gripped the sheet, and her knuckles whitened as she stiffened beneath the covering. Her knees drew upward and she rolled to one side, the groan she tried to suppress becoming audible.

Molly sat down beside her abruptly. "Let me rub your back. Maybe it will help." Her strong right hand massaged deeply into the taut muscles, low against Amanda's spine and she was rewarded by a sigh of gratitude.

"Thank you." The pain seemed to be easing, as if it ebbed and flowed like the tide at the ocean, Molly thought, and in a moment, she rose and brought a small table from the corner of the room. A basin stood on it, several towels were folded on its lower shelf and she placed it beside the bed, in readiness for whatever might occur next.

From the kitchen, she heard low voices and then Tom appeared in the doorway, carrying a pan of steaming water. "Here," Molly said, indicating the basin. "Pour some in and put the pan on the floor. I'll need more towels I think and a clean sheet to put under your wife."

"All right." Eager to follow orders, Tom left the room with haste and reappeared only moments later with the requested items. "Anything else I can do?" he asked.

Molly looked up at him and smiled, feeling distinctly ignorant as she faced the next few hours. "I'll let you know," she said, hoping the words held more comfort than she felt capable of giving.

With a look of relief in his wife's direction, Tom pulled the door closed, and Molly was left to undertake a beginner's lesson in childbirth, firsthand.

Chapter Five

"You wanta be careful, Stormwalker." The words were delivered as a warning, but Tom Green's voice bore no trace of anger.

"Because?" Jesse sought out the briefest query he could come up with. His own ire had been provoked by the man's words, but having been offered them in a friendly manner Jesse answered in like form.

"John Cross said he saw you following the woman out of town the other day. And he told folks he'd spotted your horse out at her place another time, and you need to know that she's been the topic of gossip these days."

"Seems to me that someone's awfully interested in my doings lately," Jesse said bluntly. "But the truth of the matter is, I've done nothing wrong, and I've certainly meant her no disrespect. She needed help, I needed a hand, and we've solved a couple of mutual problems. If the good folks in town want to make something of that it doesn't seem there's much I can do about it."

"Maybe not. But I thought you ought to know what the talk is."

"All right. You've told me, and I've been warned."

Tom looked at him warily. "My wife says Molly Thompson is a good woman, but the folks in town don't know what to do with her."

"And what is that supposed to mean?" Now the frustration turned to anger, and Jesse felt a black fierceness envelope him. "She's done no harm to anyone. If anything, she's the victim in everything that's happened to her. If the good folks of this town can't see that, I don't recognize much hope for any of them." He came close to biting his tongue, so violently protective were the words he held within.

"They're just ordinary people who look the other way when there's trouble." Tom dropped his head, as if shamed by his thoughts. "I did the same thing. I knew she was there, and there's no excuse for my ignoring her presence when George Thompson was intent on keeping her prisoner in her own home."

"You knew she was being abused by her husband?" Jesse heard the growl erupt as Tom flinched at the tone of his voice.

"I wasn't sure." As excuses went, it was pretty poor, Jesse decided, but he had to give Tom credit for admitting it. It wasn't proper to interfere between husband and wife. It was an unwritten law. In fact, the law of the land almost prohibited such interference.

"Can I ask you something?" Tom murmured, glancing up again to meet Jesse's gaze. His own was hesitant and Jesse recognized the regret the man offered as an apology.

"How did she get scarred?" Jesse's mouth twitched at Tom's startled awareness.

"I suspect it's none of my business, but Amanda has asked what I know, and I couldn't tell her anything."

"Why doesn't she ask Molly herself?"

"I suspect she will before the day is through."

"Did he do that to you?" Amanda breathed deeply, awaiting the next pain, and Molly held the woman's hand in a sympathetic grip. She felt the flush of embarrassment darken her skin, there where the scar was most prominent, and then felt a familiar flash of anger at the fate she'd been dealt by life.

"No. Not exactly. I was burned by a jar of raspberries. It exploded in my hand, and by the time I got the rest of me uncovered, my face was blistered. The berries stuck like glue."

"I don't remember hearing about it." Amanda clenched her fingers tightly around Molly's palm as a pain began to ascend to a peak. Her moan was soft, as though she would keep her pain within the walls of this room.

"I've heard that taking deep breaths helps," Molly whispered. She bent over Amanda's huddled form. "Here, let me rub your back."

They touched in the way of women, hand-to-hand, mouth-to-forehead, Molly whispering assurance, Amanda grasping for comfort. And then the pain was gone, for this short moment only a memory.

Molly continued to speak, softly and soothingly, as if she would take Amanda's mind from the pain she awaited. Her voice was flat, the words explaining the scar were almost a repetition of the explanation she'd given Jesse. For the second time, she'd revealed this pain to another, her rejection by the man she'd chosen to marry and live with.

The man whose death had freed her from a life of servitude and abuse.

"He was cruel." Amanda offered George Thompson no excuse.

"Yes." Molly could only agree, knowing that only another woman could read between the lines to the depths of the man's degradation.

"I'm so sorry," Amanda whispered. "Sorry that I didn't come forward before and befriend you. Forgive me." Her pain washed over her anew, and Molly shushed her words with hands that relieved her pain, words of assurance that gave succor.

It was only an hour later when the baby made its appearance, and at the first cry, Tom Green was in the room, his stride long as he approached his wife. "Amanda." His voice was broken as he knelt by her bed, and Molly could only smile at the look exchanged between husband and wife. Amanda Green was one of the fortunate few.

Tending a newborn babe seemed to come about naturally, and in another hour, the mother and daughter were nestled in the middle of the bed, Amanda weary but triumphant.

"What shall you call her?" Molly asked, leaning over the bed to whisper a goodbye. "Have you thought of a name?"

Amanda's smile shone with happiness. "We thought Noelle would sound very like Christmas. But I didn't think I'd hit the day so exactly when I first thought of what she would be named. It's a sign, don't you think?"

"Noelle." Molly allowed the soft syllables to roll from her tongue, and smiled as she considered the beauty of their origin. "It's lovely, Amanda."

Amanda's eyes closed, briefly to be sure, but it was a sure sign of the weariness that came about in the aftermath of childbirth. Even as unknowing as Molly was of such things, she sensed the woman's need for sleep.

"We're leaving," she said quietly. "You should rest now."

There was no argument given, only a smile that trembled a bit. "Thank you so much, Molly." The words were heartfelt.

"I didn't do much, only what you told me," Molly said with a dry laugh. "I think you could have done this on your own."

"I'm glad I didn't have to," Amanda admitted. "I'll do the same for you someday, perhaps."

"Not likely." Molly stood erect and her heart felt heavy within her. Not for her the joy of childbirth. Never would her body shelter a babe such as this one before her. No man would ever want to couple with her and beget a child within her.

"Molly. I'm ready to take you home." Behind her, Jesse waited, and his voice prompted her to turn and smile.

"All right, I'm ready." He held her coat and she shrugged into it, then walked ahead of him to the back door. Tom opened it and the gust of cold wind almost took her breath. Snow blew in gusts beyond the porch, and Jesse's horse waited at the hitching rail.

"I didn't think about it when I brought out your gelding, but I can get one of my saddle horses out for Mrs. Thompson to ride if you think it's a good idea," Tom offered. "Will you have any trouble making it on yours? Just watch your back."

"I will, Tom. And this is fine. We can ride together," Jesse assured him. His hand was firm on Molly's elbow as he guided her from the porch to where his horse waited; and with one quick movement, he'd lifted her into the saddle. In another lithe maneuver he'd swung up behind her, lifting her to sit on his thighs. She perched there, her back straight, her heart thumping an irregular beat, while he nonchalantly turned his mount in a half circle and waved a quick farewell in Tom's direction.

The wind was strong and he bent low to speak directly into her ear. "If you're not comfortable there, I can turn you across my lap, keep you shielded from the wind a bit better."

She shook her head, aware only of the heat of his body behind her, as if she sat against a wood-burning stove and its warmth was infiltrating her every pore. He tugged her back, his long arm holding her close, and she shivered at the feel of hard male muscles against her back, of the length of steely purpose gripping her firmly.

"What did Tom mean?" she asked, sensing his sudden stillness, as though he ceased to breathe.

"I'm not sure what you're talking about," he said after a moment.

"Oh, yes you are. He was warning you about me, wasn't he?"

"No. Not about you. About what my being seen with you was likely to do to your reputation." The words were stark, frightening almost, but she persevered.

"I don't have any reputation to uphold. I'm more concerned that the folks in town don't think you're being used by me, Jesse. You've only been helpful and kind, and I don't want them to think badly of you."

"And if they do? What then?" His words seemed almost flippant, she thought, not typical of Jesse Stormwalker, whose usual demeanor was stern and unbending. At least she'd thought it to be, until the past weeks. Now she knew a different man, one she could easily take into her home and heart. A man she yearned for in a way she'd never thought to feel toward any example of masculinity.

"Then I'll have ruined your reputation and caused you irreparable harm. I never intended that," she told him.

"If there's any blame to dish out, I'll take my share. I'm the one who has come to you time and again, spent time with you and asked your help."

"I should have left you with your dogs that first day. We wouldn't be in this fix if I'd used my head."

"No. Don't say that, Molly. Look what I'd have missed out on."

She turned her head, trying and failing to see his face. "I don't know what you mean."

His laughter was low—seductive, she thought. "Are you certain? You don't remember the kisses we shared? The times we touched?"

She nodded. "I remember." And how could she not? For the only time in her lifetime, she'd been offered true affection at the hands of a man, had learned what pleasure might be brought about by a man's presence in her life.

"Don't regret that, Molly," he said softly against her ear. "Just know that I'll take care of things. I won't let anything happen to you."

She was silent, digesting his vow. He held her close and she relished the security of his embrace, knew the bliss of his arm holding her fast against his steadily beating heart. And found regret beating a path to her door as the ride came to an end and she was lifted from his saddle and ushered onto her back porch.

"Go on in," he told her. "I'll take care of my horse and be right with you."

She was sitting on the floor when he came in, the box of pups in front of her, a bowl of milk before her. As Jesse entered the kitchen, she picked up one of the wiggling creatures and placed it before the shallow bowl, ducking his head with a quick motion into the rich milk.

The dog tried to sit up on his haunches and tilted instead to one side, his tongue licking rapidly at the end of his nose. One ear tilted upward as he tasted the milk and Molly held him again to the bowl, repeating the simple lesson.

"He's catching on," Jesse told her, struck almost speechless by the graceful movements of the woman he watched. Even in this mundane bit of play, she exhibited a touch of beauty he could not help but be drawn to. He crouched beside her, his eyes intent on her expressions, the quick smile that touched her lips as the pup licked her hand, the flicker of her eyelashes as she became aware of his scrutiny.

And then she looked up at him. "Jesse? What are we doing?"

"I don't know about you," he drawled softly, "but I'm enjoying the view."

Her face took on an aura of delight, as if she found it difficult to believe he found her so appealing, and then the look vanished and she frowned. "I'm frightened," she whispered, even as she lifted her gaze to his. Yet there was no fear in the solemn expression she offered, only a questioning entreaty that begged for his response.

"Don't ever be frightened of me," he said quietly. "The last thing in the world I ever want to do is cause you pain, Molly."

"I know that. I don't want your business to be damaged by me."

"I'm already scorned," he said with a smile of indifference. "No one can hurt me. No one but you."

She bent her head, her hand touching his as it rested on his knee. And then she lowered her face to press her lips against the wide, dark-skinned width of skin. He felt it to his depths, as if a brush of magic had bestowed a blessing on his very essence. His heart lifted in a surge of desire he could not control, and in a moment, he'd placed the pup back in the box and lifted Molly to stand before him.

His arms encircled her, his hands lifted her face to his and he touched her lips with a blend of passion and gentle yearning she welcomed with a sigh. Her lips parted beneath his, her mouth opening to his caress as would a blossom open to the sun. He tilted her head a bit, angling for a closer fit, blending their lips and tongues in an aching, tender union he had never thought to find.

She inhaled sharply, her hands pressing against his chest, and he released her, fearful of forcing himself on her, aware that she had suffered great damage at the hands of George Thompson. He would not, could not give her less than the love and respect she deserved. If she found it impossible to accept his loving, he would wait. If she could never come to him freely, gladly—he would take what she was willing to offer.

And yet his heart ached for what might be their destiny, for those moments of pure pleasure he knew he could find in her arms.

"Molly?" He gathered her close again, his touch circumspect, his hands holding her close, but allowing her the choice to stay or go.

She chose to nestle nearer to his hard, masculine body, fitting her breasts to his muscular chest, her rounded hips into the cradle of his manhood. He was hard, his body ready to claim her and he knew she felt the degree of his arousal, knew the moment she became aware of the need so mutely expressed by the automatic thrust of his loins against hers.

Her whisper was soft, her words an invitation. "I told you I would be here for you, Jesse. I meant it. If you want me—"

His big hand lifted to press against her mouth, and he shushed her words with a passionate refusal of her offer. "You know I want you, sweetheart. But unless you're willing to marry me, I won't ever have the right to take you to my bed."

She tilted her head back and her eyes shone with a passion that delighted him. "Oh, I want you. You know that already. I just don't know if I'll be able to give you what you need from a woman. I'm damaged goods, Jesse."

"No" His single word of rebuttal was firm, almost harsh as he gripped her shoulders and shook her with an utter rejection of her claim. "You've been hurt. Your body shows the result of a man's cruelty. But no more, Molly. From this time on, we begin a new part of your life. If I have to repeat it a hundred times a day, then so be it.

"I'll never hurt you. I'll take care of you and look after you, and love you till the day you die." He held her before himself, his fingers gripping her with a firm hold she didn't even attempt to evade. "I don't make promises I have no intention of keeping. You can believe every word I tell you."

Her eyes filled with tears and he lowered her to the

floor, aware suddenly that he'd been holding her on her tiptoes, his grasp lifting her high. "I've frightened you now, haven't I?" he asked. "And when I've only just told you I'd do no such thing." He bent his head and his face was buried in the mass of waves and curls atop her head. The scent of soap, of fresh skin and the seductive aroma of her woman's flesh met his nostrils and he inhaled deeply.

Without speaking the words anew she offered him again whatever he chose to take from her. Her head fell back and the long, sleek line of her throat was exposed to his view, the final surrender of her body into his keeping.

"I won't bed you now," he said. "Not until we're married and I own the right to you."

"I won't marry you, Jesse. Not until you've seen what you're accepting into your bed."

He held her away, his eyes narrowing as he digested the words she spoke. "What do you mean?" And yet, he knew the direction of her thoughts, knew her intent even before she lifted trembling hands to unbutton her dress.

"If you want me, you'll know firsthand what ugliness you'll be faced with every day of our lives together."

Jesse felt a thrill of discovery, a triumphant lift of his spirits that made right and proper this solemn moment. She would expose herself to him, openly and without shame, that he might acknowledge her pain and suffering, and be given the opportunity to accept all that she was—without reservation. He knew that no matter the damage done to her body, it had not touched the soul that dwelt within that slender frame.

And so he allowed her to continue the course she had chosen to take, watched with dark, yearning eyes as she slid the sleeves of her dress down her arms, standing before him as might a virgin on her wedding night, offering herself to the man she had chosen.

The dress rested against the lush line of her hips and her fingers touched the fabric of her vest, that bit of clothing that had been purchased for utility's sake, not for the opportunity to enhance the beauty of the woman who wore it. She tugged it free from the waistline of her dress and began the arduous task of pulling it over her head. Her movements were hesitant now, as if she had begun to rue her actions. Yet, as he caught a glimpse of the determination that visited her features, he recognized she would not back from the road she had chosen.

The vest caught on her chin and she ducked her head, pulling it over her hair, the mass of golden waves that had first caught his eye, had first made him aware of the soft beauty of blue eyes and tempting form she owned. And then she stood before him, her body exposed to his gaze, the crests of her breasts puckered and drawn up into bits of flesh that drew him nearer, bringing to life a yearning deep within his heart. His hands clenched and his fingers twitched, aching to reach for her, as though he could not bear to leave that vulnerable flesh untouched.

His hand lifted to her, one index finger pressing beneath that small nubbin, then circling it with a careful movement that he feared might send her into a panic of fear. It was not to be, for she only looked down at what that finger did, moving with gentle care over her flesh, careful not to touch the darkened place where he yearned to press his mouth.

"Can you feel this?" he asked, needful of the knowledge. For if she'd been damaged to the extent he feared, she might never know the pleasure he could bring her with the pressure of hands and mouth against her breast.

She shivered and her eyes widened as they sought his. "Yes, I can feel it."

"Is it good?" His tone was guttural now, and he rued the passion that would not allow him this moment without the pain of restraint. For no matter what happened here, tonight, he would not take her to bed, would not shame her by accepting the generous offer she had placed before him.

Her nod was quick. "It's good," she whispered, and then closed her eyes as though she must dwell upon the sensation he brought to life with the movement of his hand. He cupped her then, held that soft, yet firm roundness in his palm, careful not to press it too tightly, watching as her mouth opened a bit and her breathing increased by increments.

The flesh was rough against his palm, but he cared little for that, only that he was able to bring pleasure to the scarred area, that she was not immune to the touch of his hand. His head bent and he held her within his palm as if her breast were an offering and he the man who would accept it as his due.

His mouth opened to enclose the puckered flesh, his tongue drew on it with a careful pressure and he heard the gasp she could not contain. "Jesse?" His arm circled her waist quickly, holding her fast against himself.

"Jesse?" She repeated his name as if it were a mantra, a chant of delight he could not mistake.

His head lifted and her eyes opened, wide and wary, yet filled with a new knowledge he recognized. She was aware, awakened to him as a lover. She would accept him, acknowledge him, offer him her body. A groan of triumph rose from his chest, resounding through the room, and he gathered her close, his palm forming a healing circle about her arm, blessing her scarred shoulder with gentle touches, and then his mouth followed the path his hand had taken. His tongue touched the scarred skin, his eyes took in her pain, the shame of a woman's knowledge of her own short-comings.

With an aching tenderness, he accepted her flaws, took them upon himself as only a small part of the woman he had chosen. For there was more to Molly Thompson than the scars she bore or the sorrow she'd lived with. She was brave, loving, and filled with an in-domitable spirit he could only admire.

He stood erect before her now, his eyes moving slowly and carefully over the exposed skin she'd offered for his scrutiny, and then he lifted his gaze to hers. A touch of apprehension dwelt in the depths of her blue eyes and he hastened to assure her lest she sense a single moment of hesitation on his part.

"You're beautiful, Molly. You're all I ever wanted in a woman. I'd thought not to marry, not to have a wife of my own, and had made that decision a firm one. And then I met you, and I knew from that first glimpse of blue eyes that I must have you." He smiled, aware that his confession was giving away his weakness, and uncaring even of that.

"I've fought against my instincts, tried my best to leave you alone, and haven't been able to turn away. We'll be married as soon as it can be arranged."

He watched as a flush rose from her breasts, climbing to cover her throat and then upward to skim the surface of her face. "I want you to be certain," she whispered. Her arms crossed over her breasts in an instinctive movement, as though she had only now recognized the exposure of her body to his scrutiny.

"You will be my wife, Molly." The words left no element of doubt and she only nodded as though she accepted his edict, willing to place herself in his hands.

For she had, indeed, already done so. She had allowed his hands to examine her skin, had given him leave to look at her with eyes that measured and absorbed each increment of her scarring, and then had watched as he offered a tender touch of acceptance through the kisses he'd bestowed upon her breast and shoulder.

"It's late," she whispered. "You should go home now."

He offered her no choice. "I'm not leaving you tonight," he said firmly. "It's too late for anyone to be out and about, and too stormy for me to head for home now."

"Where will you sleep?" The words beckoned him, coaxing him into an intimacy he yearned for, and yet he shook his head.

"With you, in your bed, Molly. But I won't ask for more than a kiss perhaps, or my arms around you, or your warmth against me through the night. Will you trust me for that?" Her eyes widened as though she considered his words at length, and then she nodded her agreement.

"All right. Whatever you say."

"No, it will be as you say, sweetheart. You'll never again have to do as a man dictates. You are a woman with the ability and strength to make your own decisions. I won't take that from you."

In an hour they were curled in the middle of Molly's bed and she could only remember the last time a man had shared this space with her. That night, over six months ago when the masculine being named George Thompson had occupied her bed—a man who had scorned her, yet ravished her with cruel intent.

Tonight another held her close, not a base creature

such as George, but a man who cherished her and sought her comfort.

They watched the sky through the window, noted the clouds that had begun to scatter, the moon that had climbed high into the darkness. "The storm is over," Molly said quietly. "It's Christmas, Jesse." She laughed softly. "And I've seen my first miracle tonight."

"Miracle?" He waited for her explanation.

"Oh, yes. It was a miracle such as I'd never thought to experience. When that baby girl was born I knew Amanda's joy—secondhand, to be sure—but I shared it with her. I've always known it would not be my destiny to have a child of my own, but God was gracious in granting me the sight of a Christmas child coming into this world."

"And you think you'll not be blessed with a child of your own?" he asked quietly.

She was silent. "Do you think— "

His head moved against her hair. "I think," he murmured, and felt the shiver that passed through her slender body.

In the east, the night was fading, the heavens turning muted shades of pink, the lightening of darkness coming gradually, as did the appearance of dawn at this time of the year. The rooster in the yard crowed a challenging call and Jesse laughed softly.

"He's waking his harem," he whispered. "Time to get up, ladies." His yawn was quick and he laughed, the movement of his chest a comfort against her back. "But not for you, my sweet. You've not even slept yet, tonight."

They were the last words she heard, her eyes closing, her body warmed by his heat, her heart held inviolate in his hands.

Chapter Six

"We didn't light the candles last night," Molly said. "Do you suppose we can go in the other room after a while and do it?"

"We can do anything we please," Jesse told her arrogantly. "This is our day to enjoy, our first Christmas together. If lighting the candles is what you want to do, then that's the plan."

Breakfast was late, the cow and chickens having taken up the first hour of their awakening. The crusted snow had forced Jesse to plow through it ahead of her, taking shorter steps to accommodate her stride, allowing her to step into the holes left by his boots. Inside the barn the horses had snorted agreeably as Jesse and Molly entered through the door, and together they'd performed the everyday chores that awaited them.

The pups' care had been next, all of them gathering around the shallow dish of milk, as if their eyes had been suddenly opened to the abundance available. Their tails wagged ferociously, their small bodies rounding almost visibly as they partook of the bountiful supply of sustenance they'd been offered.

And then they'd been carried outside for a short stretch of time, during which they seemed to discover that the great outdoors was the proper place to do their morning duties. Molly laughed with delight at their scampering, the quick squatting in the snow as they found the place Jesse had swept clear for their early ablutions.

Back in their box, they curled together in a heap, almost indistinguishable from each other as they sank into a deep sleep. Molly petted them, as if she hated to leave them alone, her love for the innocent creatures apparent.

And then she left them to wash her hands and put together breakfast for Jesse. Now, sitting together at the table, they ate the simple meal she'd prepared.

"We were too tired to worry about candles last night," he said with a laugh, recalling their plan for the day. "I couldn't believe that you held out so long as it was. I think your first experience at childbirth wore you out."

"It was wonderful. Amanda was so sure of herself, of me, of everything that happened. I only watched and did as I was told." She sipped her coffee and then placed the cup on the table. "When Tom came in to her, he made a beeline for the bed and fell down on his knees beside her and buried his face next to hers."

She felt the awe of that moment once more and knew that the explaining of it did not justify the beauty she'd seen played out before her eyes. "They looked at each other and I almost cried," Molly said. "He told her he loved her without saying a word, Jesse."

"He's a good man." Jesse made the statement with feeling. "I think we've made friends with good people."

"We may need their friendship before we're done. I

just don't want them to be exposed to scorn because of me."

"Tom Green won't care. He's a man of principle, and his wife is a woman who can be depended upon."

"I care," Molly whispered, her confidence in the future still shaky.

From outside the house a voice called out and Jesse rose from the table. "Jesse Stormwalker. Are you in there?"

He rose from the table and shrugged into his coat. "Stay here," he said firmly. "I mean it, Molly. Don't come outdoors." And then he left her, opening the kitchen door and, after stepping onto the porch, pulling it shut behind himself.

Weaponless, he faced two men who seemed intent on causing a problem this morning. Molly watched through the window as one swung down from his horse, and she viewed with horror the heavy gun that swung from his side.

Their voices were a drone she could not understand, Jesse's calm and assured, the other man's harsh and demanding. "You can't shame a woman this way and get away with it." Molly heard the words clearly now, and no matter that Jesse had given her an order, she rose from the table and went to the door.

Her shawl snatched from the hook, she stepped out to stand beside him. "He hasn't shamed me, sheriff," she said quietly. "He stayed here because he couldn't get home in the snow last night. We were at Tom Green's place till after midnight. His wife had her baby and they called on us to help."

The lawman stood still, his gaze narrowing as he touched her face with eyes that missed not an increment of her scars. "You don't want to make charges against Stormwalker?" he asked.

"Why should I?" Her mouth twisted in a smile of triumph. "He's going to marry me, and that was decided before he spent the night. He hasn't hurt me, or shamed me or done any of the things to me that my legal husband did for three years. You didn't care then what happened to me. Why should you come out here now and make a fuss because a good man like Jesse is interested in my well-being?"

The sheriff shot a glance at Jesse and nodded. "I'd say you've got a woman who knows how to speak for herself, Stormwalker." He eyed Molly closely. "If you're certain you haven't been coerced into anything, I'll have to take your word for it, ma'am. I heard that Stormwalker's place was empty and I was told I might find him here, so I came out to check things over."

"Well, whoever told you he wasn't home was right, but whoever it was had no business interfering where there was no need." Molly took a deep breath. "I know that folks have been talking about me, and I understand that I've not been as circumspect as I might be. But then no one in town ever gave two hoots and a holler before about whether I lived or died, so I don't hold much stock in their concern now."

The sheriff nodded agreement. "As I said, Stormwalker, you've got you a woman who can hold her own. I believe we'll be on our way, Deputy." With a nod at the mounted horseman beside him, the sheriff climbed back on his horse and turned back toward town.

Jesse's arm circled her waist as he steered Molly back into the house. "I told you to wait inside," he growled, and then turned her to face him, leaning back against the closed door.

"So you did," she said sharply.

"Will you always be so independent?" he asked, his eyes searching her face, his brow furrowing as he spoke.

"Probably." She uttered the single word in reply and then watched him closely. Her mouth opened in a moment and the query she tossed in his direction was one he obviously did not expect.

"And will you always be so bossy?"

He laughed, his head tipping back, the chuckles and amusement he could not contain spilling over her with abandon. "Probably," he admitted. He ducked his head quickly and caught her unaware, his mouth capturing hers in a kiss that began as a joyous blending of lips and fast became a passionate, heated measure of desire that would not be contained.

She clung to him, unabashedly drawn to him as a moth is charmed by the flame that lures it near. He was all she had ever wanted, all she'd ever yearned for, and she was his. His in a way in which she'd never belonged to George Thompson.

She would be Jesse Stormwalker's woman.

He left for town an hour later, intent on stopping first to feed his stock and tend to the chores at his farm. Inside his barn, a welcoming committee stood beside the first stall. Joe Beamer held the bridle of a pretty little mare.

"I'm hoping you'll have time to work with this little lady, Stormwalker," he said quietly. "I brought her out, and it looks like I should have waited till you knew I was coming."

"That's all right," said Jesse, his dark eyes passing judgment on the other three men who watched him. "I can put her up and have her back to you in a week or so. She shouldn't be any trouble."

"I'd say you got enough trouble, Stormwalker," said one of the men, a cowhand, named John Cross.

"What's that supposed to mean?" Jesse asked harshly.

"You've just come from that woman's house," said John Cross, waving his hand at Jesse's horse. He made a production of his accusation. "She's been compromised, and everyone in town knows it."

"If you're talking about Mrs. Thompson, you need to know that she just delivered a baby for Amanda Green. We've just come back from there. Mrs. Thompson needed a ride home, and I took her and dropped her off."

"Yeah, but this isn't the first time you've been there," John persisted. "You need a lesson, half breed."

"You think so?" Jesse's words were belligerent, and in a moment, one of the other men walked behind him, gripping him and pulling his arms high against his back.

"This isn't the time or place, John," said Joe Beamer. "I came out here in good faith to do business with Stormwalker and you've made a problem I've got no issue with."

"Well, that's your choice," John Cross said. "This redskin needs a lesson and he's about to get it."

Something was wrong. Molly knew it in her bones, knew beyond a doubt that Jesse was in danger. How or what was not the issue, only that he needed her and she must go to him. Her horse was saddled quickly, her hands used to the chore, her horse obedient to her will. And after donning her warmest clothing, she headed for his farm. If he were not there, he might have gone to town. Either way, she would find him.

Some deep-seated urge to be in his proximity forced her to head for the places he might well be.

He should have returned to her by now, she decided, and the fact that he hadn't made her wary of what might have happened to him. His farmhouse was empty, his barn silent, his wagon gone, and a feeling of dread almost overwhelmed her. She knew her next stop would be the livery stable in town.

She rode there without hesitation, awaiting the presence of the man who owned the building and the business it contained.

He appeared in the wide doorway, and faced her in silence.

"Is Jesse here?" she asked quietly, her heart beating in a quick rhythm, her voice trembling. .

"What do you want with him?" The man was a giant, seemingly able to protect himself and even Jesse, should the need arise. But Molly was too aware of the idiosyncrasies of menfolk, and even the bulk of this man's powerful body might not be enough to keep Jesse from harm, should he be waylaid by a group of men.

"I need to find him," she said, her heart aching for the sight of the man she loved.

"Come on in." With a broad palm the giant waved her past himself into the depths of the stable, and she brought her horse to a halt next to him. He grasped the reins and she eased herself to the ground and gave over the mare to his keeping.

"Where is he?" She knew with a certain surety that Jesse was here. His essence called to her. His very presence crept into her heart and soul, and she stepped from her horse's side and headed for the back of the big stable.

"You're headed in the right direction."

"Thank you," Molly said, aware that the man was willing to tend her horse and apparently able to guide her to Jesse's side. The mare was ensconsed in a stall, a bag of grain holding her attention as Molly moved into the darkness at the back of the stable.

"The door on your left. Don't be worried. He looks far worse than he really is."

And what that was supposed to mean, she had no idea, only that Jesse had not returned to her, and had he been able, he would have fought the very elements to seek her out over the past hours.

He lay on a cot, a wet cloth covering his face. She knelt beside him with a broken groan of anguish. "Jesse." Her voice quavered, and she cared little. Her hands shook with a palsy of sorts, and she only held them still so he would not notice the trembling she could not control. It made little matter to her whether or not Jesse recognized her fear for him, for she only cared in this moment that he was alive, that he breathed, and that his body seemed to bear no harsh remnants of abuse.

She bent to kiss him, moving the cloth aside. Her mouth opened against his, tasting his blood, and then moved to his bruised cheek, her kisses falling on the abused skin there.

"I love you, Jesse," she whispered. "Please come home with me and let me tend you. What have they done to you?"

He groaned and she lifted from his body, fear for his well-being and anger at the hands that had damaged him vying for her attention. "Who did this?" she asked as the livery owner entered the small room behind her.

"Three men, cowhands from a neighboring ranch.

Troublemakers, all three of them, and the sheriff has them in custody. They thought they were in their rights, that Stormwalker had disgraced you by staying with you overnight."

"How? By bringing me home after I'd delivered a baby for Amanda Green? And staying because the storm would not allow him to continue on?" Rising from the floor, she backtracked to where her mare was installed near the front of the livery stable.

"Where are you going ma'am?" He followed her and Molly cast him an angry look.

"You just look after Jesse. I'll be back to pick him up and take him home when I return."

She knew little of the protocol of this sort of thing, only that the man she loved had been hurt and no one had cared enough to stand up for him. Only this livery owner who called Jesse his friend, and even now risked his business by giving support and succor to the man who lay in his tack room.

She lifted herself to her mare's back and picked up the reins. "Have him ready for me to take home, will you please?"

"Whatever you say ma'am." And he would. Beyond a shadow of a doubt, she knew that Jesse would be in her bed before this day was done, that she would tend him whether or not the men of this godforsaken town cared one way or another.

The sheriff's office was open, the door ajar, and within its depths, three men stood, watching as she rode up before the hitching rail. Her horse remained where Molly left her, trained to stay where she was left standing, and in a moment, Molly had entered the office, her eyes glittering with anger and more than a touch of a woman's feeling of responsibility for those she loves.

"Who are they?" she asked, pulling her gloves off, halting before the sheriff's desk.

"It won't do you any good to know who they are, Mrs. Thompson," the sheriff said quietly.

"Oh, yes it will. I'll know their names when I put a bullet into them."

"You ain't gonna shoot anybody, ma'am. I'm not gonna let you."

"You can't stop me," she said. "Someone has hurt Jesse terribly and I won't rest until I set things to right."

"He wouldn't want you to be doing this," the sheriff told her harshly.

"He's not able to speak for himself right now," she said, "and it seems I'm the only one who cares what happens to him."

"I care." The speaker was a short, round gentleman, dressed nicely, as if he might have been on his way to church when this occurrence had called him to a meeting with the sheriff. "He's going to be all right," the man told her gently. "I've already looked him over. He took a couple of hard punches, but Jesse Stormwalker is a strong man. It'll take more than three cowards coming at him to keep him down."

"I know that," Molly said. "But while he's not able to tend himself, I'll do it for him, whether anyone in this damn town cares for him or not. I'm serving notice right now that I care and I don't intend to let him suffer because he was kind to me." She turned to face the sheriff and the other man standing next to the desk.

"I've already given you chapter and verse of what my connection with Jesse Stormwalker is."

"We've got the men who waylaid him and they're in my jail," the sheriff said.

"I want to see them." She stood firm, her chin high, her eyes bright with a shimmer of angry tears. Yet the look of an avenging angel filled her being and the rotund man who watched her held out his hand as if he would lead her to a chair.

"Come, sit over here," he said.

"I want to see them," she insisted, and then turned to the hallway that led to the jail cells.

"You can't go back there," the sheriff said hastily.

"Don't even think about stopping me," she told him. Her gun rested heavily in her pocket and she lifted it from its hiding place and held it before her. "I'll shoot anyone who gets in my way." She walked past his silent figure and down the hallway to where three cells stood, each holding an occupant.

Three more scraggly-looking examples of manhood would be hard to find, Molly decided, pointing her gun at the first man.

"You gonna let her shoot me?" he whined in the sheriff's direction.

"What's gonna stop her?" the sheriff asked. "She's the one with the gun."

Molly lifted it and pointed the barrel at the whiskered man before her. "Why did you hurt Jesse Stormwalker?"

"He's a half breed." And as if that were reason enough, the man slumped onto the bunk behind him.

"He's a human being and he works hard for a living on his own land. He's good and honest and kind," Molly said flatly.

"He made you a laughingstock in town, ma'am," the

man said. "He stayed the night with you and your reputation is ruined."

"You think I care? You think your opinion matters to me? You're as rotten, dirty coward, and you run with a pack of coyotes who are just about a rotten as you are. You were afraid to meet him head-on, so you ganged up on him."

The gun did not waver and Molly stood firm, the wall behind her a support she leaned against. "If I ever see you anywhere near my place or Jesse's I'll shoot to kill," she told him. "And that goes for your friends there, too. I'm not afraid to defend those I care for, and Jesse Stormwalker is first on my list. I'll marry him if he'll have me."

"Hear that?" the scrawny man shouted at the sheriff. "Hear what she said? She's all set to marry up with a half breed."

"I heard her," the sheriff said agreeably. "I reckon that's her choice."

"I'm taking Jesse home with me," Molly told the five men who watched her and her gun with vigilance. "If I see anyone make any threatening moves near my place or Jesse's while I'm tending to him, I'll shoot, and trust me gentlemen, I know how to use this gun."

"I believe you ma'am." The short man behind the sheriff nodded his compliance. "Can I help you get Mr. Stormwalker into a wagon or buggy or whatever you're going to take him home in?"

"Whatever it takes. I'd appreciate the assistance," she told him, sliding her gun back into her pocket. "I'm ready to leave." Looking back at the men in the cells, she shot one final arrow in their direction. "I hope you have enough sense to leave town in another direction. Don't come near my place, or Stormwalker's, either, for that matter. I'll be watching for you."

"I'll take care of that," the sheriff said. "Now how about you heading back to the livery stable and letting someone load up that man for you? I think he could use a soft bed and a kindly woman to look after him for the next day or so."

"I can provide both," Molly told him, stepping into the street and lifting herself into the saddle on her mare, and was not surprised when the men followed her closely.

They found a sleigh for her to borrow, hitched her mare to the traces, and loaded Jesse into the seat beside her, where he slumped against her side. She covered him with the quilt she'd carried behind her saddle. Muttering beneath his breath, he murmured her name, and she shushed him quietly.

"I'm taking you home. Just sit still and close your eyes."

"I'll follow you out and help you get him into the house," the sheriff said.

"I don't need you," Molly told him. "I can do this by myself."

"Better listen to her," Jesse said softly. "She's a tough one."

"I can see that." Standing back, the lawman watched as Molly lifted the reins and snapped them over her mare's back. The sleek animal leaned forward and pulled the sleigh without any visible effort, breaking into a quick trot within twenty feet of the livery stable. Molly settled into the seat and allowed only a quick look at Jesse.

"You'll be fine," she said. "I'll take care of you."

"Now, I'll hafta marry you," he told her, humor lacing the words, even as he winced at the harsh sunlight after coming out of the darkness of the stable.

"You had to marry me before this. You've committed yourself to me, Jesse Stormwalker. I'm yours, whether you like it or not."

"I like it," he said, one big hand sliding across the seat to clutch at her hand. It slid and rested against her thigh and she covered it with her own.

"You'd better. You're stuck with me."

He mumbled a few words she could not decipher and leaned his head to rest against her shoulder. "I'm tired. I think I'll sleep a little."

They made it into the house without a hitch, Jesse stronger than she'd thought. He leaned on her heavily, but she knew her own strength and held him fast, one arm around his waist, the other grasping his hand as they climbed the two steps to the porch and then on into the bedroom.

It was to be his bed, a place she yearned to occupy, although the circumstances today were not ideal. Jesse stood by the foot of the bed while she stripped him of his trousers and shirt, and then sat down, too weary to hold himself upright. Molly knelt by his feet, removing his stockings and lifting him to the mattress. He was covered with the sheet, head resting on a soft pillow, and she folded his things and placed them neatly on a chair.

"I'm going to feed the dogs, and then I'll be right back," she told him, and earned a murmured thanks from his bloodied mouth. Returning with a soft cloth and warm water, she washed him, then rolled him to the center of the big bed and lay down beside him.

His head fit nicely in the crook of her shoulder, she thought, and his hair still smelled clean, like the rainwater she knew he used for washing. She kissed the smooth expanse of his brow, curled her palm around the line of his jaw, feeling the hard firmness of his strength exhibited there. He was young, and strong. He would heal within days, and she would never leave him again. Jesse Stormwalker was *hers*, and no one would ever deny her the right to be with him, in whatever way she chose.

He met her kiss with lips that firmed beneath hers, opening to touch her with his tongue, nibbling at the line of her upper lip. "I love you," he said, and she wondered if he would remember the words on the morrow. It mattered little, for he meant them today, and he was not a man to change his mind without just cause. His mouth drew her back again, and she kissed him with a thirsty need she could barely control.

"I think you like me," he said softly, and laughed beneath his breath.

"Yes." She breathed the word against his face, her eyes closing in a moment of thankfulness. "I like you."

"Dogs?" he asked and she knew what he wanted.

"I've fed them. They're fine."

"Which one do you want?"

"All of them," she whispered. "I want them all, Jesse. And you, too."

"It's a done deal," he told her, and even with the aching, painful hurts he had obtained over the past day, his grip on her was firm, his arms strong as he held her next to him.

"I'll take care of you," he promised.

"Not today. Right now it's my turn."

"Right," he said agreeably, turning his face into her throat and inhaling deeply of the sweet scent of woman she exuded.

Chapter Seven

A month later Jesse moved her, bag and baggage, into his house. Both wagons loaded, they made a slow trek from the old Thompson place now up for sale, to the farm that bore the name of Jesse Stormwalker on a sign hanging at the end of the lane. He pulled his wagon to a halt, watching as she drove ahead of him, but unable to pass the sign without looking up at it.

One day it would carry two more words.

Jesse Stormwalker & Sons. The thought of that day brought a thrill to the depths of his soul, and again his eyes sought the woman who moved toward his house. The woman who would make a home of that empty place where he'd only existed until the first time she'd appeared.

His reins fell in a soft movement against the backs of his team of horses and they obligingly leaned into the traces and bore the load without hesitation. By the time Molly reached the back of the house, he was behind her and she shot him a quizzical glance.

"What were you doing back there?"

"Making plans," he said with a secret smile. "I'll tell you all about them one day soon."

She nodded with the assurance of a woman who is loved, and he hastened to make his way to where she waited, lifting her down from the high seat, and allowing her slender form to brush against his body for a few short moments. He was primed, ready to claim her, and yet he felt a patience he'd not thought himself able to muster as he considered the time ahead.

They would be married on the morrow, in the small church in town. Tom and Amanda would stand up with them, the three children joining the group. Amanda had insisted on being a part of the wedding, even though Molly expressed doubts about the whole idea.

"You've only just borne a child," she said impatiently. "I'd never forgive myself if something happened to you because of me."

"And I'd never forgive myself if I weren't there to stand beside you," Amanda said firmly.

"You'd might as well not mess with the woman," Tom told Molly. "She's a bullhead from away back." And yet there was in his voice a warmth that could not be mistaken, and a joy he did not attempt to hide as his gaze touched upon his wife.

Now, they were bringing the final load to be distributed within the four walls of Jesse's house, and unless he was mightily mistaken, the horseman riding across the field to the west bore a startling resemblance to Tom.

One hand lifted in a wave of welcome as Jesse stepped toward the man. "I didn't know you were coming by," he said.

"Amanda chased me out the door. Said I needed to lend a hand over here." His eyes scanned the loaded wagons. "I'd say she was right." He dismounted and tied his horse, then turned to the first wagon, his hat gently tipped for Molly's benefit as he met her gaze.

"Morning, Miss Molly," he said with a grin.

"Good morning, Tom. Give Amanda my best, will you?"

He nodded briefly, then turned back to Jesse. "Let's get this stuff unloaded and in the house."

They'd only brought the things that Molly did not associate too closely with George. His own belongings were in the shed, his remaining clothing that had not been cut up for rugs burned on the pile where Molly got rid of all her rubbish. She'd brought things from her mother's house, bedding and dishes, what few George hadn't broken.

The Christmas tree, candles half-burned, remained in the sitting room. Molly was unable to remove it yet. Jesse would tend to it later, he'd said, for she could not bring herself to consign it to the burn pile. He would remove the candy and save the candleholders for another time. For there would be more Christmases to come, more candles to light, and perhaps even store-bought decorations to hang on green branches.

But this first tree, this emblem of his caring and concern for her would remain forever in her memory, glowing with the love of the man who had made her Christmas possible.

She thought of the things she'd brought from the old farmhouse. Her own belongings were scanty, her clothing not worth talking about, Jesse had said. He'd already planned to take her to the general store and find dresses and undergarments for her use. She did not argue. Whatever Jesse wanted to do was all right with her. In fact, she gloried in the knowledge that he had her best interests at heart and all of his attention was devoted to her comfort.

She felt cherished, coddled beyond belief, and luxuriated in the love he bestowed upon her without measure.

They'd slept separately last night, although he left her reluctantly late in the evening, after extinguishing the shimmering, glowing candles, only to return at daybreak, teasing her into cooking breakfast while he did the chores. She'd met him at the back door, garbed in her nightgown, aware of his gaze running the length of her body, his flaring nostrils as he bent to kiss her willing mouth, and the grasp of warm hands as he drew her against the chilly fabric of his coat.

Now they were to spend the last day of their lives as two separate individuals in this house, where tomorrow they would begin the sharing of bodies and souls. Molly yearned for the hours to pass, hesitant of what was to come, but trusting in Jesse to make the transition for her from woman to wife in a manner that would please her.

In an hour Tom had finished his chore and was on his way back home, the furniture and boxes scattered throughout the house. Molly went from one room to another, sorting out her belongings and finding homes for them among Jesse's. Her paltry collection of underclothes were side by side with his in one drawer. Her dresses hung beside his shirts on hooks against the wall, and her house shoes sat next to his newest, shiniest boots at the foot of the bed.

Her mother's china bowl and pitcher were settled in a prominent place in the bedroom, on a table which seemed to have been built for the purpose. The feather bed was made up with fresh sheets from Jesse's collection, Molly having decided she would not chance sleeping on a sheet George's body had contaminated.

Jesse laughed at her words, but agreeably helped her fluff the feather tick and turn it before she tucked the sheets around it. She found pillowcases her mother had embroidered for her hope chest and pulled them on Jesse's pillows. They'd been kept in the bottom of her trunk, for she'd been unwilling to allow George to sleep on her mother's handiwork.

She'd left the rugs behind, much to Jesse's delight, for she'd seen the smug smile of satisfaction he wore as she'd kicked them into a corner, as though she dismissed the final touches of her past with a flourish.

"Do you want to go to town?" he asked her, watching as she surveyed the kitchen. Everything was as clean as soap and water could make it, and they'd eaten a tasty meal of soup and corn bread. Now he seemed to feel the need to take her out in public and she could not deny him this gesture of defiance in the face of the town.

"All right," she said, even as her heart stuttered at the thought of what might greet them. She freshened up her hair, careful to appear the part of a sedate woman, but Jesse only smiled as she buttoned her dress to the collar and tugged her sleeves to cover her wrists.

"You're laughing at me," she said accusingly, only to receive a quick denial.

"Never," he told her. "I'm enjoying you, and that's a big difference, sweetheart."

The trip went quickly, and indeed, Molly wished for a bit less speed on the part of the horses. He went first to the livery stable, hailing the owner from the depths of the large barn and spoke at length with him in a quiet tone as though they shared a secret. Disappearing into the dark cavern of the barn, the two men laughed together in a conspiracy that baffled Molly, but in moments had reappeared, pulling a shiny new sleigh behind them.

"What do you think of that?" Jesse asked her, his smile restrained but proud.

"It's lovely," she said, taken aback by the implication of the gesture.

"It's my wedding gift to you. Sort of Christmas present and wedding combined, I think. Come on over here and try it out."

Lifting her from the wagon, he led her to the red-and-black enameled vehicle and placed her on the cushioned seat, lifting a lap robe from beside her and shaking it open to spread over her lap. "Will you be warm enough?"

"I think this will work better if we have a team of horses harnessed in place," she said soberly. "And yes, I'll be warm enough."

"That's easily fixed, ma'am," the livery owner said with a wide grin. "Congratulations to the both of you. I hear there's gonna be a wedding tomorrow. Am I invited?"

"Do you want to be?" Molly asked with an uptilted chin and an unbelieving smile.

"You'd better believe it, ma'am," the giant said. "Wouldn't miss this for the world. Mr. Stormwalker here is one of my favorite people in the world."

And wasn't that an enlightening statement, Molly thought. Perhaps Jesse had no idea of the loyalty he'd earned from the menfolk hereabouts.

In a few minutes the horses were harnessed to the sleigh and they headed into town proper, drawing up before the general store with a flourish.

Their welcome was not as warm as she'd have liked,

but then she hadn't really expected much better. A few of the ladies came out the door before she was lifted from the sleigh and made their disdain known by sniffs and uplifted noses before they made their dignified departures.

Inside the store they were greeted cordially by Mr. Sheldon. "I heard there's to be a wedding," he said jovially, almost echoing the livery owner's words.

"Where'd you hear that?" Jesse asked.

"It's the talk of the town," Mr. Sheldon said pompously. "The sheriff told it all over after he came out to the Thompson place the other morning. Folks are kinda divided about it, Stormwalker, but then I suspect you knew that would be the case."

"I don't give a damn who likes it or not," Jesse said harshly, and Molly shot him a surprised glance. He was not given to cursing and only the knowledge that he felt protective of her made his words palatable.

"Well, there's some folks planning on coming by the church," Mr. Sheldon said. He leaned over the counter. "Now, what can I do for you folks?"

It seemed he could do a great deal, and inside an hour he had decked out Molly in a collection of clothing such as she'd never expected to own. An assortment of soft, sheer garments to be worn beneath her dresses were stacked before her, and she felt the urge to cover them with a piece of brown paper wrapping to conceal them from the masculine eyes who seemed to watch her every move.

Four dresses had been chosen from the folded offerings on the shelf, one of them chosen for the wedding, and only her adamant refusal had swayed Jesse from adding to the stack. He'd found a warm cape for her and a bonnet with a wide brim to keep her from the elements.

Shoes in her size had fortunately been hiding in a box beneath the counter and she'd blushed as Jesse slid her feet into them and stood back to cast a measuring eye on them before he gave his approval.

Molly fidgeted, clasped her fingers before her waist and finally uttered the words that brought a halt to the proceedings. "That's enough, Jesse. I won't take another thing." Her mouth took on a mutinous pout and he examined it for a moment before graciously nodding his agreement.

"If you say so." Turning to Mr. Sheldon, he placed a dark complected hand on each of the stacks of apparel and spread his fingers especially wide over the feminine undergarments he'd chosen for his bride. It was a proprietary expression, filled with masculine arrogance, and Molly blushed anew at the unspoken gesture of possession.

"I'll just wrap this all up and write up a bill for you, Mr. Stormwalker," Mr. Sheldon said, his eyes already flashing as if they were estimating the total of Jesse's generosity.

Molly lifted a hand as a thought occurred to her. "I'd like something for the new baby," she said hesitantly, glancing into Jesse's face.

"Whatever you want," he said quickly. "A dress? Or maybe a blanket?"

"Something fancy. Something Amanda would not think necessary."

He smiled, acknowledging her woman's desire for beauty. "Get what you like."

And so she did, choosing two small dresses, and then a white shawl, the needlework so fine, the texture so dainty it might have been blended into one luxurious piece by the power of cobwebs.

"We'll need some supplies, too," Jesse said, after nodding approval of her choice. "Miss Molly will choose what she wants while I sort through some things over on the other side."

And so Miss Molly gave orders to the storekeeper as she'd never been allowed to do in the previous visits to this place, although Mr. Sheldon had been more than kind to her in the past few months. Now he viewed her with a new respect and she could not help but revel in the knowledge that her marriage would bring about a change in more than one area of her life.

Perhaps her fears would be set to rest. Maybe the townsfolk would be more accepting than she'd thought. And maybe not, she thought with a sad little sigh. It mattered little either way, she decided. Marrying Jesse was her choice, and she would not veer from the path he had laid out for them to follow.

The stack on the counter only grew as she pointed to one staple, then another, unsure of what was in the tall cabinets in Jesse's kitchen. "Don't forget lard," he murmured over her shoulder. "And I'm almost out of sugar."

"Did you find what you wanted?" she asked, looking up at him, her eyes feasting on the sharp profile, the dark skin, the hair that hung to his collar in a fall of ebony.

"Yes." His reply was brief and she stepped back as Jesse moved ahead of her to pay his bill. He showed some small item in his palm to Mr. Sheldon and she heard a murmur of approval from the man as he added an amount to the total he was figuring.

"I'll put it on your account," he told Jesse.

"I can pay cash." The words were sharp, as though he would not infringe on the white man's policy of credit where Indians were concerned. It was well known that cash on the barrelhead was the accepted method of payment in certain segments of town.

"No need. We'll settle at the end of the month."

Jesse's nod was slow, but accepting of the terms, and then he stood back as the storekeeper wrapped up the purchases they'd chosen.

The sleigh was heavily laden when they left town. The wagon would be delivered by the livery stable when the weather broke, since there was already another at the farm for their use. Bells on the harness rang as the team trotted a path against the snow that had become compacted on the road.

Tomorrow. Tomorrow, I'll be his wife. Molly sang the words in her mind, only a bit of trepidation marring her happiness. Jesse would not hurt her. She *knew* it, yet there was that lingering memory of pain, of the power of a man to bring about shame to a woman's heart and soul, and she wished that the first encounter between them might be done with and behind her.

The wedding was short, a simple exchange of vows, overseen by Tom and Amanda, the tiny baby girl a vocal addition to the ceremony. She nestled in her mother's arms and made soft noises, edging toward wakefulness. A soft cry escaped her rosebud lips, as if she must give her benediction to the event, and Molly could not help but smile. It seemed fitting.

Jesse took her hand in his then, awaiting the pastor's words of commitment, his sure, certain touch easing a golden band onto the appropriate finger of her left hand. Her eyes widened at the sight, the ring catching the sun's rays within its shimmering circle as he pressed it into place.

It was what he had chosen in the general store while she shopped, what he had shown to Mr. Sheldon at the last, and then tucked into his pocket. And, miracle of miracles, it fit as if it had been made for the slender hand that wore it now.

"I have nothing for you," she murmured, looking up with shining eyes into his dark countenance.

"Ah, but you have," he said, denying her claim, and as his meaning became known to her, she felt a flush of color rise to her face and had she but known, her expression of bewilderment gave way to one of expectation.

Several of the townspeople were there, shyly examining the couple, their congratulations seeming sincere. Jesse was aloof, Molly nervously eager to meet their approval, and it was only the strength of Jesse's hand at her waist that allowed her to smile and acknowledge the ladies who offered good wishes.

They left town with a flourish, Molly tucked into the sleigh, Jesse tall beside her, his somber face a stern warning to those who watched. He would not allow his wife to be an object of scorn, would not take well to having her given short shrift by the people of this town. And so they rode down the street in a dashing red-and-black sleigh, the bright paint gleaming in the rays of a winter sun.

The farmhouse awaited them and Jesse lifted her from the seat, ushering her into his kitchen before he tended to his vehicle and the animals. Molly went inside, drawn by the sound of the four puppies who welcomed her. She gathered them into the front of her dress, uncaring of the havoc they might wreak on the new garment, and carried them outdoors.

Frolicking in the snow, they performed as was expected of them, and with soft words of praise, she picked them up and carried them back to the big box, making them wait as she brought milk from the pantry.

"You've taken on a permanent job there," Jesse said from the doorway. "If you'd known, two months ago, what you were getting into, would you have stopped and picked them up?"

She looked indignant and sounded almost angry at his query. "Of course I would. How could anyone pass by and allow tiny creatures to die unattended?"

He allowed a bit of cynicism to surface. "A lot of folks would have ignored them. They represented a great deal of trouble, Molly. Not everyone is as kind as you."

"Or you," she whispered, looking up from the milk she poured.

He denied her words with a shake of his head. "I'm not kind."

She rose and stood before him. "You'll never convince me of that, Jesse Stormwalker. I know you, maybe better than you know yourself."

His dark eyes softened as they searched her face. "Maybe you do at that."

The day passed slowly, Jesse tending to chores almost as if it were any other day in his life, as though he'd set aside the fact that this was their wedding day. Perhaps so that she would not think he made more of it than he should. That he accepted their joining as a fact to be accomplished.

"I'll make a pen for the dogs tomorrow," he told her as they ate a late supper. "With wire over the top they'll be safe from critters, and they'll stay warm enough if I put it in the barn. I'll just turn them loose from there a couple of times a day and get them used to being outdoors."

"All right," she said, feeling a touch of sadness at his words. She would miss the moments spent with those small, round bodies tucked beneath her chin. And as if he sensed her mood, he smiled and laughed softly.

"You can visit them anytime you please, Mrs. Stormwalker. They'll still love you." His eyes narrowed as he focused on her, his mouth firmed and she caught a glimpse of dark color edging his high cheekbones. His hand clenched on the table and for a moment she cringed inwardly at the gesture. And then his fingers spread wide, reaching for her, grasping her chilled flesh within his palm.

"I think it's time for bed," he said softly, although no trace of yielding touched his stern features. He lifted her from her chair, led her to the bedroom beyond the kitchen and closed the door behind them.

She stood in the middle of the room, looking at the already familiar bits and pieces of furnishings. A quilt, from the hands of his mother…the china pitcher and bowl from hers. The nightgown he'd placed across the bed, awaiting her disrobing. And behind her, he waited, silent and watchful.

She jerked as his hands touched her shoulders, shivered as he reached in front of her to tend to the buttons on her dress, and then leaned her head back against his shoulder in a gesture of surrender she knew he would not mistake. The dress fell to the floor, the soft undergarments exposed to the light of a single candle he'd placed on the bedside table earlier. And the nightgown was left in a crumpled pile at the foot of the bed.

Across the room hung a mirror and she saw the shadowed figures in its depths, a man and woman, dark hands against pale skin, black hair falling against golden waves.

His head bent and his mouth touched the tender spot where her neck joined her shoulder, opening against the skin. With a sigh of submission, she turned in his embrace, lifting her arms to encircle his neck.

"Only because you want it to happen," he said quietly. "Not because you must."

"I know," she whispered. "I want to be your wife, Jesse."

"Then you will be," he said, his voice deepening as he scooped her into his arms and settled with her on the bed. He lay almost on top of her, leaning on one elbow, his free hand opening the line of buttons on her vest. It was spread wide in moments and his mouth found the rounding of her breast, his tongue touching the puckered crest with care.

"All right?" he asked, murmuring against her skin.

"Yes. More than all right," she whispered in return. She lifted her hands to his head, guiding him to where her flesh yearned for his caress. He obliged, his mouth opening over her, his hands careful as he cupped first one breast, then the other, as if he offered them as a gift to himself, accepting them into his keeping.

With ease, he took her clothing from her, and with a speed that amazed her, he undressed himself, only to return to her with his body already hard and firm, his manhood prominent against her belly. "All right?" he asked again.

And again she nodded, almost unable now to speak aloud. He would take her, open her body to his and claim the part of her she'd never given before. Always it had been a violation of her dignity, a taking of her pride, a painful reminder that she was helpless beneath the man who used her with cruel strength.

Now she knew the difference, she found, for Jesse only led her down the path, did not bring fear to her heart, allowing her to set the pace of her own seduction. His hands were warm, tender, his kisses coaxing, his big body careful not to hold hers too firmly in place, lest she feel trapped by his passion.

He offered her a loving so precious, so slow and thorough, she could not be other than charmed by his tenderness, taken prisoner by the chains of desire he wrapped about her slender form. She lifted to him, enclosing him within the embrace of limbs that clung to his hips, her arms clasping the strong muscles of his shoulders, her mouth gasping out words of surrender as he sought her pleasure with hands and lips and the pressure of his body against hers.

And then found the pleasure to be a gift he could offer with gladness...opening her to receive the gasping, groaning peak of ecstasy she had never known existed before this moment. He waited, watching her, and hesitated. For that short moment, she trembled in his embrace, and he drew back, his forehead pressed to hers, his breath shuddering in his lungs, and uttered the query for the final time.

"All right?" If she shook her head, he would cease, even if it took every bit of self-control the man could muster. As surely as she knew her name, she knew that Jesse would accede to her wishes. But her needs were as great as his, her heart pounding at a rate beyond measure, and she could only nod, tugging at him impatiently as he hesitated at that last moment of choice.

He eased his way into her body, even as his words penetrated her heart. "I love you." They were not spoken lightly, she knew, recognizing them as being unfamiliar to his lips. He'd only found them to be true during the last few days, and now he offered them to her as a final gift.

His manhood swelled within her, surging against the walls of her narrow passage, seeking the final moment of his own release. And then he shuddered, his great body pressing her against the feather tick, holding her fast in the embrace of a man sated and trembling with a passion fulfilled.

Holding her fast, he rolled with her, cuddling her beneath his bowed head, his mouth tender as he bent to kiss the scars she wore on her face. "A sign of courage," he said softly.

"He said—"

"What he said no longer matters," Jesse told her. "You are beautiful, Molly. Every bit of you." Placing her on her back beside him, he leaned to caress the puckered flesh on her arm and shoulder, bent to whisper words she could not understand against the ruined skin of her breast. Words in his native tongue that sounded guttural, yet expressed a tender meaning, the syllables ones she would seek the meaning of another time.

But now he lifted his head, and his eyes were fierce. "What I say is what matters, and I say you are lovely beyond measure. Never doubt that."

And in that moment, she accepted his tribute as her just due, content to believe that his love for her was true, that she could depend on his strength.

They slept then, curled beneath the quilt, enclosed in a cocoon of loving that promised to last for all time, for all the days of her life.

Epilogue

Stormwalker Ranch
Late summer 1894

"Aren't you going to wait and see first?" Molly's words were placid, as if the matter was of little importance, but her smile delighted the man who watched her.

"It doesn't matter, sweetheart. Boy or girl, that sign is gonna still involve the whole bunch of us. If I have to I'll just add the daughter thing to it."

"You're not happy with the way it looks now?" she asked, teasing him gently.

"I'll be happier when I can add a letter *S* to the last word up there."

"You want another boy, don't you?" Her chin lifted sharply. "And you said it didn't matter. You lied, Jesse Stormwalker."

"Naw," he said, carefully denying the accusation. "I can just as easily leave it as it is, if you like."

"I don't see all the fuss over a stupid sign anyway," she told him, pouting nicely as he lifted her from the chair she'd occupied for the whole long length of the morning and most of the afternoon, as though she were too weary to exert herself. And then as he held her clasped in his arms, allowing for the heavy weight of her pregnancy that kept him at a distance, she frowned, looking down distractedly.

"I think we have a little problem, Jesse." Even as she spoke, the floor was awash with an outpouring from her body that made him jump back in surprise.

"Well, you sure decided to keep things lively today, didn't you?" His grin was wide as he bent to kiss her.

"None of that," she said sharply. "That sort of thing is what got me into this fix to begin with."

"Complaining?" he asked softly, leaning to brush his mouth against her neck, directly beneath her ear, where a sensitive place coaxed his tongue to linger.

She shivered and was unsuccessful in suppressing a tender smile. "Never. You know better than that."

"Tell me that again in a couple of hours," he said gloomily. He ran a hand distractedly through his hair. "Do I have time to ride over and get Amanda?"

"You'd better have. I'm not too good at this yet."

"But you're getting there, sweet. Another couple of babies and you'll know the routine right well." His drawl was teasing but the worry she spotted in the depths of his eyes brought forth the need for comfort.

"I'll be fine, Jesse. Just ride on over and I'll get things ready for Amanda. Emily is sleeping and David is playing with the new litter of puppies. I'll have time to put some soup on for your supper."

He shot her a look of exasperation. "Forget the damn soup. Just get to bed and rest till I get back."

She nodded docilely. And then when he was gone she

became a virtual whirlwind of activity. At least as much as her awkward body would allow. And by the time he'd returned with Amanda in tow she was more than ready to retire to the big bed. The soup was begun, onions and meat simmering on the back of the stove and the vegetables were ready to add in a couple of hours.

She told him as much as Amanda led her away, her voice trailing back to where he stood. "Stubborn woman," he muttered, his heart heavy as he remembered the long hours of labor she'd endured with the last two childbirths. They'd had this out before, and he'd won the battle both times, refusing to leave her as she labored in a silence he feared.

Better that she cry out or groan or curse him for his part in this. But she instead held his gaze with her own, her hands clasped tightly in his, her face pale, her body trembling as she faced the harsh reality of bearing his child.

"Damn, I'm going to stay away from her from now on. No more of this," he muttered, watching down the lane for the doctor to make an appearance. And even as he spoke the words, he recognized the futility of his vow. He could no more keep his hands from the small woman he'd married than he could cease to breathe. She was his life, the very heart and soul of his home.

And his fear was great.

The evening stretched out into an interminable length of waiting. And then, when he'd felt hot tears of defeat overwhelm his soul, when her pain seemed to be more than she could bear, more than he could watch without cursing aloud, he sensed a change in the atmosphere within the room.

"That's it," Amanda said softly. "Once more will do it, Molly." And with her words of promise, the babe was born, squalling and howling his anger for all to hear.

"A boy?" Molly asked breathlessly, and at Amanda's affirmative smile, she cast her own beaming, radiant laughter in Jesse's direction. "Don't mention another baby for at least two years," she said fervently. "Now go put up your new sign."

Her eyes closed, and he bent to kiss her. "I love you," he whispered. "Thank you, Molly, for my son." His lips touched hers again and his voice was husky with an emotion he made no attempt to hide. "Thank you for loving me, sweetheart." He knelt beside the bed and held tightly to her, one arm across her waist, the other sliding beneath her head.

"The sign?" she asked, smothering a yawn.

"Forget the damn sign. I'll put it up one day next week. I just needed to yatter at you over something this morning. You could have had twin girls and I wouldn't have cared, except that you were safe and the babies were healthy."

Her brow lifted and she shot him a glance that made him sit up and take notice. "Twin girls? Now that might make it easier, having two at a time. We'll think about that."

"No." The single word was spoken firmly, adamantly, and he glared at her. "I heard you the first time. No more babies for at least two years."

She whispered, a soft query he bent low to hear, and as she repeated the words, his heart sang with joy. "Can we still practice?" she asked, her smile coaxing, her mouth promising pleasure beyond his sweetest dreams.

His heart was in his eyes, his desire a kindled flame she could not mistake, and his words confirmed his love.

"Practice? You betcha, sweetheart. You betcha."

* * * * *

Available from Harlequin Historicals and
CAROL FINCH

Call of the White Wolf #592
Bounty Hunter's Bride #635
Oklahoma Bride #686
Texas Bride #711
One Starry Christmas #723
"Home for Christmas"

Other works include:

Silhouette Special Edition

Not Just Another Cowboy #1242
Soul Mates #1320

Harlequin Duets

Fit To Be Tied #36
A Regular Joe #45
Mr. Predictable #62
The Family Feud #72
Lonesome Ryder? #81
Restaurant Romeo #81
Fit to be Frisked #105
Mr. Cool Under Fire #105

*Bachelors of Hoot's Roost

Please address questions and book requests to:
Harlequin Reader Service
U.S.: 3010 Walden Ave., P.O. Box 1325, Buffalo, NY 14269
Canadian: P.O. Box 609, Fort Erie, Ont. L2A 5X3

HOME FOR CHRISTMAS

Carol Finch

This book is dedicated to my husband, Ed,
and our children—Kurt, Shawna, Jill, Jon, Christie
and Jeff. And to our grandchildren, Brooklynn, Kennedy,
Blake and Livia. Hugs and kisses!

Prologue

Oklahoma Territory
December 1889

Seth Gresham pulled up the collar of his sheepskin coat to ward off the icy chill, then nudged his horse into a faster clip. Despite the Blue Norther that had come sweeping across the prairie a deep sense of gratification warmed him inwardly. He was riding across *his* land, the one place that he could call home after thirty-two years of wanderlust. He had made the wild Land Run in April—along with thousands of other hopeful settlers—to claim his own homestead. His days as a bounty hunter, who dealt with the worst scoundrels who preyed on society, were behind him. He was a man of property and the folks in this new territory didn't treat him like an outcast. Seth had acquired a little respect and had things going his way—for once.

So why had he been feeling restless and twitchy lately? Damn if he knew. But he'd become oddly discontented and the walls of his cabin had been closing in on him. Which was why he'd saddled his horse, braved the cold and told himself that he should check on his closest neighbor, Mitch Ramsey, who had staked the quarter section that joined him on the east.

Dismounting, Seth stared at the log cabin he had helped Mitch construct. It was only a third the size of Seth's new home, but Mitch claimed it would suit him dandy fine. In exchange for helping with the building project, Mitch had shared his knowledge of livestock to ensure Seth's cattle herd thrived.

Seth smiled wryly as he ambled toward the inviting glow of the lantern light that flickered in the window. He had to admit that sometimes he came to visit Mitch under the pretense of asking for advice he didn't really need. He just got lonesome for the sound of someone's voice. Mitch Ramsey was a natural-born storyteller that Seth counted as friend, father figure and mentor.

After using the signal of knocking three times on the door, he heard a wheezing sputter and cough. Seth frowned worriedly as he stepped inside, then closed the door quickly to block off the cold draft. When he heard a loud moan he stared toward the bedroom.

"Mitch? You okay in there?" he called out.

"Not very okay." Mitch's voice trailed off into another coughing spasm.

Alarmed, Seth walked into the room and stared down at his bedridden friend, who sported several days' growth of whiskers. His gray hair was standing on end. His face was flushed and perspiration popped out on his wrinkled forehead. Hiram, the older man's devoted hound, lifted his broad head and whined in sympathy for his ailing master.

"Came all the way from Mizzou," Mitch wheezed, then shivered under the pile of quilts. "Worked my fingers to the bone to make a new start in this territory. Ain't no justice in this world if you have to fit me for a pine box before my first Christmas here."

Seth pulled up a chair then reached out to brush his hand over Mitch's clammy forehead. "How long have you been down? And when's the last time you ate?"

"Been in bed three days," Mitch said, then coughed. "Don't feel like eatin'."

Faced with the prospect of losing the first good friend he'd ever made, Seth quickly rose and took charge. "I'll fix you something to eat, then I'll chop firewood."

"No need for that," Mitch choked out. "You already chopped enough wood to last me all winter...if I make it that long."

Seth's brows jackknifed in alarm. Ordinarily Mitch was teeming with enthusiastic optimism and he had the stamina of a man half his age. At fifty-five Mitch had been the picture of good health. And then suddenly, here he was, making mental arrangements for his journey into the hereafter.

"You'll be fine when we get some warm food down your gullet," Seth said encouragingly.

"Easy for you to say since you don't have one foot in the grave," Mitch contradicted, then heaved a dismal sigh as he glanced down at his faithful, flop-eared hound. "I'm bequeathing Hiram to you."

"Mitch—" Seth tried to object but Mitch waved him off with a feeble flick of his wrist.

"I can rest easy knowing Hiram will be well tended." He sighed audibly as he stared up at the ceiling. "I wish I had the chance to make amends with my daughter before I fly off to the Pearly Gates. We parted on a sour note and I don't feel right about it. That'll probably haunt me through eternity."

Now there was a subject that sorely aggravated Seth. Miss Olivia La-Di-Da Ramsey had yet to descend from her tufted throne to pay her father a visit. If Seth had parents, he'd damn sure make a point to see them occasionally. But since he didn't, he regarded Mitch as the father he never had. *He* came by regularly to check on Mitch. *Olivia* couldn't be bothered.

"If I was granted one wish for Christmas, it'd be to see my pretty little girl one last time."

Seth tried to visualize the female version of Mitch and wondered if *pretty* was the proper adjective to describe the chit. He sincerely doubted it.

"I need to tell Livie how much she means to me," Mitch croaked. "Is that asking so much?"

"No, it isn't. I'd ride off to fetch her myself, but I don't want to leave you alone."

Mitch's gray head rolled back and forth on his lumpy pillow. His lashes fluttered down momentarily then soulful hazel eyes zeroed in on Seth. "If I asked you to bring her to me, would you do it?"

"Of course, but I don't see how I can be two places at once."

"I can hold out until you get back," Mitch said, then coughed hoarsely. "It'd be a comfort knowing you are escorting her to me, a comfort knowing she'll be in good hands. I'd have something to look forward to, something to inspire me to get back on my feet."

Seth's mind buzzed with possible arrangements. He could ask Widow Hadley to come by to check on Mitch. She lived three miles south with her two sons, and Seth had noticed the spark of interest she showed when Mitch was around. Although Seth was uneasy about leaving his homestead and livestock unattended, he supposed he could pay the Hadley boys to stop by his place on their way into town.

"I'll ride out first thing in the morning," Seth promised as he spun on his boot heels. "But I'm not leaving until I've cooked up something to tide you over." When Mitch opened his mouth to protest Seth flashed him his trademark stare that had stopped men in their tracks when they tried to cross him. "Do not argue with me, old man, you won't win."

A faint smile curved the corners of Mitch's mouth upward. "Damn, boy, that look of yours could freeze water. Where'd you learn to do that?"

"In places you don't want to know about. But if I'm going to do this favor for you, then you're going to eat whether you're hungry or not."

Seth walked off, serenaded by another round of wheezing coughs and groans. He made a mental note to stop by the physician's office on his way through Guthrie to have Doc Potter make a house call. If Seth was going to have to endure the company of Mitch's snooty, ungrateful daughter then the man had damn well better be alive and kicking when he got back!

Chapter One

Olivia Ramsey glanced up from taking an order at Williams Café when a tall, rugged-looking stranger entered. Raven-black hair, which was sorely in need of trimming, and an unshaven jaw gave the man a formidable appearance. His hat sat low on his forehead and his piercing green eyes landed squarely on her. Olivia felt her defenses leap to full alert when the man scrutinized her with blatant disapproval. Another jolt pelted her when the powerfully built stranger made a beeline toward her. She had the oddest sensation that this dangerous predator had her in his sights and he'd like to do her bodily harm. Why? She couldn't imagine. She'd never seen this hard-bitten hombre before in her life.

If Olivia hadn't sworn off men three months earlier she might have been intimidated by the swarthy-looking man, who stood six foot two and weighed a solid two-hundred-and-some-odd pounds. But because of her mortifying experience with the man she had loved since adolescence, Olivia gave no ground and refused to kowtow to any man—not even one whose foreboding presence caused a hush to descend over the patrons at the crowded restaurant.

If this stranger thought she would quail before his menacing glare, he'd come to the wrong place—and to the wrong woman. Olivia jutted out her chin and stared into those icy green eyes that rivaled the temperatures outside. "Take a seat, sir," she said authoritatively. "I'll be around to take your order when I finish with these gentlemen. It's first come, first serve around here."

She expected her clipped tone to be obeyed immediately. Instead, the stranger quirked a dark brow, as if amused by her attempt to put him in his place. She had the unmistakable feeling that he was the kind of man who didn't have a place and wouldn't stay in it, even under penalty of death. For some reason he seemed unswervingly determined to have her undivided attention.

"Olivia Ramsey, you're coming with me."

Olivia blinked, startled. The man's decree sounded as if he was placing her under arrest. She glanced down to see if there was a silver star pinned to his massive chest. If there was, it was concealed by his heavy sheepskin coat.

"It's not against the law to take customers' orders," she scoffed. She hitched her thumb toward the empty table in the corner. "*Go...sit...down or get...out.* I don't care which."

"I'm taking you to Oklahoma Territory to see your ailing father and we're leaving now," Seth decreed as his gaze locked with those extraordinary—but defiant—blue eyes that matched him stare for unblinking stare.

For a man who had learned to be prepared for anything during a decade of tracking wily criminals, he had to admit that he had not been prepared for the startling impact this snippy female had on him. Sure, Mitch had raved incessantly about his attractive daughter, but Seth had chalked it up to fatherly pride and affection. This shapely female—with her curly mane of fiery golden hair that was piled on her head and porcelain skin so creamy and smooth that it begged to be caressed—made everything male in him respond.

Seth did not appreciate his vivid physical reaction to this ungrateful, disrespectful—he could go on and on—female who had defied her father's wishes and refused to join him on the one-hundred-sixty acres he'd staked in the Land Run. No doubt, Miss Couldn't Be Bothered felt it was her mission to remain behind in Missouri and break as many hearts as possible, just for the sport of it.

While Seth stood there, disliking Olivia for what she *was*—and liking her too damn much because of the incredible way she *looked*—she tossed her head and stared down her pert nose at him. "Excuse *you*, you are in my way," she said loftily.

Although she tapped her foot and fisted her hands on her curvaceous hips—indicating that she had lost patience with him—Seth didn't budge from the spot. He had come for Olivia and he was not returning home empty-handed.

Olivia glanced toward the kitchen door. "Amos! This man is bothering me. Kindly fetch the shotgun."

The prickly female didn't waste time with half measures, Seth noted. She went straight to last resorts. He'd be sure to remember that during future dealings with her.

"Nice try," he said as he clamped his hand around her forearm to escort her out the door. "Like it or not, you're coming with me and we're burning daylight."

Olivia jerked her arm from his grasp and glared pitchforks at him. "Touch me again and you'll lose the use of that hand. Amos!"

Seth's attention shifted to the rail-thin proprietor who appeared at the kitchen door, toting a sawed-off shotgun that was guaranteed to scatter enough buckshot to maim half his customers.

"You aren't welcome here, mister," Amos snapped. "If Olivia don't want ya here then git out."

Another hopeless admirer, no doubt, Seth presumed as he watched the scrawny man brace himself, prepared to come to Olivia's defense. Seth suspected she was accustomed to using the power of sex appeal to control men. No telling how many men this woman kept at her beck and call. But for sure and certain, *he* wasn't going to be influenced, just because she happened to be the most strikingly attractive woman he'd ever clapped eyes on.

When Olivia smiled triumphantly he gave her the full benefit of the evil eye. "There's more than one way to skin a cat," he muttered as he watched several male customers reach for their pistols.

"The only cat in danger of getting skinned appears to be you," she taunted.

Seth gnashed his teeth and stared her down. Damn, but he'd like to wipe that gloating smile off her lips—or kiss it off. The impulsive thought startled him and he glared even more fiercely at her. "Your ailing father *needs* you."

"My father hasn't been sick a day in his life," she countered. "If anything, this is some ploy to meddle in my life again. Now skedaddle before Amos fills you full of buckshot."

It went against Seth's grain to retreat without the prissy Olivia in tow. But he didn't want to cause a disturbance that would land him in jail and delay his departure.

His male pride smarting, and annoyance spurting like a geyser, he spun on his boot heels and stalked off. He might have to take a fallback position for now, but Olivia Almighty Ramsey hadn't seen the last of him—and that was a promise!

Seth waited until he was outside before reaching into his pocket to check his timepiece—for fear one of Olivia's besotted, trigger-happy admirers might mistakenly think he was going for one of the pistols that hung on his hips. Six-thirty, he mused. Well, when her royal highness got off duty he would be waiting to escort her to her father. Then he'd see how bold and sassy she was when she didn't have a café full of men to back her up.

Olivia inhaled a steadying breath when the ominous stranger exited. What was there about that domineering man that instantly rubbed her the wrong way? she wondered as she took a customer's order. She contemplated that question for a few minutes, then decided it was her unwanted attraction to the rough-edged man that irritated her most. She also hated to admit that she envied his take-charge attitude.

Olivia had no idea how much her father had paid his hireling to deliver her to Oklahoma, but she doubted a man like that did anyone favors—for free. The man, however, appeared to take his duty very seriously. She had to admire him for that, in a frustrated sort of way.

What a pity that Jacob Riley, the man she'd dreamed of marrying, didn't possess that kind of unfaltering devotion.

Thoughts of Jacob's cruel betrayal sent anger and shame ripping through her. *You can't trust him, and you're a fool to try*. Her father's words rang sharply in her ears, as they had so often the past few months. *Jacob isn't good enough for you, and the sooner you figure out that he has no substance or scruples the better off you'll be*.

The truth had wounded deeply and Olivia had felt like a fool of the highest order. Turned out that Jacob was only interested in her physical appearance and had no intention of marrying someone beneath his lofty social station. Discovering that there was nothing endearing about her character and personality had come as a crushing blow to her self-esteem. After Jacob's betrayal she had sworn never to give her heart to a man again. She'd learned her lesson about men the hard way. She was never going to care so much for a man that he had the ability to hurt her. Love, she had decided, was a silly romantic notion and she wasn't going to stumble into that bottomless pit again.

Her gaze drifted to the door, visualizing the brawny stranger who'd come and gone. No one was going to drag her off to see her father until she was good and ready. And she wasn't good and ready yet. Mitch had proved to be right about Jacob Riley, and Olivia couldn't bear the mortification of hearing him say, "I toldja so. You should have listened and made the Run with me instead of staying behind."

Mitch's blunt remarks had ignited her temper. They had argued long and loudly. She'd become disrespectful and her father had become curt and demanding. They had parted on an extremely sour note eight months ago.

Olivia intended to reconcile with her father and apologize, but she wasn't ready to do so yet. Not until she'd regained her dignity and the thought of being jilted didn't hurt quite so much.

And that business about being sick? Olivia smirked at the flimsy excuse. Mitch Ramsey was a bundle of energy in constant motion. Always had been. She didn't think he was ill, just determined to see her uprooted. Although she wouldn't mind making a fresh start in the new territory, she didn't want the townspeople thinking she was leaving because Jacob had discarded her. That would feel like a demoralizing retreat, and she wouldn't give that miserable, two-timing scoundrel the satisfaction!

A mischievous smile pursed her lips as she delivered a tray of food to her waiting customers. Maybe she would enlist the services of her father's formidable hireling and sic *him* on *Jacob*. She'd feel ten times better if Jacob was as bruised and battered on the outside as she felt on the inside. That would definitely go a long way in healing her injured pride.

Too bad Olivia had been raised not to be that spiteful and vindictive. She could have paid Jacob back—in spades.

Seth had made good use of his time by sneaking into the bedroom window of Olivia's cottage that sat on the edge of town. He'd felt uncomfortable about rummaging through her wardrobe to cram gowns and undergarments into a carpetbag, but he figured he'd probably have to hold her at gunpoint to get *her* to do it. But no matter what, Olivia was making this trip.

Clearly, she wasn't the least bit concerned about Mitch's ailing condition. She was too self-absorbed with her own beauty to show Mitch the slightest concern. But she damn well better *act* concerned when they arrived at Mitch's cabin, Seth thought bitterly. He'd twist her arm a dozen different ways, if necessary, to make certain that this uncaring brat of a daughter appeared to care that her father might not survive the winter.

Seth carried the carpetbag out the back door in the cover of darkness and tied it to the spare mount he'd brought with him. Reversing direction, he strode inside to jot a short note that would quell the concern of Olivia's many admirers.

The missive read, *Decided to visit my father. Olivia.*

Seth propped the note against the lantern on the dining room table then glanced impatiently out the window. With his luck an entourage of doting suitors would escort Olivia home and he'd have to fight them off with a stick.

To his surprise, he saw Olivia ambling—alone—beneath the last lamppost on the edge of town. He smiled in supreme satisfaction, pleased that his male counterparts had enough sense to avoid this shapely female like the plague.

"It must singe your haughty pride that you can't convince even one man to escort you home in the dark." Seth smirked as he monitored Olivia's approach. "There *is* a modicum of justice in the world, after all."

When Seth heard footfalls on the porch he positioned himself beside the door—an effective tactic he'd employed a dozen times while apprehending outlaws. Nothing better than the element of surprise to catch a thief—or a mouthy witch who was so full of herself that she was about to burst.

When the door creaked open, Seth sprang into action. To squelch her resistance he nuzzled the barrel of his pistol between her ribs, clamped his hand over her mouth and pulled her full length against him so she couldn't break and run.

The unwanted jolt of attraction pelted him when he felt her lush contours molded familiarly to his. The scent of jasmine clogged his senses. The tantalizing distraction gave Olivia the chance to gouge him in the midsection and bite a chunk out of his hand.

"Ouch, damn it!" Seth yowled as he struggled to restrain the woman who had attacked like a rabid wolf and defied the pistol rammed against her ribs. "Hold still or I'll shoot you!"

"No, you won't," she snarled as she squirmed for release. "My father won't pay you if you bring me back dead."

That much was true, Seth mused as he hooked his arm around her waist and lifted her off the floor. If Mitch were clinging to life by a slender thread, hanging on to the hope that he'd be reunited with his daughter, grief and disappointment *would* kill him.

When Olivia grabbed a breath and screamed bloody murder, Seth covered her mouth with his hand. "Stop doing that or I'll lose what's left of my temper," he growled.

"It's *my* temper you'd best worry about," Olivia growled back. "Now I'm really good and mad! I'll have you—"

Silence at last! Seth thought as he stuffed his kerchief in her mouth, then hastily tied it in place with a strip of leather. Despite her muffled protests—and she had plenty of them—he tossed her over his shoulder and headed for the door. He didn't even flinch while she pounded her fists against his spine. Olivia's vicious behavior was proof enough that beneath the enchanting face and ripe womanly body beat the heart of a full-fledged hellion.

Seth was pretty sure Olivia was cursing him to the farthest reaches of hell as he tossed her onto the horse. Too bad she didn't know that he'd been to hell and back more times than he cared to count. No doubt, she would have been delighted to learn that he'd brushed shoulders with the eternally damned on occasions too numerous to mention.

He tied her feet to the stirrups and her hands to the pommel then he mounted up. Serenaded by her muffled tirade Seth trotted west. He waited an hour for Olivia to cool down before he leaned over to remove her gag.

"I will have you arrested for assault and kidnapping," she sputtered furiously. "How dare you abduct me!"

Roosting sparrows squawked and scattered from the surrounding trees when her voice hit a shrill pitch. Seth winced at the offensive sound emitted by this ill-tempered female.

"Pipe down. If you weren't such an ungrateful, inconsiderate brat of a daughter I wouldn't have the misfortune of escorting you to your father. And if my friend dies before we arrive, I'm likely to be so aggrieved that I'll take it out on *you*." He shot her a sinister glare for effect. "Just so you know in advance, I've no intention of setting a leisurely pace to accommodate you. So make the best of it and keep the complaining to a minimum. If there is one thing I despise it's a whining female."

There was enough moonlight beaming down on her golden head for Seth to view the murderous glower aimed at him. "And just so *you* know, if you lay another hand on me during this trip I will bite it off, one finger at a time. I will *not* be the fringe benefits of my father's ruthless hireling!"

Seth snorted at the very thought of cozying up to this fire-breathing dragon lady. "I'll make *you* a promise—"

"A man making a promise he says he'll keep?" she cut in sardonically. "That would be worth its weight in manure."

"Be that as it may, you have my word that the very last thing on my mind is manhandling you for pleasure or spite. Let's just make the best of this trip, shall we?"

"No, we shall not," she muttered shrewishly. "I'm freezing to death. The very *least* you could do is offer me your sheepskin coat."

Determined to be gallant—though why he wanted to prove to this little snip that he could be, if he felt like it, he didn't know—Seth doffed his warm coat and draped it over her shoulders. "There. Happy now?" he asked snidely.

"Not even close." She scowled as she shrugged off the jacket that was so thick with his appealing male scent that it nearly suffocated her. "Never mind. It smells like you. That's almost as bad as having the likes of you touch me." She shot him another scathing glare. "And where, may I ask, did my father dig you up? He used to keep company with a better class of people."

He stared at her for a long moment while he donned his coat. "Are you always this mean and nasty, Olivia?"

"You may call me *Miss Ramsey*," she insisted aloofly. "And the answer to your question is no. I'm usually much worse. You just caught me on one of my good days."

Olivia felt a strange flutter in her chest when the man broke into a crooked grin. She hadn't intended to amuse him with her snippy retort, but she obviously had. She'd have to try harder to annoy him so he'd turn her loose.

"You must be adopted," he said, then flicked her a wry glance. "You aren't anything like your father. A pity that."

"You are right about that," she mumbled as humiliating torment assailed her. "He was right and I had to find it out for myself."

His thick brows furrowed questioningly. "Beg pardon?"

"Nothing," she said dismissively. She wasn't going to wallow in hurt and rejection again today.

Olivia shivered from the evening chill and her teeth chattered, reminding her that there was no place colder than the back of a horse when the winter wind swirled around you. To her surprise, she saw her abductor rifle through his saddlebag, and then drape a quilt over her shoulders.

"You might as well tell me your name so I won't have to bother sifting through wanted posters when I have the sheriff swear out a warrant for your arrest," she sniped.

"Seth Gresham," he said, seemingly unruffled by her threat. He picked up the pace, causing her to bobble uncomfortably in the saddle. "Your father is a good friend who staked a homestead next to mine."

"So you make extra money by kidnapping all your friends' offspring and toting them to the new territory for Christmas?" she asked caustically.

"No, I only have one friend and I'm not getting paid for this." He stared solemnly at her. "And if worse comes to worst and Mitch doesn't make it, I'll buy the land you inherit so we won't have to be neighbors."

That pretty much indicated what he thought of her. Not that she cared. Cold, weary and frustrated, Olivia slumped forward to rest as best she could atop the horse. No doubt, Seth intended to show no compassion during this journey and didn't plan to stop for the night. She might as well grab forty winks while she could.

Chapter Two

Despite Olivia's prediction, Seth called a halt at midnight. He slept fitfully on the bedroll that he'd placed as far from Olivia as he could get—and still make certain she didn't steal off into the darkness. Weary, Seth stared into the distance, wishing he could sprout wings and fly home. Of course, all this persnickety witch needed was a broom, he mused as he shot Olivia a disgruntled glance.

Seth didn't want to be on the rugged cross-country trail again, not after endless years of living in the wilderness. He didn't want to be with this woman, either. But out of the kindness of his heart, and his friendship with Mitch, he was *stuck* with Olivia for the duration of the journey.

And damn it, every time he glanced in Olivia's general direction, his gaze kept lingering on her strikingly attractive profile. It just wasn't fair that such a mean-spirited, self-centered shrew should be so incredibly alluring, he thought resentfully.

Olivia the Terrible awakened the next morning complaining—and she kept it up until long after they'd eaten their meager lunch of trail rations. She groused that the pemmican was too dry, the temperature too cold and the horse's gait so rough that it jarred her teeth. She called him every name in the book—and added several off-color adjectives that he doubted most respectable females would dare to voice. He swore she was griping just to antagonize him.

It dawned on Seth around three o'clock that afternoon that he had expected the woman to use her pretentious charm to manipulate him into reversing direction or releasing her. Her hostility just didn't seem to fit his first impression of her. But what the hell did he know about women? Nothing, that's what. Sure he'd dealt with flirtatious prostitutes, had been snubbed by uppity socialites and he had matched wits with a few cunning female outlaws in his time, but he'd already spent more consecutive hours with this termagant than any woman alive.

"Don't talk much, do you, Mr. Gresham?" she commented as they splashed across a narrow creek.

"Who could get a word in edgewise while you're whining and complaining?"

She shrugged him off, as if the barb had no effect on her. "It has occurred to me that I should change tack."

"And you're giving me fair warning?" he said, and snorted. "Mighty sporting of you, Miz Ramsey."

Here it comes, he predicted. She'd bat those long, thick lashes at him, flash a few enchanting smiles and he was supposed to melt into mush. Not damn likely. She couldn't pull that off after needling him incessantly about the discomfort of riding horseback for hours on end and surviving on tasteless trail rations.

So naturally, he was caught completely off guard when she twisted sideways in the saddle, looked him straight in the eye and said, "Could you please explain to me why men are such worthless, self-serving bastards?"

Seth's jaw sagged, then he snapped his mouth shut and stared her down. "You mean me personally, I presume." Obviously she wasn't changing tack at all, just planning to insult and antagonize him from a different direction.

"Is it even possible for men to feel with their hearts instead of their...? Well, you get my drift."

Seth gaped at her, having no idea whatsoever where she was going with this line of questioning. He was so befuddled that all he could think to say was, "Huh?"

She tossed him an exasperated glance. "What is it that men actually care about? Loyalty to one woman obviously isn't on the list. Apparently men perceive women as serving only one purpose. Well, I'm tired of being reduced to a sexual object and treated as if my feelings count for nothing."

Having never participated in this sort of conversation with a woman, he wasn't sure what to say without setting her off again. "I think I liked it better when you were haranguing me," Seth muttered.

"Well, I'm tired of that game. I want to play another one to while away these monotonous hours in the saddle."

"Twenty questions?" he said, then snorted. "No thanks. I'd rather talk to my horse. He's not as snippy as you are. And he's nowhere near as insulting, either."

"Look, Mr. Gresham—"

"Seth," he corrected.

"Fine, *Seth*, I'm only asking you to help me understand what makes the male of the species tick."

"We do not *tick*. We just get along the best we can and play the hand we're dealt." He shifted awkwardly on the saddle when she kept staring at him. "I don't know what you want from me. I'm only doing Mitch a favor because I care about him. He didn't say a thing about my having to explain why men are the way they are."

Seth sighed in relief when she let the matter drop. But a mile later she said, "I just don't get it."

He frowned, bemused, when Olivia slumped in the saddle. She looked forlorn and frustrated and he had no idea why.

"Look, why don't you just tell me, flat out, what's bothering you and I'll do what I can to fix it. Just trim the fat, Miz Ramsey, and give me the boiled-down version."

Something peculiar twisted in his chest when those beguiling sky-blue eyes, tormented by some hidden pain, focused on him and her lush bottom lip trembled noticeably.

"Is it me? Am I so unworthy and unlovable?"

It was on the tip of his tongue to reply with a heartfelt *yes*, but it suddenly occurred to him that she might have gotten her heart broken. That explained the bitterness and hostility, the need to strike out and hurt, as she had been hurt. Maybe she was projecting this shrewish persona to keep folks—men in particular—at arm's length. Maybe she wasn't as bad as he'd first thought. The least he could do was give her the benefit of the doubt, he decided.

"Does this bastard who wronged you have a name?" Seth asked with sudden insight.

The shiny tears that welled up in her eyes really got to him, especially when her posture slouched in defeat. He felt helpless for the first time because he had no experience consoling a woman who had been jilted or betrayed—he didn't know which.

She blinked back the tears and tilted her chin to a challenging angle. "I'm sure Papa told you all about it, you being his best friend and all. Frankly, I'm surprised you haven't thrown my humiliation in my face yet."

"I have no idea what the hell you're talking about," he replied. "You should know your own father well enough to know that he delights in regaling folks with tales of his experiences, but he's not much for gossip. All I know is that you and Mitch had some sort of falling out and you haven't written to him in three months. He's been in contact with a few of his friends to keep tabs on you."

His gaze instinctively dropped to the full swells of her breasts when she inhaled a deep breath and let it out slowly. Seth forced his attention back to the troubled expression on her exquisite face.

"Papa didn't tell you that I'd been in love with Jacob Riley since I was old enough to tell the difference between men and women? He didn't tell you that he warned me that I was pinning my hopes on a foolish dream of marrying the most attractive, wealthiest bachelor in the county? That I was the last to know that he only saw me as a temporary conquest?"

When Seth shook his dark head, Olivia inwardly groaned in humiliation. He honestly *hadn't* known what had caused the rift between her and Mitch and had provoked her stubborn refusal to leave Missouri to make the Land Run in the new territory? Well, blast it. Nothing like babbling your most mortifying secrets to a virtual stranger, she thought in frustration.

Now that she'd exposed her idealistic foolishness to her traveling companion, she might as well admit to it and then steer the conversation to something else. "My father was right about Jacob," she said regretfully. "I was walking on air when he turned his attention to me. Like an idiot, I fell for his silver-tongued promises and pretentious charm. I thought my long-held dream of becoming his wife had finally come true." Olivia steeled herself against the tortuous emotions roiling inside her and continued. "I returned to the boutique where I was working to find my best friend and Jacob closeted in one of the fittings rooms. They were…"

Her voice faltered as the betraying image exploded in her mind. She had kept Jacob at arm's length, wanting their first romantic encounter to be their wedding night. But seeing Jacob with Angela Beckham assured Olivia that she had only been a prospective conquest and that the man of her dreams had turned elsewhere when she refused to succumb to him. Olivia wondered if she would ever forget how it hurt to discover that the man who held her heart had so little loyalty and affection for her that he would seduce her friend—who had turned out to be no friend at all. Shocked, resentful and feeling horribly insecure, Olivia had quit her job of designing and sewing fashionable gowns because she couldn't face Angela on a daily basis.

"How am I supposed to trust again when the two people I thought were my friends betrayed me?" she asked, deflated.

"I don't know the answer to that tough question, but I can tell you from firsthand experience that life isn't always fair. Furthermore, blind trust can get you killed —or hurt badly, inside and out." He smiled sympathetically. "So this Jacob character was the impossible challenge you'd been chasing. When you finally had him within your grasp, you discovered he was a heartless womanizer and your friend was as infatuated with him as you were."

Olivia noted that Seth had a unique way of filtering through information and stripping it down to the bare bones. And he was probably right on target. Jacob had been a long-held challenge for her. She had made a crusade of trying to attain the unattainable. In the end he had shattered her fantasy and she'd lost a friend and her rewarding job in the process.

"Mind if I offer some free advice?" Seth asked a few moments later.

"Sure, why not?" A faint smile pursed her lips as she added teasingly, "I will, of course, take it at face value."

When he chuckled, a warm tingling sensation trickled down her spine. Seth had an engaging laugh. Deep, resonant, good-natured, appealing.

"You might not be the shrew I mistook you for," he said, "but if you ever find yourself unemployed you can sell sass by the barrel."

"It's my newly acquired protective armor," she explained with a careless shrug. "Male repellant. I have no more use for men, and I've vowed never to become susceptible to that kind of pain again. Once was plenty, thank you very much."

"Which brings me around to my bit of advice," he interjected. "I've met several Jacobs during my travels. They seem to think their wealth affords them all sorts of privileges. Most of the Jacobs of the world are shallow and self-indulgent. There isn't room for concern for anyone else." He tossed her an apologetic glance. "I hate to annoy you by agreeing with Mitch, but you're better off without the man."

"It's embarrassing to have to admit to being so blind and stupid," she muttered. "I fell in love with the illusion I conjured up and I refused to listen to Papa."

"Don't be so hard on yourself." Seth veered south to follow another of the endless creeks that meandered through the hilly terrain. "While I tracked murderers, shysters and thieves for bounty—" He cut her a quick glance, expecting to see the usual expression of distaste that he encountered with so-called decent folks. To his surprise, Olivia simply waited for him to continue. "I can't tell you how many times I heard people comment that they had no idea the person they *thought* they knew was capable of committing such dastardly crimes. Seems that no one really knows other folks as well as they think they do."

"My father said something to that effect, and I told him that he had no clue what he was talking about," Olivia confided. "I even went so far as to prophesy that I'd have Jacob's ring on my finger by Christmas, thereby proving Papa was about as wrong as he could possibly get."

Seth nodded in understanding. "So that's why you were reluctant to pay your father a visit or correspond with him."

"He'll never let me live it down," she murmured. "I more or less told him to go satisfy his sense of adventure by making the Land Run and leave me to live my own life. We didn't part company on the best of terms last April and I've been too ashamed to write and tell him what happened."

Seth smiled to himself. He could easily visualize this feisty female squaring off against her father—even if she was only twenty years old and probably thought she was wise in the ways of the world. Seth couldn't fault her for that because he'd thought he was pretty damn smart at age twenty. At thirty-two, he knew better. He felt decades older than Olivia, but he reckoned that getting your heart trampled could hurt as much as having a desperado plug you with a bullet. Some scars just weren't as visible, but the pain was long-lived.

"Have you ever been in love?" Olivia asked, jostling Seth from his pensive musings.

"No, can't say that I have."

Olivia peeked up at him through a fan of sooty lashes and said, "Consider yourself lucky. I wouldn't wish getting jilted on my worst enemy. Although I *am* spiteful enough to wish Jacob would fall for some wicked temptress and discover how much it hurts to be used for selfish purposes *after* she took him for all he was worth and ran off with someone else."

Seth snickered. "Remind me to avoid hell if the devil enlists your help in dishing out punishment to the eternally damned. You're so creative that it's frightening."

His heart stalled in his chest when Olivia tossed back her head and let loose with the first honest-to-goodness laughter he'd heard from her. The uninhibited sound gave him a warm, fuzzy feeling. If he wasn't careful he might actually start *liking* Mitch's lovely daughter.

That had disaster written all over it, Seth cautioned himself. Olivia had sworn off men—for good reason—and she probably had no intention of taking up residence in Oklahoma Territory. He couldn't regard her as anything but a casual acquaintance. Not that she would ever be interested in the likes of a man who lacked social graces and had spent years associating with the worst excuses of humanity.

"Would you mind untying my hands now that we're so deep in the middle of nowhere that I couldn't possibly find my way home?" she requested. "It was bad enough that you kept me tethered last night so I wouldn't escape, but it serves no purpose now, does it?"

Seth's first reaction was one of mistrust. Experience had taught him never to be fooled by a captive who had suddenly become chummy and chatty. For all he knew Olivia could have concocted that elaborate tale to prey on his sympathy—before she hightailed it off in the opposite direction.

"We appear to have something in common," she commented as she watched him stare warily at her. "Complete lack of trust."

Seth slid his dagger from its sheath on his thigh, then leaned over to cut her hands loose. He figured she was bright enough to know it wasn't a show of faith on his part, because he had already assured her that he had the experience and know-how to run her to ground if he was forced to it.

When she flashed him an impish grin he half expected her to gouge the horse in the flanks and charge off, just to challenge him. She was *that* feisty and spirited, he speculated. No doubt, her father had left her to her own devices long enough for her to develop a staunch independent streak. But she didn't bolt away, just to annoy him. She just kept smiling as they rode abreast.

"I have no idea what's going on in that quick mind of yours, Ramsey, but that smile makes me nervous," he said.

"It shouldn't. I just realized that, stranger or not, you're the first person I've confided in. Venting my frustrations is exceptionally gratifying." She heaved a gusty sigh. "I feel better than I have in months."

"Good, let's pick up the pace then. There's a stage station near Grand River where we can sit down to a warm meal."

When she smiled again, another corner of Seth's hardened heart cracked. "If I don't have to serve the meal or clean up afterward, then I'm all in favor. Race you—"

Her voice drifted in the wind as she thundered uphill, causing Seth's mount to bolt sideways. Taking control of his skittish horse, Seth charged after Olivia. He decided she was not only a spirited but complex female and he'd probably never have the chance to figure her out completely. But continuing the journey with her had become more appealing—after he'd gotten to know her better.

That was good, he decided. And that was bad. It would be difficult to remain emotionally detached when Olivia wasn't trying so hard to aggravate him.

Several hours later an uneasy sensation prickled the back of Seth's neck as they trekked through the wooded hills of the Cherokee nation to reach the stage station. Just to be on the safe side, he grabbed his Winchester and laid it across his thighs. That sixth sense he'd acquired over the years kept niggling at him as he panned the copse of trees to the northwest. His body tense with wary anticipation, Seth reined his horse away from Olivia's. If there was someone lurking in the trees—and there were always outlaws lurking in Indian territory—he wasn't about to give them a skillet shot. Once the bushwhackers realized a woman accompanied him they would make Seth their primary target, allowing Olivia the chance to escape—he hoped.

"Seth? What's wrong?" Olivia questioned as he put more space between them. "Why are you—?"

A flash of color caught Seth's attention. Sure enough, thieves were lying in wait. "Get down!" he shouted at her.

She tried to look every direction at once. "Why—?"

Two rifle blasts simultaneously split the air.

"That's why," he muttered as he jerked his Winchester into firing position.

Seth fired off three quick shots then swore inventively when the two desperadoes split up. He reined back to Olivia, who was sprawled on her mount. Her eyes were as wide as saucers and her face was as white as salt. He grabbed the reins from her knotted fist, gouged his steed in the flanks and raced headlong for the cover of the nearby creek.

Another shot rang out, whizzing past his shoulder.

"Get down yourself!" Olivia railed at him. "You're a sitting duck!"

"That's the idea," he said as he plowed through the underbrush. "Better me than you."

She reared up in the saddle to flash him an annoyed glare. "If you think I'll let you take a bullet for me—" She shrieked in alarm when another shot flew over her head and thudded into a nearby tree. "Dear God! What do they want from us?"

Seth was off his horse in a single bound, jerking Olivia to the ground and protecting her body with his own. "In these parts, you can lose your life for the money in your pocket and the horse you're riding on. Now *stay down*, damn it!"

He grabbed one of the pistols on his hips and handed it to her, butt first. "If someone comes at you, shoot him," he ordered.

"What are you going to be doing while I'm shooting whatever moves?" she asked suspiciously.

"Evening the odds."

When Seth tried to whirl away Olivia clutched his arm. "Can't we just hide and wait?"

"A strong offensive attack is the best defense," he said as he pried her fingers off his forearm. "Don't let your guard down until you hear me call to you. And do not move from this spot. Mitch will have my head if I shoot you by mistake."

Difficult as it was to leave her hunkered down in the underbrush, looking uncertain and bewildered, Seth scuttled through the trees and circled the creek to find an advantageous position. Having fought most of his battles alone, he'd never had to worry about risking someone else's life during a showdown. It made him edgy and he kept darting glances toward the spot where he'd left Olivia.

His senses leaped to full alert when he spied two scruffy-looking desperadoes closing ranks on the abandoned horses. When he heard rustling in the bushes beside him, he suspected there was a third member of the gang trying to get the drop on him. Still on his knees, Seth whirled toward the sound, prepared to aim and shoot.

He removed his finger from the trigger and cursed foully when Olivia's golden head rose above the bushes. "Damn it to hell, woman, I thought I told you to stay put!" he growled.

"Well, I thought it over and decided that I didn't agree with your plan of action," Olivia whispered as she scuttled up beside him.

Seth resigned himself to the fact that Olivia was one of those rare females who refused to be ordered around, even in the midst of battle. Apparently, she had overcome her initial fear and decided he needed reinforcements. Now that was a first. Ordinarily, bystanders scattered like a covey of quail, leaving him to fend for himself when all hell broke loose.

Unwillingly impressed with Olivia's fortitude and irrepressible spirit, Seth handed her the other loaded pistol. "Let's show 'em our firepower and maybe they'll retreat," he murmured. "On three. One, two…"

Seth cast Olivia an exasperated glance when she jumped the gun and began blasting away. And he thought *he'd* had trouble following orders while he was in the army?

After firing off a round of shells with his Winchester— while Olivia awkwardly handled both pistols at once—the bushwhackers reversed direction, much to Seth's relief. He sprang to his feet and whistled to his horse. The roan gelding trotted obediently to him.

"Now where are you going?" Olivia wanted to know.

"To drive home our point." Seth swung onto his horse then shook his finger at her. "And this time, if you move from the spot where I left you, *I'll* shoot you myself!"

Olivia rose to a crouch to watch Seth thunder across the clearing, guiding his well-trained mount with his knees and firing his rifle—just over the heads of the retreating ambushers, to make certain they kept running in the opposite direction.

You had to admire a fearless warrior who spit in the face of danger and kept right on going, Olivia mused as she watched Seth in action. Whatever else this man was, he knew how to deal with unexpected trouble. In fact, he'd seen it coming before it actually arrived. How'd he do that? she wondered. She hadn't seen or heard a thing until bullets started flying.

Several minutes later, Seth returned, looking a bit mussed up and breathing heavily. Dried leaves and grass clung to his coat and breeches. If she wasn't mistaken, he had run the scoundrels to ground and pounded some sense into them.

Olivia was a mite disappointed that she hadn't been on hand to witness the conclusion of their battle with outlaws. This was the most excitement she'd had in her life. The fact that she had been compelled to come to Seth's defense went a long way in bolstering her self-respect. Maybe Jacob Riley thought she existed to serve only one purpose to a man, but she had discovered that she counted for something more. Once she had overcome her instinctive fear of danger, she felt the need to fight back.

Of course, knowing Seth was on her side might have accounted for her burst of daring, she allowed. The man was a sight to behold when he was engaged in a gun battle.

Olivia glanced up when Seth skidded his horse to a halt in front of her and she took note of his agitated glare. She flung up her hand to forestall the scathing lecture he looked as if he was set to deliver.

"What did you do with those scoundrels?" she asked.

"Tied them to trees and ran off their horses. I figure it will take them a day to work themselves loose." His gaze narrowed on her. "The next time I tell you to—"

"Nice work, Gresham," she cut in before he could gather a full head of steam to chastise her. "Now, how far away is that stage station you mentioned? All this excitement worked up my appetite. I'm starving."

He opened and shut his mouth like a drawer, then rolled his eyes at her. "Were you *born* this stubborn and defiant?"

Undaunted, Olivia smiled up into his disgruntled frown. "'Fraid so. Now you know why Papa sent you to fetch me. He must have thought he was getting too old to deal with all my shortcomings himself." She strode off to fetch her horse, then threw over her shoulder, "Thank you, though, for trying to protect me from harm. I'll be sure to tell Papa about your amazing feats."

Seth simply sat there in the saddle, watching the daredevil female stride toward her grazing horse. He was astounded that she felt compelled to race to his rescue, even at the risk of her own life. She had proved—quite convincingly—that she was no shrinking violet. Of course, Seth had figured that out from the start. The woman definitely had the heart of a lioness, he decided as he nudged his steed to rejoin Olivia.

Chapter Three

After three days of constant companionship, Seth was certain that he had observed Olivia's every mood and had seen her at her best, worst—and everything in between. He was, however, unprepared for the panicky feelings that overcame him the afternoon when she disappeared into thin air.

He had stopped at the general store in Okmulgee, the capital of the Creek Indian nation, so she could purchase a heavier coat. While she was trying on the garments Seth strode into the bakery to pick up two loaves of bread. When he returned to the store Olivia had vanished.

His first thought was that she had skipped out on him. His second thought—one far more alarming—was that someone had made off with the woman he had been sent to guide and protect.

An indignant feminine screech sent Seth plunging down the boardwalk to locate the sound. Another muffled squawk led him to the alley. Two burly ruffians were pawing at Olivia while she tried to fend them off. He felt the tug of admiration, watching her fight for all she was worth while he rushed to her rescue.

Seth slammed the butt of his pistol against one drunkard's head and he pitched facedown in the dirt. Seth spun around to bury his fist in the other scoundrel's soft underbelly, then clipped him in the chin. The ruffian staggered backward then plopped on the ground. Both men, who reeked of liquor and smelled worse than skunks, lay sprawled in the alley, groaning in pain.

Assured that the riffraff had been incapacitated, Seth whirled to watch Olivia clutch modestly at the torn bodice of her gown. Her face was flushed from exertion and her eyes blazed hot enough to peel paint. She stormed over to give the downed men a swift kick in the seat of the pants.

"Like I said, bastards one and all," Olivia burst out on a seesaw breath.

She stamped up to Seth and tilted her face to a determined angle. "I'm *not* leaving town without a bath to wash off the filthy stench and that's that!"

You had to admire a woman who got mad rather than getting scared, he decided as he studied the waterfall of golden hair that had come unbound during the tussle. His lips twitched when she flashed him a challenging stare, jabbed her forefinger at his chest and said, "Do not even think of objecting to a delay."

He held up his hands in supplication. "Wasn't planning on it." He looked her over closely, noting the scratches on her bare shoulder and the discoloration on her neck. "You okay, Liv?" he asked in concern.

She huffed out a breath and her defensive posture sagged. When she bobbed her head jerkily, several more fiery tendrils tumbled over her heaving breasts. "I'm sorry about taking my anger out on you. I did plenty of that when we first met."

Seth reached out to rearrange the silky strand of hair that

fell across her flushed cheek and fought the urge to bury his hands in those silky tendrils—for starters. Willfully, he restrained from touching her again. "I may be one of the bastards, but remember that I'm *your* bastard until I deliver you safely to your father."

When one of the men dragged himself to his knees, Seth's pistol cleared leather in nothing flat. The deadly click of the trigger indicated that he meant business. "Don't get up because your first step will be six feet straight down," he threatened without taking his eyes off Olivia. "As for you, Liv, take as much time as you need to bathe and change clothes. In fact, I think we'll spend the night at a hotel."

As she let loose with one of her radiant smiles, the world seemed just a little brighter. Seth's heart practically melted in his chest and dribbled down his rib cage. He decided it wouldn't take much for him to become one of Olivia's hopeless admirers. She simply had a fierce impact on a man.

To his amazement she pushed up on tiptoe to press a quick kiss to his lips. And that was the defining moment when he realized he was never going to be satisfied until those dewy lips were opening beneath his and he could taste her deeply, thoroughly.

The traitorous thought promoted him to stiffen in resistance. This was Mitch's daughter, he reminded himself. Mitch trusted Seth to bring her home safely. Yielding to these lusty cravings that made him ache to touch and taste her possessively would be the worst form of betrayal to the only true friend he had.

When Seth leaped away like a scalded cat, all too familiar feelings of disgrace and rejection lambasted Olivia. Tender wounds that had only begun to heal ripped wide open. She reminded herself that Seth had come to her rescue once again because he felt responsible for her, not because he had the slightest interest or affection for her. He was more or less her bodyguard and guide and that's where his obligations began and ended.

She was the one who had stepped over the line when overwhelming feelings of gratitude and relief bombarded her. Plus, the strength and power he emanated made her feel safe and protected. She'd let her guard down around him because he'd become a man she could talk to, lean on and enjoy. In addition, she had been duly impressed by Seth's amazing ability to defuse what might have been another appalling situation. She predicted Seth Gresham had been hell on outlaws during his heyday as a bounty hunter. Twice now, she had seen him become an indomitable warrior.

She might not have been so sassy and defiant toward him at first meeting if she had seen him in action first, she decided. The man was definitely a force to be reckoned with.

When Seth shifted uncomfortably from one foot to the other and stared at the air over her head, Olivia realized that she had become quite proficient at making a fool of herself. Hadn't she learned her lesson with Jacob? Obviously she never said or did the right thing while in the company of men.

Feeling properly put in her place, Olivia strode from the alley to locate a suitable hotel. There and then, she promised herself not to make any amorous advances toward Seth again. Nor would she offer the slightest display of gratitude or affection. She had made a thoughtless, impulsive mistake and she'd probably lost what little respect Seth had gained for her.

Truth be known, she had spent the past few days admiring Seth's survivor skills, fighting a fierce physical attraction and wondering what it would be like to kiss him.

Damn her and her secret fantasies! She'd begun to feel at ease with Seth and now she'd spoiled the makings of a friendship because of that reckless kiss. He probably thought she made a habit of throwing herself at men.

Disheartened and embarrassed, Olivia clutched her torn gown as she veered into the hotel to request a room. Thankfully, Seth left her alone for a few minutes to gather her composure. But her ever-faithful bodyguard was one step behind her when she ascended the steps.

Seth set her belongings inside the door and then backed off. "I tied up the men who assaulted you. While you're bathing, I'll march them over to the town marshal's office."

She noticed his evasive gaze drifted over her shoulder, rather than meeting her eyes directly. No question about it, she had made him uncomfortable with that unwelcome kiss.

"As soon as the water is delivered for your bath, make sure you lock the door. I'll be back with supper."

That said, he pivoted around and exited the room, leaving her to suffer her most recent humiliation in silence.

"I swear, Livie, you stumble from one disaster with men into another," she chastised herself.

In a matter of three days she had managed to spoil her first real friendship with someone of the male persuasion. "Good going," she grumbled as she waited for the servants.

After delivering the prisoners Seth entered the bathhouse, while Olivia was in the hotel room—naked, gloriously naked. The arousing thought and the scintillating image floating in his brain put a scowl on his face as he scrubbed himself squeaky-clean. Damn it, he'd been doing a fine job of maintaining his perspective until Olivia had kissed him unexpectedly. Since that moment, unruly desire had been gnawing at him. He didn't want to want her. Hell's bells, he was doing Mitch a favor, giving the older man something to live for while he was bedridden.

Well, so much for noble intentions, Seth mused in exasperation. Now that kiss was right there between them and the forbidden craving he had managed to control was threatening to slip its leash.

Muttering, Seth reached over to retrieve a bucket of cold water and poured it into his tub. It helped—somewhat. Grabbing a towel, he dried off then fastened himself into a clean set of clothes. He made fast tracks to the telegraph office to contact Doc Potter and check on Mitch. After he received the discouraging reply that Mitch's condition hadn't changed, he entered the café to order their meal, but the news about his friend didn't do much for his appetite.

Tray in hand, Seth inhaled a bolstering breath and headed for the hotel. He was going to make small talk during supper then camp out on his bedroll on the floor—as far from the bed as he could get. He would pretend that kiss never happened, he told himself fiercely. If ever there was a woman who was off-limits *she* was it. And if he had the sense God gave a termite he wouldn't let himself forget that.

Determined of purpose, Seth called upon the relentless determination he'd relied on during his years in pursuit of desperadoes. But no matter what, he was *not* going to get close enough to that bewitching siren to tempt himself. He would remain impersonal and detached—and hope that he and Olivia could regain the easy camaraderie they had developed the past few days.

But the moment she opened the door, looking refreshed and enchanting, Seth knew that if he let his guard down for one second that he'd get lost in that endearing smile and those mesmerizing eyes that left him swearing that he was staring into a boundless blue sky.

And so he concentrated on eating his meal so he could keep up his strength and relayed the message from Doc Potter that Mitch was holding his own. Then Seth sprawled on his pallet and faced the wall. He wasn't sure how many sheep he counted before he fell asleep, but the number must have been in the thousands.

"Seth?"

Olivia's voice jostled Seth from the most erotic, forbidden dream he'd ever had. His body throbbing, he opened his eyes to see the woman who'd had the starring role in his arousing fantasy hovering over him in the darkened room. Dear God in heaven! How much torment did a man have to endure?

"Are you all right? You were moaning in your sleep."

Of course, he was moaning in his sleep. She might have been, too, if she'd shared his dreams. Seth shifted self-consciously on his pallet. Desire still throbbed through him, fiercely reminding him that he'd envisioned his naked body joined intimately with hers.

"Why don't you sleep on the bed and I'll take the pallet," she offered. "You paid for the room, after all. It's only fair that you should spend half the night in comfort."

Crawl into a bed that was thick with her clean, alluring scent? No thank you, thought Seth. He was having enough trouble controlling these traitorous sensations without doing *that!* "I'm fine. Go back to sleep. I'm sorry I woke you."

Dressed in her chemise and pantaloons, she sank down cross-legged beside him. "You didn't wake me. I've been lying there, trying to figure out the best way to apologize for making you uncomfortable when I kissed you. It seems I have a gift for making a fool of myself."

"Look, Liv—"

When she pressed her fingertips to his lips to shush him, he stifled a groan. He wanted to feel her mouth melded to his so badly he could almost taste her, remembering exactly what she tasted like—sweet, intoxicating and *forbidden*. He was already hard and aching and the intensity of his desire for her was enough to make a grown man whimper.

"Please, let me finish." He heard her sigh in the shadowy darkness. "My emotions were in a tailspin after that unnerving ordeal with those drunkards. Odd as it may sound to you, you've become the safe place I've turned to. I was impressed with how quickly and efficiently you came to my rescue. While it's true that I've had men fight over me before, I've never had anyone fight *for* me. I was touched and grateful, but kissing you was improper and impulsive. I could tell it made you uneasy. You tiptoed around me all evening, as if I were a ticking bomb and you weren't sure when it would go off."

Only because he didn't trust himself with her, knowing impossible temptation was a hairbreadth away and that he was dangerously close to betraying his best friend, his father figure. *Her father.*

"Go back to bed." His voice was gruff and abrupt and he cursed himself soundly when she shrank away from him.

Seth expelled a harsh breath and raked his fingers through his tousled hair. He was going to have to be bluntly honest with her, he decided, because she was getting the wrong impression. Jacob, the jackass, had her feeling vulnerable and insecure already. Damn if Seth was going to contribute to her feelings of rejection and mortification.

"Here's the deal, plain and simple," he said, clutching her arm when she tried to rise. Red-hot sensations scorched his fingers so he released her quickly. "I may be as tough as nails when dealing with the kind of men who ambushed us and assaulted you, but I'm not immune to you. One look in the mirror should make you aware of how attractive you are."

When he saw her chin tilt to an offended angle he recalled how sensitive she was about being seen only for her beauty and not the person she was inside. "I told you earlier that I'm one of the bastards. There's no getting around that."

"But you're *my* bastard," she said, a hint of a smile in her voice. "It was that endearing comment that contributed to my impulsive need to kiss you."

"Well, there you go," he said teasingly. "That kiss was obviously as much my fault as it was yours. My irresistible charm just got to you in the aftermath of an adrenaline rush."

Her quiet laughter went through him like sensual lightning and his body hardened again. That was forbidden temptation for you, he decided. It didn't take much to ignite fiery sensations that had you fighting like hell for control.

"So, you think your charm got to me and you backed away from my kiss because you find me physically attractive?" she asked, baffled. "No wonder I don't deal well with men. I don't understand them at all. I thought you were deeply offended because I kissed you to repay you for rescuing me."

Seth reached up to torment himself by brushing his index finger over her cheek, marveling at the soft texture beneath his hand. "There is little to understand about men, Liv. You're beautiful and I want you. I was lying here dreaming of having you, even when I know Mitch would skin me alive for just entertaining such thoughts. And what kind of friend would I be to you if I acted on my selfish needs? It's clear as day that you're still carrying a torch for Jacob What's-His-Name."

"Who?"

She leaned down to kiss him and fire flared in his veins. Self-restraint flew out the window as his arms closed around her, pressing her supple body into his aching contours. He realized instantly that his dreams were no match for the erotic reality of holding her close and that he was in serious trouble. He told himself—while he kissed the breath clean out of her—that he'd reacted so fiercely because he'd been a long time without a woman. But he knew better. The protective and possessive feelings he'd felt earlier assured him that he was emotionally involved, not just going through the routine he'd honed countering attacks from outlaws.

When Seth finally came up for air he released his left hand, which was clamped familiarly on her derriere. He was shocked to realize that he'd pressed her into the cradle of his thighs, letting her feel what she was doing to him. "Damn it, Liv," he ground out. "Go back to bed before we both do something we'll regret."

"You maybe, but don't speak for me," she murmured breathlessly.

Olivia's mind reeled as unprecedented desire pinwheeled through her. A multitude of sizzling sensations shimmered inside her, making her crave more of him. She realized that she'd never really been kissed before—not with that kind of intensity and focus. But being thoroughly kissed by Seth was an epiphany that shattered her long-held fantasy of Jacob Riley in one second flat.

She hadn't been in love with Jacob at all, she thought in amazement. She'd been in love with the idea of seeing her childish fairy tale come true. It had nothing to do with *Jacob*. He had simply been the image of the kind of young man a woman would pin her dreams on. Good family, wealthy and attractive. She hadn't looked deeper to see what was in his heart and soul.

Olivia sank bonelessly beside Seth and blinked as if she'd emerged from a trance. "Sweet mercy, I didn't even love him," she mumbled in disbelief.

"What?" Seth said hoarsely.

She looked down at the brawny form of the man stretched out beside her. "Have you ever wanted something so badly and waited forever to have it, only to discover that the prize didn't measure up to the anticipation?"

"Yes." Seth could certainly identify with that. He'd saved and scrimped for years to build the nest egg that allowed him to make improvements on his new homestead and purchase a cattle herd. And for the past few months he'd been plagued by the nagging feeling that something important was still missing in his life.

"Well, that's what Jacob was to me," she explained. "Turned out that he was only the *illusion* of perfection that I conjured up. I wouldn't want him now, even if he crawled on hands and knees and begged forgiveness for betraying me with my best friend."

"Good, because that blockhead doesn't deserve you," he assured her.

He watched with relief and regret as she rose gracefully to her feet. "Thank you, Seth. In a matter of days you've made me feel better about myself than I have in months." She halted on her way to bed, then glanced back at him. "And Seth?"

"Yeah?"

"You were right. It *was* your irresistible charm that grabbed hold of me and wouldn't let go," she said, then added playfully. "So kissing you, out of the blue, wasn't *my* fault at all. It was *yours*. I simply couldn't help myself."

Seth grinned in the darkness while he listened to the rustling sounds of Olivia flouncing around, trying to make herself comfortable. It occurred to him that he and Olivia hadn't traveled all that many miles together, but they had definitely come a long way from her sweeping condemnation of the male persuasion and his less than flattering first impression of her. Now they understood each other better—and he liked her way too much.

He also wanted her something fierce.

Seth rolled onto his side and told himself that he'd spent years cultivating self-discipline and self-control. He wasn't going to jeopardize his friendship with Mitch or take advantage of Olivia's emotional vulnerability. He might yield to the temptation of an occasional kiss, but that was as far as it would go....

Just listen to him, would you? He was already making bargains with himself and bending the rules to accommodate the cravings that had been tormenting him since he'd been spending day and night with this alluring female. *What next, O Great Master of Self-Restraint? A few caresses when your hands itch to touch her? You better set a fast pace to Mitch's homestead or you'll spoil his one and only Christmas wish.*

On that unsettling thought, Seth squeezed his eyes shut and promised himself that no matter how much the want of this woman got to him, he wouldn't ruin the first honest-to-goodness friendship he'd acquired in two decades. And besides, Olivia deserved someone who knew how to be gentle and kind. Not someone who had grown up in a world of death and violence.

Face it, Gresham, even if you have a new lease on life, you still are what you are and you aren't good enough for Olivia. She deserves to be loved, and you don't have the first clue what love is about.

Chapter Four

Olivia stared across the rugged terrain, amazed that the world seemed a better place than it had in months. The troubled doubts about her self-worth and self-esteem that had been hanging over her head like a black cloud had eased up. Even the biting winter wind didn't diminish the warm glow of satisfaction that settled inside her. Oh, certainly, she was still apprehensive about her reunion with her father, but Seth had made her realize that not all men were devious, manipulative creatures. Seth Gresham was a man you could count on when the chips were down. He was honorable and courageous. He also possessed a noble streak that had kept him at a respectable distance since he'd kissed her— and she had discovered the meaning of explosive desire. Other men might have taken advantage of the situation and her vulnerability, but Seth's loyalty to her father had kept him at arm's length.

Much to her disappointment.

Having gotten a thorough taste of him, feeling that sinewy body pressed familiarly to hers, she realized that she had the power to arouse him. Of course, she wasn't so naive nowadays to think she had some exclusive effect on him, but he had made her feel irresistible and desirable—and insanely curious about the intimacy shared between a man and woman.

She glanced sideways to see Seth staring at the scudding clouds that had thickened during their morning ride. She felt comfortable with *him*—yet oddly restless. He made her feel protected—yet he didn't treat her like a senseless nitwit whose needs and opinions were unimportant. In short, he was a man she was pleased to call friend, companion—and perhaps something more if he weren't so blasted conscientious and loyal to her father.

Olivia shook her head and smiled at the direction of her wayward thoughts. Less than a week ago she'd had no faith whatsoever in men and she had been filled with anger, bitterness and self-doubt. Now, here she was, mulling over the prospect of seducing Seth because he inspired erotic yearnings that intensified with each passing day.

"You've been awfully quiet this morning," Seth said, breaking into her thoughts.

"Just thinking."

That wry smile that hinted at his dry sense of humor kicked up the corners of his chiseled mouth. Olivia was reminded of how well she'd gotten to know his expressions and mannerisms—gotten to know him—during their constant togetherness.

"Thinking, huh? Is that a wise idea?" he teased. "Wouldn't want to strain that pretty little head of yours, ya know."

"I try to think at least once a day to keep my wits sharp," she countered good-naturedly. "You should try it sometime, Gresham."

And that was another thing she liked about Seth, she mused. They had developed a playful camaraderie and, thanks to him, she'd become less sensitive and defensive to comments about her looks. She was at ease with him, relaxed. And yet, she felt poised on the brink of needing to explore this physical attraction that intensified with each passing hour.

"You've been doing enough thinking for both of us," he commented, tossing her a wry grin. "Since you're so good at it, I'll provide the brawn and you can provide the brains on this trip."

There it was again, that subtle reassurance that she counted for something, that he respected who she was. He'd been doing that a lot since they'd had their heart-to-heart talk two nights ago in Okmulgee. Apparently he had figured out what she required to get back on emotional track and he tried to provide it. She'd like to hug the stuffing out of him for being so aware and considerate of her needs.

And so she yielded to the spontaneous impulse. She leaned across the space that separated them, hooked her elbow around his neck and gave him a playful squeeze.

"What was that for?" he asked after she had uprighted herself in the saddle.

"Just because you're you."

When he glanced at her, goggle-eyed, Olivia wondered if he was harboring a few self-doubts of his own. Aware of his former occupation—and the stigma that some so-called decent folks attached to men who were guns for hire—she suspected he had been treated as a social pariah who wasn't much better than the ruthless criminals he tracked down.

"Tell me about yourself," she requested abruptly.

His broad shoulders lifted in a nonchalant shrug. "Not much to tell. My unwed mother left me outside a church in Chicago when I was four and took off for parts unknown. I grew up on the streets, struggling to survive, learning to defend myself with whatever improvised weapons I could lay my hands on. I did a stint in the Army of the West during the Indian uprisings and decided I didn't deal well with obeying orders without question."

"So you took your well-honed skills and went into business for yourself," she said thoughtfully. "Well traveled, self-reliant and unafraid of dangerous adventure. Not to mention a strong sense of justice that probably inspired you to put all the bullies of the world behind bars."

Seth blinked, startled. "Damn, Ramsey, you're astute. I never thought of it that way, but maybe I was retaliating against the bullies in the streets that worked me over until I got big enough and tough enough to chop them down to size." He glanced at her momentarily then looked away.

He'd been doing that a lot lately, she recalled. She wondered why. It was as if he couldn't make eye contact for more than a few moments without becoming uncomfortable.

"Guess I'd just had my fill as a kid of watching some folks get away with lying, stealing and murder. I had the training and skills to do something about it, so I did."

"Even though you weren't fully appreciated for the dangerous risks you took to protect society," she surmised. "I for one admire you for that. I also envy your extensive travels, if not the life-threatening encounters you faced. As for me, this is the farthest I've been from home." She stared directly at him. "*You're* the only adventure I've ever had."

He chuckled at that. "Damn, woman, if that's the case then you really do need to get out more."

"Obviously," she agreed. "While you were out cleaning up the world for society, I just sat there designing and sewing fashionable gowns." Her smile faltered. "I loved the job, until the owner—and my best friend, Angela—fell prey to Jacob's charms. Then I had no choice but to find other work. So I became a waitress. Not much adventure in that."

"And I spent years wishing to be more than a human tumbleweed. Now that I've staked a claim in Oklahoma Territory I finally have a roof over my head and property to call my own. It's better than finding myself a moving target or staring down the spitting end of a six-shooter," he commented. "This is the first Christmas in twenty-eight years that I've had reason to celebrate. My previous life wasn't one that I'd wish on anyone else, believe me."

Olivia could only imagine the lonely hours Seth had logged in the past two decades. It made her feel petty and childish for fantasizing about Jacob Riley all those years. At least she'd had a home and parents to watch over her until she could make it on her own. Although she'd lost her mother to typhoid ten years earlier, her father had cared and provided for her. Mitch had only ridden off to satisfy his need for adventure *after* Olivia had a life of her own.

Her Christmas holidays had been filled with gifts, love, laughter and family. She wondered if Seth had ever received a gift or if he had anyone to share the festive season with him.

"This being your first Christmas in your new home, what is it that you wish for?" she asked curiously.

"Me?" He looked so surprised and perplexed by the question that a wave of sympathy washed over Olivia.

"Of course, you," she said sassily. "What do you want for Christmas, besides having me out of your hair after days of forced companionship?" She snapped her fingers, as if struck by inspiration. "That's it, isn't it? Your Christmas wish is *not* to have to put up with me for days on end."

Right, Ramsey, you've been tough to take. Staring into that pretty mug of yours and having someone to talk to be-

sides my horse is a tough job, but someone has to do it. His smile turned pensive. "I don't know what I'd wish for Christmas. I've acquired all I thought I'd ever want. It would be selfish and ungrateful to expect more. But I guess my only wish would be to see your father back on his feet."

The prospect of losing her father before she had the chance to reconcile with him made her anxious often during their journey. She had battled her share of *should haves* and *what ifs* for days. Now she was eager to see him again. She would nurse him back to health, she promised herself. She would care for Mitch, just as he had always been there for her. No one was ever going to come between her and her father again. Especially not the likes of Jacob Riley. He hadn't been worth the conflict that had erupted between father and daughter eight months earlier.

"Thank you for being my father's friend," she murmured.

"When you only have one friend, you don't take him for granted or do anything to spoil the friendship."

Which implied that all these affectionate feelings that assailed her when she glanced at Seth were to be left unfulfilled, she mused as they trotted ever westward. Good thing Seth hadn't asked what *she* wanted for Christmas, because she wasn't sure he could deal with her growing infatuation. Sure enough, it would be in direct conflict with the unfaltering loyalty he felt for her father.

Now there was irony for you, she thought as they rode over hill and dale. She envied the unswerving devotion Seth had for Mitch. Maybe Seth was right. Maybe she *was* an ungrateful brat. But all the same, why couldn't a man feel that kind of loyalty and affection for *her?*

Seth scowled in frustration as he watched huge snowflakes swirl in the icy wind. Two more days of relentless riding and he would have been home to check on Mitch. He would have been able to put Olivia out of sight and try to weed these traitorous thoughts of lust from his mind.

Damn, he thought as he watched the snow pile up around him. Sometimes a man just couldn't catch a break.

"Are there any towns hereabout where we can stop to warm up and wait out this storm?" Olivia asked as she shivered atop her horse.

"No, unfortunately," Seth grumbled as the wind picked up and began to howl through the leafless cottonwood trees that reached up like bony fingers to the darkening sky. "The closest town is the new territorial capitol in Guthrie, which is a good fifty miles away. Once we're there we're only four miles from home. We'll try to make it as far as we can before we camp out for the night."

Seth noted that Olivia didn't look all that pleased with his plan, but she voiced no complaints, just huddled inside her new coat and got that determined look on her face that indicated she intended to make the best of a difficult situation.

Her expression reminded Seth of her father. During their endless hours and days together Seth had come to realize that Olivia was made of amazingly sturdy stuff. He could tell this arduous journey was wearing on her, but she had tried to match him step for step. He admired her for that. He was asking a lot from a woman who had never braved the elements and had to live on trail rations for what must have seemed like forever to her.

This jaunt was a vivid reminder of Seth's endless forays into the wilderness to track desperadoes. He'd done it hundreds of times before. It also reminded him that he was thankful those grueling experiences were behind him. Now, if he could only put these ill-fated feelings for Olivia behind him then he could get on with his new life.

Three hours later the mounting snow made traveling difficult. Seth had to slow their pace, for fear one of the horses might step in an unseen hole and come up lame. Riding double might conserve warmth, but it would wear down an already exhausted horse. Seth resigned himself to the fact that he would have to halt much earlier than planned and dig into the south side of a ravine to wait out the snowstorm.

He wouldn't have minded a white Christmas if he were nestled up to the potbellied stove in his cabin, but cuddling up with the woman—who scrambled his good sense and played hell with his male body—kept him on edge.

Well, he would just have to keep reminding himself that she was off-limits.

"I'm sorry to complain," Olivia shouted over the whistling wind, "but I'm so cold that I can't stop shivering. Can we stop for a few minutes to walk about?"

Seth directed her attention to the grove of cedars at the base of the ravine. The smile of gratitude she flashed him shot straight to his groin. Damnation, he'd never been so affected by a woman's smile. He was definitely getting soft, he diagnosed. Two years ago, back in those days when he functioned on pure instinct and training, nothing got to him. He'd never allowed emotion to rule his mind.

Now, the lure of this particular woman penetrated his ironclad defenses. He'd reached the point that he would do just about anything to make her happy.

"Thank God!" Olivia dismounted stiffly then worked the kinks from her back.

When she staggered forward and her legs nearly folded up beneath her, Seth's hand shot out to steady her. Fire leaped through his blood when she instinctively huddled against him to ward off the icy chill.

"I—I'm s-so c-cold," she mumbled against his coat. "I-I'm n-not s-sure I—I'll ever b-be warm again."

He was burning from inside out and he was wondering if *he* would ever be the *same* again. He could have stood there for hours, snuggling up to her—as if it were his right and privilege—and never complaining about the frigid temperatures.

Seth hadn't realized that he'd wrapped her so tightly in his arms and rested his chin on the crown of her head until she shifted closer. White-hot flames flickered through his overly sensitive body.

Seth sprang away from her lickety-split. "Come sit over here. I'll find some dry kindling to start a fire."

"Let me do that. I need to move about before the blood freezes in my veins. You'd best tend the horses before the storm descends in full force."

Seth smiled at the bossy streak that indicated Olivia was accustomed to doing things her way. Then he reminded himself that he usually did things his way, so who was he to object?

He watched her scratch around to unearth several fallen tree limbs then dust off the snow. She worked diligently to gather enough wood for a fire while he unsaddled the horses. Seth shook his head, amazed at how wrong his first impression of Olivia had been.

After Seth tethered the horses in the shelter of the trees, he unrolled the tarp that served as their makeshift tent. The thick cedars, canvas wind block and the V-shaped ravine made it possible for them to shield themselves from the unpleasant effects of blowing snow. While he stacked up wood for the campfire, Olivia sat down—legs drawn up to her chest, arms locked around her knees—and wrapped her bedroll around her quivering shoulders.

"I can't begin to imagine how you survived so many

harsh winters in the wilderness," she remarked as she watched Seth hunker down to light the fire.

"Got used to it," he replied.

Olivia smiled to herself. *She* was getting used to having Seth around, knowing he was capable of providing whatever they needed to survive the strenuous journey through barely civilized country. She'd grown accustomed to the sound of his voice, content in knowing he was always close by. His ruggedly handsome face was the first thing she saw each morning and the last thing she saw at night—and she liked that.

The warm feelings that just being with Seth incited in her were more profound than those she'd felt for Jacob. The man didn't begin to compare to Seth Gresham. Too bad Seth wouldn't allow himself to progress beyond friendship with her because she had begun to want far more from him. He was her grand adventure, and she found herself yearning to make the most of their short time together.

She watched him move with that trademark economical motion, studied his brawny profile and remembered how safe and protected she'd felt when he'd hugged her close to warm her up. A wistful smile pursed her lips, wondering what it would be like to spend the entire night snuggled up against his powerful body, wondering what it would be like to experience passion and set all her bottled emotions free.

"You okay, Ramsey? You look a little dazed."

His deep, resonant voice jostled her from her secret fantasy. She had never thrown herself at a man before, but she was seriously considering seduction. Not that she knew how or where to start, but just looking at Seth made her want to try.

And what was wrong with wanting to have a reckless

fling for Christmas? Seth was her first true adventure in life. She was intrigued with him, and she'd learned the hard way that pining for a fairy-tale kind of love was a waste of time and emotion. She wanted the here and now, wanted to live in the moment and savor all it could offer.

"Ramsey?" he prompted when she continued to stare speculatively at him.

She knew why he'd taken to calling her by her last name—an attempt to keep things light and impersonal between them, even while they were living in each other's pockets.

He squatted down in front of her and reached out to tilt her chin up to study her at close range. "You aren't feeling sick, are you? Feverish? Your father would never forgive me if I toted you home in the same condition he's in."

"I am feeling severely chilled," she said, taking the perfect opening he'd provided.

For years she'd dreamed of baring herself to Jacob on their honeymoon, with romantic candlelight flickering around their featherbed. But stretching out beside Seth, learning him by taste and touch, while huddled on a pallet during a snowstorm was beginning to have tremendous appeal.

Resolved to see at least one whimsical dream come true, Olivia unbuttoned her coat and tossed it aside. When she unfastened the second button on her calico gown Seth's eyes bugged out and his whiskered jaw sagged to his chest.

"What in the hell are you doing?"

She put forth her best effort and tossed him a smile that was meant to be pure seduction. "You're a smart man, Seth. Figure it out yourself."

Chapter Five

Olivia watched his smoldering eyes drop to the lacy chemise exposed by her gaping gown. Well, at least she had his undivided attention. Good. Now, if she could just make him forget how honorable and noble he was for a few minutes, maybe her attempt at seduction wouldn't be a humiliating flop.

"You're trying to seduce me," he croaked. "I told you that I can't—"

She didn't want to hear that her father stood between them so she flung her arms around his neck and kissed him for all she was worth. She hoped her enthusiastic technique compensated for her lack of experience because the thought of disappointing Seth was intolerable. She wanted him to want her so much that he quit holding back. She wanted to feel the fire he'd ignited inside her that one time when he'd really let loose and devoured her with those full, sensuous lips. She wanted to explore every inch of those muscled planes and contours that were concealed beneath his bulky clothes.

And then she wanted him to touch her in return.

"Aw, damn, Liv, I've been fighting to keep my distance," Seth growled as he reared back to break their scorching kiss. "And you're still stuck on someone else. You're going to regret this."

Olivia locked her arms around his neck, refusing to let him retreat. Not again. Not this time. She stared him squarely in the eye and said, "I told you I'm over that faithless philanderer. *You* are all I want for Christmas."

She watched his Adam's apple bob as he swallowed hard. She could tell he was battling conflicting emotions. Wouldn't you know the man who had intrigued her was teeming with so much self-control that he wouldn't reach out to take what she was freely offering him?

He didn't move, just stared down at her from beneath thick black lashes. Rejection bombarded her, accompanied by enough embarrassment to put a blush on her cheeks— a blush that had nothing to do with the cold temperatures.

Olivia recoiled, clutched her gown and stared everywhere except at Seth so he wouldn't see the tears that clouded her eyes. When she reached out to retrieve her discarded coat, his hand folded over hers. Her befuddled gaze leaped to his rugged face. When he guided her hand inside his coat, she felt the thundering beat of his heart.

"This is what you do to me. It's not because I don't want you like hell blazing. I do," he insisted hoarsely. "I told you that days ago."

The tears swimming in her stunning blue eyes hit Seth right where he lived. He couldn't bear to see her upset, especially when he knew he was the cause of it. Before he could stop himself he curled his free hand around her neck and drew her head to his. He'd only meant to give her a chaste, consoling kiss. But her dewy lips parted beneath his, inviting him inside, and he was lost. His entire body clenched as he absorbed her scent, her taste and the feel of her curvaceous body molded to his. He'd never been any woman's fondest wish before—Christmas wish or otherwise. No woman had ever looked as him so adoringly, so trustingly, so determinedly.

It was his complete undoing. He wanted this woman more than he wanted breath, more than he'd ever wanted anything in his life. Right or wrong. Hell to pay or not. *He wanted her.* It was as simple and as complicated as that. She was worth whatever repercussions he had to face for this fleeting moment when his secret fantasy merged with reality.

When she looped her arms over his shoulders and leaned closer, Seth crushed her desperately in his arms. His head was spinning like a cyclone and desire surged over him like high tide. He was so aroused that he shook with the need to possess her and to be possessed in return. When she matched him kiss for soul-searing kiss and clawed impatiently at the buttons of his shirt, good sense and self-control abandoned him in the time it took to blink.

His hand glided beneath her chemise to cup her breast. When she moaned softly the earth shifted beneath him. Never in his life had he wanted to please anyone the way he wanted to pleasure this woman who had the astonishing ability to turn him wrong side out and leave him obsessed with forbidden hunger. He wanted to banish Jacob from her thoughts and brand his memory—and this moment—on her mind forever.

To that dedicated end he willed himself to slow down, to savor every magical sensation. He filled his hands with her silky flesh and kissed her as gently as he knew how. He resented the rough calluses on his hands, the stubble of whiskers—everything that detracted from her sensual pleasure. He couldn't stop the icy wind or blowing snow, but he could wrap them in a sheltering cocoon of quilts and bedrolls and block out the world around them. Seth knew he wouldn't be satisfied until she was wearing nothing but him and he had memorized each luscious curve and swell of her body by touch, by taste, by heart.

"Sweet mercy!" Olivia gasped when he suckled her breast.

"I'm sorry. Did I hurt you?" he murmured against her quivering flesh, then flicked his tongue lightly over the rosy crests.

"No, I just didn't expect…"

He smiled devilishly when her voice dissolved into a breathless gasp. He caressed her tenderly with his fingertips and felt her tremble in helpless response. When she arched toward him, he kneaded her breast with one hand and let the other glide up her leg to sketch featherlight circles on her inner thigh. He felt her flesh quiver, heard her breath catch again. It gave him immense pleasure to know how wildly she responded to his touch.

When she whispered his name and her nails bit into the side of his neck, he knew she experienced the same profound need that thrummed inside him. He wanted to be the man who healed her broken heart and reassured her that she was incredibly desirable. He wanted to be the one who made her world right again.

Seth cupped his hand over the soft curls between her legs, then glided his fingertip over her moist flesh. He felt the fire of her passion burning his hand, compelling him closer to her sultry heat. Dipping his finger inside her at the same instant that he plunged his tongue into the soft recesses of her mouth, he imitated the profound intimacy he wanted to share with her.

To his delighted amusement she clutched at him urgently and emitted all sorts of wild, unintelligible noises. Then she clamped her hands on the sides of his face and stared at him with such astonished wonderment that he felt the last corner of his heart crumble in his chest.

Whatever she wanted, whatever she needed, he would provide it. The spacious cabin he'd built with his own hands was hers for the taking. The quarter section of land that he'd claimed by outrunning thousands of would-be settlers was hers, too. His herd of livestock and his favorite mount were at her disposal. Whatever he had was hers if it made her happy.

She could have him, too, if that's what she wanted.

And it looked as if that was *exactly* what she wanted— at least for the moment—for she shoved the coat off his shoulders and made fast work of unfastening his shirt and long underwear. Her hand grazed his laboring chest and he swore her scorching caress had raised blisters on his flesh. Seth forgot why breathing was so crucial. He could have survived quite nicely on the exquisite sensations her caresses aroused.

He didn't put up a smidgen of resistance when she set to work relieving him of his holsters, dagger and then his breeches. The moment her hand curled around his rigid arousal Seth felt uncontrollable desire swamp and buffet him, drag him to the teetering edge of restraint. He folded his hand over hers, stilling the scintillating caresses that were driving him ten kinds of crazy.

"Easy, darlin'," he cautioned on a ragged breath. "It won't take much to make me lose control. You deserve better than that."

Her smile turned impish as she brazenly measured him from base to tip. "That's what I want, *darlin'*, to see you lose control—for once. What I *deserve*," she added provocatively, "is to have you right where I ache for you the most. Now. Right this very minute…"

When her lips slanted over his and she caressed his throbbing manhood, Seth swore he was on the verge of passing out. His body forgot it had a brain attached to it and his good intentions of taking his time with Olivia went up in smoke. Ardent needs enflamed him, leaving him burning hotter than a thousand suns. Feeling frantic and impatient, he hooked his arm around her waist and rolled above her to settle between her thighs. She was breathing hard as she lay pinned beneath him, her full breasts exposed to his hungry gaze, her eyes blazing with the passion they had evoked from each other.

"Now," she insisted urgently. "I want you *now*."

"Demanding little thing, aren't you?" he teased as he shifted so he could ease her skirt up the shapely columns of her legs.

"Exceptionally demanding. I'm afraid you'll change your mind if I give you time to think."

"Too late. I'm long past thinking," he whispered as he braced his arms on either side of her shoulders and moved deliberately toward her.

Olivia met his scorching gaze, memorized every bronzed feature of his face and then melted into a puddle of helpless abandon when he angled his head to kiss her. He'd never kissed her quite so desperately before and she responded instantaneously. She felt his hard length gliding inside her, filling her, consuming her with indescribable pleasure. When he retreated, suddenly aware that he was her first lover, she clutched at his hips, refusing to let him withdraw.

"If you stop now, I swear I'll strangle you."

"I thought—"

His voice fizzled out when she gyrated her hips against him. He groaned in unholy torment and she moved suggestively beneath him again. She felt his resistance crumble, felt his muscular body surge helplessly toward hers. When he plunged inside her, hard and deep, heat radiated through every fiber of her being and need exploded like fireworks.

Sensation after staggering sensation converged on her and she closed her eyes to focus on nothing but the hot, wild intensity that mushroomed inside her. This unique, powerfully built man, who had, day by day, burrowed into her heart and taught her to trust again, was sweeping her away with each possessive thrust. Even while his muscular body weighed her down she swore she was flying in the wind.

"Look at me, Liv," he demanded hoarsely.

Her lashes swept up to see him staring at her as if she were his absolute focus. For certain, he was the entire focus of her mind and body. She wondered if he thought she was pretending to be with the man who had inspired her silly fairy tales, even after she had assured him it wasn't true. It seemed that he needed the reassurance that *he* was the one she wanted to introduce her to intimate passion.

"All I see and feel is you," she whispered as she arched eagerly toward him. "Only you, Seth."

His relieved smile warmed her heart and touched her soul. When he lifted her exactly to him and set a frantic cadence of passion the world spun into oblivion. She clung to him as staggering desire pelted her. She matched each demanding thrust and held on for dear life when spasms of nearly unbearable pleasure buffeted her repeatedly.

Her breath gushed out in gasping spurts and stars exploded in her mind when Seth groaned her name and clutched her tightly to him. They were flesh to flesh, heart to heart and soul to soul for that glorious space in time. He shuddered above her and held on to her as if she were the only stable force in a universe that had spun helplessly out of control.

It was a long blissful moment before the hazy cloud of passion parted and Olivia remembered they were huddled together in a tangle of quilts and bedrolls. She also noticed that darkness had descended, leaving the impression that they were the only two living souls left in a world blanketed with snow.

Not one smidgen of remorse hounded her as she gradually returned to her senses. She wouldn't trade a fortune in gold for the immeasurable ecstasy that she had shared with Seth. Considering all the things that had gone wrong with her life, this was the only thing that felt *right. He* felt right.

When Seth tried to shift sideways, she clamped hold of him. "Please, not yet," she implored.

"I'm crushing you," he murmured in concern.

"Can't think of a better way to go." She flashed him a cheeky grin. "Being snowbound is a lot more fun than I thought it would be. Hope it lasts a week."

She felt as much as heard the deep rumble of amusement in his chest as he levered onto his forearms to stare directly at her. "You are definitely the best time *I* ever had during a blizzard."

When he tossed her that adorably lopsided grin, Olivia realized that she had somehow fallen in love in a matter of days. It was the last thing she had wanted or expected to happen, considering she had lost all faith in men. And poof! Seth had come barreling into her life with his curt demands then abducted her from her own house. And in a short span of time she realized that Seth was everything she had conjured up as the perfect man. Jacob Riley had fallen miserably short of the mark, but Seth hadn't. Despite what he probably thought, this wasn't some reckless impulse. This was her mended heart showing her the way, teaching her how it truly felt to be hopelessly, deliriously in love.

And if he thought she was going to be satisfied with only one moment of incredible splendor then he was mistaken. Olivia shifted beneath him and felt him respond. Then she kissed him until the aftermath of passion became passion in and of itself. Lost in each other's arms they embarked on another wild journey into sensual ecstasy.

Much later, Olivia sighed in pleasurable exhaustion when Seth snuggled up to her and tucked her head possessively against his chest. Her lashes fluttered shut and in a few moments she was asleep, not the least bit concerned if she awakened to find herself buried beneath an avalanche of snow.

It wouldn't matter, as long as she was cuddled up in the circle of Seth's encompassing arms, for suddenly he was the only place she truly needed to be.

Chapter Six

The next morning Seth made certain he was up and gone before Olivia roused. Guilt, that scaled, fanged serpent, reared its ugly head and inflicted all sorts of nasty little bites. Despite the most sexually gratifying moment of his life, regret churned in his belly. He fought a battle royal with his conscience—and lost. That nagging voice inside his head kept whispering condemning words like *traitor* and *hypocrite*, to name only two. He knew he was nowhere good enough for Olivia and he predicted that Mitch had high expectations for the man she eventually married. Seth probably wouldn't come close to measuring up to what Mitch was looking for in a son-in-law.

He shuddered to guess how Mitch would react if he knew that Seth had deflowered his only daughter. For sure and certain, Napoleon had nothing on Seth. *His* Waterloo went by the name of Olivia Ramsey. It had taken Seth years to achieve his cautious, controlled state of existence and Olivia had shot it all to pieces in one night.

Seth stiffened apprehensively when he heard Olivia crunching through the snowdrifts.

"Morning," she murmured.

Seth didn't turn to face her, just hurriedly fastened the saddle that he'd slung on his horse. He needed to put a physical and emotional distance between them, but he wasn't allowed that luxury.

"Morning yourself," he mumbled awkwardly.

"Just as I thought," she said as she came to stand behind him. "You're avoiding me, aren't you?"

"Why would I do that?" he said, his voice carefully neutral.

Olivia grabbed his coat sleeve and turned him to face her directly. The sight of those slumberous eyes and curly golden hair tumbling over her shoulders left Seth fighting another kind of battle. He was assailed by the insane urge to pull her into his arms and kiss her senseless. But damn it, that would put him right back where he started. He couldn't allow himself to yield to the reckless impulse to do what he knew he shouldn't do—again.

"I'm not sorry about what happened between us. Besides, I'm the one who started it." She smiled wryly. "It must have been my irresistible charm that got to you. This time you're the one who simply couldn't help himself."

She certainly had that right, he mused. He knew she was trying to tease him back into good humor, same as he'd done after her impulsive kiss in the alley at Okmulgee. But there was one whale of a difference between a kiss and the phenomenal intimacy they'd shared last night—for most of the night.

"Look, Liv—"

"No, *you* look," she interrupted as she stationed herself in front of him and jutted her chin. "Don't think for one second that you were some sort of consolation prize to compensate for my humiliation. You were not my way of getting back at Jacob. Furthermore, I have no expectations and I have no intention whatsoever of making demands on you."

While Seth stood there, unsure what to say, Olivia dragged her saddle from the snowbank and struggled to hoist it onto her horse. Seth quickly took up the chore for her. He was in the process of fastening the girth strap when Olivia said, "I'm in love with you, Seth. *I* need to be able to tell you because I want to trust my own judgment after it failed me where Jacob was concerned. *You're* going to have to deal with that without feeling pressured. I know you don't return my sentiments and *I* will have to deal with *that*."

His hands stalled. His jaw sagged on its hinges as he glanced sideways at her. "You can't be in love with me."

"No? Where was I when that rule was passed out?" she asked flippantly.

"What I meant to say was that you aren't really in love with me. You just *think* you should be because we took a tumble in the hay—or snow, as the case happened to be. That's all it was—a moment when lust and curiosity got out of hand—so don't try to make more of it. Besides that, I'm the furthest thing from the kind of man you need and deserve."

She tilted her head and flashed him an amused glance. He, however, couldn't find one damn thing amusing about this conversation. "So you're saying that I'm trying to soothe my conscience by telling myself that I *must* love you, otherwise I wouldn't have seduced you and surrendered so shamelessly? And this I have to hear," she added with a smirk, "just what kind of man have *you* decided is right for me?"

Flustered by her sassy tone and challenging smile, Seth wheeled away to gather their gear. Olivia the Relentless was one step behind him. No surprise there.

"Well?" she prodded when he refused to reply.

He was stalling, of course. Olivia could tell by the way he bustled around camp. He hurriedly packed their bedrolls and dodged her stare. The fact that he looked decidedly uncomfortable was more endearing than annoying to her. *She* had accepted the fact that Seth was the man she'd waited for all her life—and wouldn't have met if he hadn't kidnapped her. *He,* unfortunately, had some crazed notion that his troubled beginnings and his previous occupation made him unworthy of her respect and affection. He'd been abandoned as a child, left with no one to turn to for help, love or reassurance, and he seemed to think it was a personal flaw that invited social alienation. In addition, he was carrying the burdensome weight of guilt because he believed he had committed the queen mother of all cardinal sins and betrayed her father's trust.

If he didn't have so many admirable traits he wouldn't be fighting such a fierce internal battle. Why couldn't he see that he possessed all the qualities that made him the man she could spend the rest of her life with—if he were so inclined?

"I'm going to hound you incessantly until you tell me what kind of man you think I need. You realize that, don't you?" she said as he stalked off with an armload of supplies.

"First off, you told me less than a week ago that love was only a deceptive illusion," he reminded her.

Olivia grimaced. "Yes, well, I was angry and bitter then. I'm over that now."

"Gee, that was quick," he said, and snorted. "Secondly, you need someone who knows how to treat a woman like a lady. Someone with polished manners, proper breeding and a respectable background. All I've done is uproot you, drag you all over creation and get you snowbound in a blizzard. Not to mention what happened last night. Some lines shouldn't be crossed—and that was one of them. That was unforgivable!"

And she thought *she* had been plagued by insecurity and battered self-esteem? Ha! "If you could see yourself through my eyes you'd know why I love you. But go ahead and keep telling yourself that you aren't the man I want or need. And, of course, I'm a bad judge of men because unrealistic illusions of Jacob Riley tripped me up. So how could I possibly know what I need, idiotic twit that I am? Right?"

Exasperated, Olivia watched Seth strap their gear in place then mount up. Stony-faced, he stared down at her. "You coming or not, Ramsey?"

"Suddenly I have a choice? A little late for that, isn't it?"

"Get on the damn horse," he growled, then rode off.

Although she wanted to shake him until his pearly whites rattled, she clamped hold of the pommel and pulled herself onto her horse. She predicted the last leg of their journey was going to be filled with stilted silence. Well, it was her own fault, she reminded herself as she followed the path Seth forged through the snow. She shouldn't have blurted out her feelings. Seth was uncomfortable with her confession—because *he* didn't return *her* affection.

Oh, certainly, he enjoyed their intimate tryst—she knew he had—but he'd only been scratching an itch. What he'd really meant to say—and hadn't, just to spare her feelings—was that *she* wasn't the right woman for *him*.

Sure enough, Seth set a swift pace and made no attempt at conversation. He also avoided her gaze and flinched at each incidental touch. In all her life she'd never seen a man take such great pains to steer clear of her. He had become noticeably impersonal and emotionally detached. He was doing the job he'd been sent to do—deliver her to her father—and nothing more.

Olivia smiled ruefully as they made their way through the bustling new capital of Guthrie then turned south toward her father's homestead. She expected Seth to dump her off on her father's doorstep and hightail it to his own house. She probably wouldn't see him again, not if he could help it.

The thought deflated her spirits.

"Well, damn it to hell!"

Seth's booming voice jolted her from her pensive musings. Olivia glanced toward the clearing that yawned before them and her mouth dropped open. There in the distance was her father—the man who was supposedly battling a mysterious illness and clinging to life by a frazzled thread. He was chopping down a cedar tree—that would likely end up adorned with Christmas decorations—while Hiram had his nose to the ground, scenting an unseen varmint.

It was just as she suspected. Mitch had conned Seth into racing off to Missouri to deliver her like a gift-wrapped package. She had lived with her father long enough to know how determined he was when he set his mind to something. Here was a shining example. Mitch had wanted her home for Christmas and he cleverly made Seth the extension of his will, the sneaky rascal.

Olivia glanced sideways to survey the outraged expression that settled on Seth's bronzed face. She heard him swear foully then watched him gouge his horse in the flanks. With snow flying around his steed's hooves, he thundered toward Mitch. Olivia trotted along at a slower pace. She steeled herself against the jumble of emotions provoked by seeing her father for the first time since their fiery argument. She wasn't sure what to say to him, especially in light of the fact that he had maneuvered Seth like a pawn.

Seth skidded his horse to a halt and bounded from the saddle. He loomed over Mitch like a storm cloud, itching to grab the sneaky old coot by the lapels of his jacket, jerk him off the ground and give him the good shaking he deserved.

"You aren't sick!" Seth all but shouted.

"I got better." Mitch grinned at him then gazed heavenward. "It's a miracle."

"The hell it is," Seth fumed.

All this time he had been tormented by an overwhelming sense of betrayal. Come to find out, Mitch had deceived *him*, sent *him* under false pretenses to fetch Olivia. "You could have just come right out and asked me to escort your daughter home. You even dragged Doc Potter into your scheme, didn't you? 'Holding his own,' Doc said when I sent him a telegram to check on your condition." His gaze narrowed accusingly. "You were doing a lot more than holding your own, you sly old weasel! I oughta grab a Yuletide log and pound you over the head with it!"

Mitch had the decency to wince. "I wasn't willing to risk having you reject my request, Seth. This was entirely too important to me."

Mitch glanced past Seth's rigid shoulders to see Olivia trotting forward. Seth watched the older man practically melt into his boots as he savored the long-awaited sight of his daughter.

"Sweet mercy, she's even lovelier than I remember," Mitch murmured.

"You wanted her here with you and I delivered her," Seth said, and scowled. "Merry Christmas."

Seth mounted up and reined away from the man who stood stock-still, his gaze transfixed on Olivia. She had halted her horse a small distance away to stare at her father—the devious old coot. Seth could tell by the expression on Olivia's face that she was unsure whether to cling to her injured pride or give in to the underlying need to mend the rift between father and daughter.

"Sweetheart?" Mitch took a reconciliatory step toward her. "I missed you like crazy. I'm damn sorry for the things I said to you."

Something deep inside Seth squeezed tightly in his chest as he watched Olivia dismount and fly toward Mitch like a homing pigeon coming to roost. Thanks to Mitch's willingness to forgive and forget, the angry words that had come between them were suddenly inconsequential.

A lump clogged Seth's throat as Mitch opened his arms and Olivia dashed straight into them to be swallowed up in a zealous embrace. That, he decided, was what family was all about. Beneath ill-chosen words and bruised pride there was still that soul-deep connection that refused to be severed.

Aware that he'd been forgotten, Seth watched Mitch squeeze the stuffing out of Olivia, clinging to her as if he never meant to let her go. He heard the broken phrases of apology tumbling from Olivia's lips while Mitch spun her in a circle and nuzzled his chin against her neck.

Seth supposed he should feel gratified that he was responsible for reuniting father and daughter. Instead he felt left out, lonely and used. He ought to be accustomed to that feeling, after years of being perceived as no more than an expendable tool utilized to dispense justice.

Well, at least he'd been betrayed for a noble purpose, he tried to console himself. He'd granted Mitch his fondest wish and made the Ramseys' holidays complete. That should count for something.

Unnoticed, Seth rode toward his cabin. He should be delighted to return to the warmth of a roaring fire and the comfort of his own bed, after nearly two weeks of riding back and forth cross-country on horseback. Should be, but wasn't.

He'd been alone plenty of times before, but he'd never felt quite so lost and abandoned as he did when he entered his empty cabin and was met with deafening silence.

Straight away, Seth strode over to retrieve a glass and whiskey bottle from the cabinet. He planned on being on the wrong side of sober by nightfall. And he might just stay there until after Christmas. Surely a few drinks would help him forget that he had betrayed Mitch's trust, just as surely as that rascally old goat had deceived him.

But first and foremost, Seth wanted to forget that Olivia no longer needed him, forget the gratitude she had mistaken for love would fade in time. She had her father to protect and provide for her. She had only leaned on Seth for comfort and support while she was vulnerable and insecure—because Mitch had seen to it that Seth had been her convenient shoulder to—

Seth jerked up his head and frowned when a suspicious thought suddenly occurred to him. "Well, I'll be damned. You're smarter than I gave you credit for, you old fox," he said to the picture of frizzy gray hair, a wry smile and shrewd hazel eyes that formed in his mind's eye.

Mitch had been discreetly keeping tabs on Olivia for months. He'd known she'd been embarrassed and demoralized. Mitch hadn't wanted to run the risk of fetching Olivia himself, for fear their previous conflict and her stubborn defiance would prevent her from making the journey.

And so Mitch had sent *Seth* to deal with her anger, hurt and resentment and deliver her to Oklahoma Territory.

Seth held up his glass to toast the image dancing in his head. "Too bad you outsmarted yourself by sending me, Mitch. Turns out that sending a wolf to guard the lamb didn't work out quite as you'd expected."

The memory of the wild passion he'd shared with Olivia hit him like a blow, right between the eyes—and below the belt buckle. Seth plunked into his chair, chugged a drink—or three—and stared into the leaping flames he'd brought to life in the hearth. He kept pouring liquor down his gullet until he couldn't see straight, couldn't think straight.

Finally, blessedly, he reached the point that he couldn't *feel* anything except dizzying numbness.

Seth didn't fall asleep on the eve of his homecoming. He simply *passed out.* And that was exactly what he craved—unconscious oblivion that would override the hurt and longing.

The evening after her arrival at the homestead, Olivia helped her father position the Christmas tree in front of the parlor window then accepted the colorful, handmade paper chain he extended to her. While she and her father decorated the tree—a family tradition they'd shared for as long as she could remember—she wondered if Seth had resettled into his normal routine and had been jumping for joy after he'd dropped her off at her father's cabin. No doubt, she was out of Seth's hair and off his hands for good—and he was glad of it.

"I suppose Seth took good care of you during the trip," Mitch commented as he grabbed a chair and climbed up to adorn the treetop with a paper angel. "Good man, Seth. He even helped me build this cabin."

Olivia admired Seth's handiwork. "He's a man of many talents, obviously," she said, then tossed her father a reproachful glance. "You shouldn't have deceived him. He didn't take it well at all."

Mitch smiled enigmatically. "He'll get over it, soon as he figures out why I specifically sent him."

Olivia frowned, bemused. "Just why did you send him, rather than come yourself?"

He shrugged thick shoulders and continued to place crude wooden ornaments on the top tiers of the tree.

"Papa?" she prompted warily.

"*What?* Can't a father wish his only daughter home for Christmas and send a dependable friend to fetch her?"

His all-too-innocent stare didn't fool Olivia for a moment. Then it suddenly dawned on her why her cunning father had sent Seth to Missouri. "He was supposed to be my *cure*, wasn't he?" she asked perceptively.

He didn't bother to deny it. "I wanted you to have the chance to know what a good, reliable man is like. They don't come any better or more competent than Seth Gresham. He might not have Jacob Riley's social graces and practiced charm—"

"No, thank goodness—" she cut in.

"—but if you want a job done right you send a professional, someone who can get you safely to your destination and overcome any obstacle thrown in his path."

"Except one obstacle," Olivia said under her breath. "He didn't know how to handle the fact that I fell in l—" She snapped up her head and glared at her father. "Dear God!"

Olivia was so exasperated by the thought that she hadn't noticed how closely her father was scrutinizing her. There was a shrewd smile playing on his lips and a mischievous glint in his eyes. She'd seen that expression often enough over the years to recognize it for what it was.

"You sent Seth to be far more than a cure for what ailed me," she accused sharply. "You wanted me to fall in love with him, didn't you? You picked him out for me!" Her voice hit an outraged pitch. "Of all the sneaky, low-down, dirty tricks!"

Olivia tossed aside the paper chains and stamped up to her father, who was still poised atop his chair. She was so aggravated with him that she considered kicking the support right out from under him. "You should be ashamed of yourself!" she scolded hotly.

Mitch didn't look the least bit repentant or ashamed. He was grinning like a Cheshire cat that had feathers sticking out of its mouth. "Can't help but love him, can you, daughter? I knew if the two of you had ample time together sparks would fly, same as they did between your mamma and me. Emma was as feisty, independent and spirited as you. The love of my life, she was, but it takes a certain kind of man to handle a sassy, quick-witted woman."

His expression softened as he climbed down from the chair and pulled her resisting body into his arms. "All I've ever wanted is to see you happy, sweetheart. You'll have children of your own one day and then you'll understand how it feels to want the very best for them, to feel the overwhelming need to protect them from hurt and harm."

Olivia slumped against him, savoring his sheltering embrace. All her defenses crumbled, after putting up such a good front the past two days. She had tried to deal with the fact that Seth didn't love her back. She'd even told him that he didn't have to. So long as he accepted her affection for him. Blast it, she should be used to unrequited love by now, but getting over Seth was a different kind of hurt than she'd experienced with Jacob. He had trampled on her pride, but losing Seth left a hollow ache in her heart. She could understand how devastated her father must have been when he lost his wife.

When a sob bubbled up in her throat and escaped her lips Mitch patted her consolingly. "Tell me true, honey, you love him, don't you? You see in him, same as I do, all the fine qualities that he has trouble acknowledging in himself."

She nodded and sniffled. "Only problem is that your scheme didn't work both ways."

Mitch reared back to stare into her blotchy face. "You know that for a fact? Did you tell him how you feel?"

"Yes," she murmured as she wiped her eyes with the back of her hand. "I told him straight out."

"And what did he say to that?"

"He said I was mistaken about how I felt and that he wasn't the kind of man I needed." Olivia backed from her father's embrace and inhaled a restorative breath. "Now, if you don't mind, I'd like to go to bed. I'm still trying to catch up from the exhausting journey."

Mitch watched his daughter retire to the spare bedroom, then glanced down at Hiram, who lay sprawled in front of the glowing hearth. "C'mon, boy. We have a late evening call to make."

Hiram didn't stir a step. He lifted dark, soulful eyes to his master, but he didn't look the least bit interested in braving the cold temperatures.

"Well fine, you stay here and guard Livie. I've got an ax to grind with my neighbor." Wheeling around, Mitch snatched his coat from the hook beside the door. In afterthought he grabbed his rifle. Never knew what—or whom—you might encounter at this time of night, he reminded himself.

Chapter Seven

Seth jerked upright in his chair when someone hammered impatiently at his door. Sluggishly, he grabbed for his pistol, but he couldn't clear leather before the portal banged against the wall. Mitch Ramsey appeared like a demon from the darkness. His trusty rifle lay cradled across his arms. His furrowed brows shot up like exclamation marks when he spied the two empty whiskey bottles at Seth's elbow.

"You're drunk," Mitch said, disgust evident in his voice.

Seth squinted at him, then scowled. "You rode all the way over here to tell me that? Waste of time. I already know it."

Without invitation Mitch barged inside and kicked the door shut with his boot heel. "For a man who is usually as sensible and practical as the day is long, you oughta know better than to take a flying leap into the bottom of a whiskey bottle."

"Spare me the lectures," Seth slurred out. "Wha'dya want from me now? Another favor? Forget it. You're already over your limit. I'm not going to be your errand boy again."

Mitch leveled him a fulminating glare. "I'm here because you made Livie cry and you're going to answer for that."

Seth wagged his finger in Mitch's general direction, wishing his vision wasn't so blurred. "The next time you decide to come storming over here to chew me out, *don't*. In case you haven't noticed, I'm put out with you, old man."

"Well then, I'd say we're even," Mitch flashed back. His gaze darted back to the empty bottles. "When did you start this drunken binge?"

"Last night," Seth mumbled. "Not that it's any of your business."

"It's a complete waste of time," Mitch insisted. "Tried it myself when the memories of Emma kept tormenting me, but it didn't help. Drinking isn't the answer because when you sober up you'll still remember the question."

Seth's pickled brain couldn't function quickly enough to keep up with Mitch's rapid-fire comments. He flicked his wrist limply, indicating the door. "Go 'way. I'm not in the mood to deal with you."

"Why not? Head about to explode?" Mitch taunted. "I wanna know why you told Livie that she didn't know what she was talking about when she said she loved you." Mitch demanded sharply.

Seth tried to raise himself from a slouch. "Is that *all* she said?" he asked warily, then snapped his mouth shut when Mitch's gaze narrowed suspiciously. Damnation, if this wasn't a good lesson in why it was crucial to keep your trap shut while you were soused then Seth didn't know what was.

To Seth's amazement, Mitch cocked the trigger of his rifle. The blast rang in his sensitive ears and he stared incredulously at the splintered wood that was six inches away from his stocking feet.

"You shot a hole in my floor!" Seth roared, then grabbed his aching head.

"I could've blasted a hole in your *chest*, ya know," Mitch

growled. "I was a damn fine soldier and a fair shot when I served with the Confederate Army. And don't think I haven't figured out what happened—that shouldn't have happened—between the two of you during that trip!"

"Well, it's your own fault, you conniving old goat," Seth flashed angrily. "You should've known better than to send a man like me. I'm nobody's idea of a gentleman, you know."

To Seth's bemusement, Mitch lowered the gun barrel, held up his hand and demanded, "How many fingers am I holding up?"

He squinted at the blurry images. "Two. Why?"

"Obviously you haven't drunk yourself completely blind, just stupid. And here I thought you were smart enough to figure out why I purposely sent you to fetch Livie."

"I know why," Seth muttered. "You were too much the coward to face her anger and resentment. So why not send me to take the brunt of it? I've had to do everyone else's dirty work all my life. Why not my *ex*-best friend's, too?"

Mitch shook his gray head and cast Seth a withering glance. "That wasn't the reason I sent you. I handed my own daughter over to you on a silver platter as my Christmas gift to *you*. And you were my gift to *her*. I wanted the two people I hold dear to have the chance to become well acquainted without distraction or interruptions. I didn't want you to have one of those splash-and-dash courtships that barely total up to a few days of togetherness over a span of six months, either."

Seth's stubbled jaw scraped his chest. He'd been *had*—to the extreme. "You were matchmaking?" he croaked.

"Well, of course I was. You were handpicked and sent off with my stamp of approval." He stalked forward to loom over Seth. "And there's gonna be a wedding on

Christmas Eve at my place," he decreed, then trained his rifle threateningly on Seth's chest. "Or your funeral. Married or buried. You choose." Mitch pivoted on his heels and strode to the door. He paused to glance back at Seth's bewildered expression. "And Merry Christmas to you, too, *friend.*"

Olivia sorted through the garments Seth had haphazardly crammed into her carpetbag before he'd abducted her from Missouri, then she donned her best gown. Mitch had invited a few friends over to celebrate Christmas Eve and she had baked three apple cobblers to serve to the Widow Hadley, her two sons, Doc Potter and several other guests.

It had been a week since Olivia had seen Seth, and she doubted that he would show up for the festivities. She had considered dropping in on him a few days earlier, but she had chickened out. She doubted that he had the slightest interest in seeing her again.

He doesn't love you, Liv, she told herself as she arranged her curly hair into a fashionable coiffure. *He's satisfied with his life, just as it is.* Too bad she hadn't gotten over him as easily as he had forgotten about her.

Olivia was in the process of mixing up a batch of eggnog when her father exited his bedroom, dressed in what appeared to be a new suit. She didn't recall that he'd made the purchase the day they had ridden into Guthrie to restock supplies. Neither did she recall seeing Mitch so fidgety before. He kept glancing at the mantel clock at irregular intervals while he paced the parlor.

Amused, Olivia tossed him a grin. "Since when does the prospect of hosting a holiday party have you wearing a nervous path on the floor?"

"Since—" Mitch pulled up short. "It's our first Christmas here, ya know." He glanced out the window then said, "Oh good, some of our guests have arrived."

Ignoring her father's peculiar behavior, Olivia followed him to the door to exchange pleased-to-meet-yous with the first wave of guests. It didn't take long to realize that the Widow Hadley was sweet on her father. The woman's gaze followed him around the room and she cleverly managed to guide him to the empty space beside her on the sofa. Not that Mitch stayed put for very long, Olivia noticed. He kept bounding up like a jackrabbit to look out the window and fetch more refreshments.

When another rap resounded on the door, Mitch said, "Get that, will you, Livie? I've got my hands full with this tray of pastry and eggnog."

Olivia swept across the room and pasted on a smile to greet another of her father's guests. When she opened the door, the shock of seeing Seth—decked out in his Sunday best, his raven hair neatly trimmed and his ruggedly handsome face smooth-shaven—held her immobile. A flood of emotion bubbled up inside her when their eyes met and a host of forbidden memories flooded over her. Heat flared in those fathomless green pools and her body instantly responded to the long-awaited sight and scent of him.

"Don't just stand there, honey, invite him in from the cold," Mitch prompted.

Olivia gave herself a mental shake and stepped aside. "Nice to see you again, Seth," she said, exasperated that her voice sounded breathless and she could feel a blush pulsing in her cheeks.

"You, too, Olivia," Seth said awkwardly.

"Now that the other guest of honor has arrived, let's get started," Mitch announced.

Totally bemused, Olivia watched the man that her father had introduced as Pastor Rogers set aside the glass Mitch handed to him then rise to his feet. Pastor Rogers strode up in front of her, as if in some official capacity, and smiled kindly at her.

"Very wise of you to select Christmas Eve as your wedding day," he said then winked. "The groom is less likely to forget your anniversary."

"Anniversary? Wedding?" Olivia echoed. Her bewildered gaze flew to Seth who stood a step behind her, looking more like the honored guest at his own necktie party. "What in—?"

"Don't rile your father," Seth murmured for her ears only. She followed his pointed gaze to the rifle hanging above the door and she realized that Mitch must have delivered a threatening ultimatum to Seth.

Outraged, she whirled toward her father, who looked so pleased with himself that she wanted to smear his triumphant smile all over his face. When she impulsively lunged toward him, Seth's muscular arm snaked out to hold her in place.

"'Better wed than dead,' he said. "Or something to that effect," Seth murmured. "He blew a hole in my floorboards and vowed to do the same to me if I didn't show up tonight. *You* might be his daughter, but I wouldn't cross him right now if I were you."

Olivia's face flamed with humiliation as she surveyed the smiling guests, who had obviously been informed that a ceremony would take place this evening. Well, they were doomed to disappointment because she was not going to marry a man who had been threatened with bodily harm if he didn't show up to tie the knot!

"No! Absolutely not!" Olivia burst out. She refused to go through with this surprise wedding and have Seth re-sent her for the rest of his life. She would not allow her father to arrange a marriage to a man who didn't love her, despite how much she loved him.

"Wedding jitters," Mitch explained to his startled guests. "My daughter is a bit high-strung."

Although the pastor and guests were staring uncertainly at Olivia, she did the only thing she could think to do. Run. She bolted toward the door and tore off across the lawn, as if the hounds of hell were nipping at her heels. She had no idea where she was going, but she knew she couldn't remain here, not after her father had embarrassed her, manipulated her and served her up like a slice of apple cobbler.

Olivia had been mortified when Jacob Riley betrayed her with her best friend. But that was nothing in comparison! A shotgun wedding, for heaven's sake? Her father had completely misjudged her if he thought she would stand for it!

"Livie, hold your horses!"

Olivia screeched to a halt then whirled at the sound of Seth's booming voice. "I am so sorry," she blurted out, humiliated to no end. "I swear to you that I had no clue what Papa had schemed up this time. I never said one word to him about…" She shifted awkwardly as Seth approached. "Well, *you* know what I'm talking about. But how could *he* have known?"

Her uneasy gaze darted toward the front door, expecting her father to stalk outside with his rifle in hand. "I'll ride into Guthrie and spend the night at one of the hotels," she insisted rashly. "First thing in the morning I'll make the roundabout stage and railroad connections to return to Missouri."

"No, you won't. That's too dangerous."

Seth appraised the frantic expression on her flushed

face, studied *her* and wondered how he'd managed to keep his distance for an entire week. Certainly, he had weighed his options, but in the end, he had accepted Mitch's ultimatum because…

"When it comes to friends," Olivia said sourly, "you can really pick 'em. As for me, I'm stuck with him because he's my father." She darted another anxious glance at the door, then peered curiously at Seth. "You could have hightailed it to parts unknown and Papa wouldn't have been able to track you down. *Why didn't you?*"

Seth took a deep breath, stared into the bewitching face that haunted all his dreams and said, "Maybe I don't want to leave behind the only home I've ever had. And maybe I've decided that settling for the gratitude you've mistaken for love is better than not having you at all. Maybe I'm tired of the world passing me by. Maybe I want to be a family man, like most of the other settlers around here. Ever think of that?"

Eyes popping, Olivia staggered back a step. "So now I'm your consolation prize to make you feel like an accepted, respectable part of the nearby community?" she howled, offended.

When she lurched around, Seth clutched her elbow. "Okay, so that didn't come out quite right. The truth is that I wasn't sure I wanted to be around when you finally realized you weren't really in love with me." He grabbed a quick breath, then blurted out, "Because loving you the way I do, I wasn't sure I could handle it. I've dealt with danger and disappointment plenty of times." He was babbling now, the words rushing out like floodwaters, but he couldn't hold them back. "But I swear, Liv, the prospect of you waking up one day and realizing that I wasn't everything you thought I was, just like with that jackass

Jacob, has been driving me crazy. Yet, I've missed you so damn much that I'd rather face your eventual disillusionment than live without you. I even tried drinking you off my mind and out of my heart, but that didn't work. I—"

When she pressed her fingertips to his lips to shush him, Seth closed his eyes, savored her touch and felt himself boil down to mush. Damn, wouldn't you know that a man with his legendary reputation for tracking ruthless criminals—that no one else dared to confront—would be brought to his knees by a five-foot-nothing female? Now there was irony for you.

"You love me?" she asked, her blue eyes shining with tears. "When did this happen?"

Seth clasped her hand and brushed a kiss over her fingertips. A wry smile quirked his lips as he studied her bewildered expression. "You mean precisely? The exact moment?"

When she nodded and smiled back at him the darkness seemed to glow with hope and infinite possibility.

"Yes, the *exact* moment," she said. "*Precisely.*"

"When I was standing in the café in Missouri, watching you stare me down like the boldest outlaw I ever faced. You tapped your foot impatiently and made it clear that you weren't the least bit intimidated by me."

Her gaze widened in surprise. "Are you serious?"

"As serious as a shotgun wedding," he assured her. "I was hooked on you the moment you said, 'Excuse you, you're in my way.' Smart mouth and all, I knew you were the kind of trouble I wanted to spend the rest of my life with. I want to see that spirited twinkle in the eyes of my own child. I want the chance to be the kind of father who never lets his kid down, the way my parents let me down." He reached out to sketch the elegant curve of her cheek.

"You taught me to feel with my heart and I haven't been the same since. But there was Jacob's memory standing between us, not to mention your misconceived affection for me and your father's machinations. I thought you needed time to sort out your true feelings for me."

When Olivia flung her arms around his neck and kissed him with everything she had in her, Seth felt the last of his apprehension bubble into a cauldron of hungry desire.

"Are you coming back inside or not?"

Mitch's voice shattered the hypnotic spell. Olivia dropped down on her heels and stepped sideways to stare at her father. "The real question is, are we going to allow you to get away with this or not? You should be shot for all your underhanded tactics, Papa!"

Olivia watched a look of unease claim her father's features. At this distance she couldn't be sure, but she swore he was holding his breath and hanging on tenterhooks. It served that conniving rascal right to stand there and stew in his own juice for a few minutes.

Mitch half collapsed in relief when Olivia nodded her assent then grabbed Seth's hand to accompany him back to the awaiting wedding guests.

"A shotgun wedding," Olivia said with a disbelieving shake of her head. "Now *there's* a fantasy that never crossed my mind."

"Good." Seth gave her hand a loving squeeze as he strode along beside her. "Sure would hate for my memory to get all mixed up with those childhood fairy tales in that pretty little head of yours," he added teasingly.

Olivia stopped short and stared deliberately at her future husband. "If I hear you mention another word about that jackass Jacob and my foolish expectations, I will nag you until the end of your days. He means absolutely nothing to me. You are the *only* man who does… Well, except for Papa and I'm perturbed with him at the moment."

Seth chuckled as he towed Olivia toward the house. "Glad to hear that. I prefer that all your fantasies center around a snowstorm in the middle of nowhere."

She grinned mischievously and said, "I've had that very dream every night for a week. As good as it was, I should warn you that I have even higher expectations for our wedding night."

A slow burn worked its way through Seth's body as he escorted his bride-to-be into the parlor to say the I-dos. He even managed to take the good-natured ribbing from the Hadley brothers, who claimed he'd been roped and hogtied and was destined to be led around by the nose by his feisty wife. But none of the playful taunts got to him because, for the first time in his life, he knew how it felt to be happy and content. Each time he glanced at the gold band he'd slid onto Olivia's finger, a little voice kept whispering, *She belongs to you now so don't mess up the best thing that's ever happened to you.*

Right there and then, Seth made a solemn promise to do everything in his power to make Olivia as happy as he felt at this moment. She was never going to have to worry about him turning to another woman because he loved her like crazy.

And he'd like to communicate these bottled-up feelings for her this very minute. Seth glanced around the crowded parlor, estimating the acceptable length of time a man was expected to endure his wedding reception before he could take his bride home—and have her all to himself.

Olivia blinked in pleasant surprise when Seth opened his front door and carried her across the threshold. The spacious, well-furnished cabin was so welcoming that she felt at home immediately.

"Well, Mrs. Gresham," he said as he set her to her feet, "what do you think?"

Olivia noted his expectant smile, understood that he needed her approval, but she had far more important things on her mind than circumnavigating the parlor to inspect the furniture. Grinning impishly, she pivoted to tug at the cravat that encircled his neck then peeled off his coat. With a careless toss, she left the garments hanging haphazardly on the couch and rocking chair.

His dark brows shot up as she unbuttoned his linen shirt and flung it toward an end table. "I'm redecorating," she replied to the question in his eyes. "I love what you've done with the place, by the way, but it won't have that homey appearance until all your clothes are draped on the furniture and I've dragged you off to bed to have my wicked way with you."

Seth chuckled as she reached for the placket of his breeches, "Patience, wife, we have all night."

"Only what's left of it, after Papa kept dragging out the reception until I was ready to take his own rifle after him," she countered. "He did that on purpose, the ornery rascal."

Seth unfastened the small pearl buttons on the front of Olivia's dress. "It seems Mitch has had an ulterior motive for everything he's done this month." He smiled dryly. "Remind me to thank him…after I can get my mind on something besides all the things I've dreamed of doing with you for an endless week."

His expression turned to molten heat as his gaze roamed freely over her. Olivia stood before him, wearing nothing but the gold wedding band that symbolized the bond between them. The look on his face held erotic promises of the passion they'd shared once before. She vowed that, from this night forward, Seth would never have cause to doubt her unfaltering affection. She would make certain that he knew this was no fleeting fancy that would fade over time.

To that dedicated end she cupped his face in her hands and drew his head steadily toward hers. "You asked me once to look at you and to be certain I knew whom I was seeing," she murmured. "Now I want you to look at me and to know that I'm the woman who's going to love you from now until long past forever."

She pressed a kiss that carried a wealth of meaning and promises to his sensuous lips and felt intense emotion expanding inside her. "I love you with all my heart and soul, Seth Gresham. *Know* that, *believe* that, because it's true. And come Christmas morning, I'll be right here beside you, still loving you, as I will be for all the days of your life."

When he crushed her to him and devoured her, savored her and held her as if she were his most cherished gift, Olivia surrendered to all the aching need and ardent passion that roiled inside her. This, indeed, would be a Christmas to remember. It was a new beginning in a new territory. It was the end of every silly childhood notion, because the reality of loving Seth, and knowing that he loved her in return, far exceeded whimsical fantasy.

As he tumbled with her onto their bed, and snowflakes danced like miniature elves on the wind, Olivia knew she had received the greatest blessing life had to offer. She had *love*, the everlasting kind that shimmered in every part of her being.

"My love, my life, my beloved wife," Seth whispered as he came to her, giving all of himself, all that he was and ever hoped to be. "Merry Christmas, sweetheart."

Olivia peered up into his shadowed face as he angled his head to seal the magical bond between them with a kiss.

In his eyes, in his lopsided smile, she saw her future shining like the brightest stars in heaven. Mrs. Olivia Gresham had it all. And not for one moment was she going to take for granted this precious gift her father had given to her.

She'd have to make a mental note to thank Mitch for that, she thought fleetingly. Her father had known exactly what he was doing when he sent Seth to her for Christmas.

* * * * *

Be sure to watch for Carol Finch's next historical,
THE LAST HONEST OUTLAW,
coming only to Harlequin Historical
in December 2004.

Available from Harlequin Historicals and
LYNNA BANNING

Western Rose #310
Wildwood #374
Lost Acres Bride #437
Plum Creek Bride #474
The Law and Miss Hardisson #537
The Courtship #613
The Angel of Devil's Camp #649
The Scout #682
High Country Hero #706
One Starry Christmas #723
"Hark the Harried Angels"

Please address questions and book requests to:
Harlequin Reader Service
U.S.: 3010 Walden Ave., P.O. Box 1325, Buffalo, NY 14269
Canadian: P.O. Box 609, Fort Erie, Ont. L2A 5X3

HARK THE
HARRIED ANGELS
Lynna Banning

To the memory of Mary Banning Yarnes
and Lawrence Yarnes

Acknowledgments

With thanks to Suzanne Barrett, Susan Renison,
Tricia Adams, Kathleen Dougherty and Brenda Preston.

Prologue

Irina Likov trudged from the railway station down the lane and across the bridge toward town. Heartsick and so alone the ache inside felt like an ax slicing into her belly, she listened to the water gurgling beneath the stone arch. Her footsteps slowed, her boots crunching in the snow. Her reddened nose dripped. Her toes had no feeling.

She had lost everything, her husband, her mother country, her hopes and dreams of a new life in America. Yuri had died of fever on the ship from Odessa.

When she saw the house, and the lights, she stopped. Snow blanketed the roof, drooped over the windows like eyebrows. Columns of smoke puffed from the chimney and vanished into the branches of a chestnut.

The windows glowed with light, and in each one hung a wreath, as if a green eye peered out from the panes. Even the door had a circle of evergreens, with a swirl of ribbon splashed in the center like a smile.

Beside the house, lights glittered from the branches of a cedar, and at the top a star winked. In the quiet she could hear her own breath rasp in and out. She took a step, listening. Another. The snow whispered as if she walked on velvet.

Her heart cried out to those who dwelt in that place of warmth and silence. *Please. Oh, please. Let me belong.*

Chapter One

Partridge, Oregon, 1907

Irina often watched the man the townspeople called the Vinegar Man through the spaces in the board fence that separated her backyard from his His name was Adam Garnett, and everything about him seemed a bit loose, slipshod, as if he had dressed with his eyes closed. As if he wore the same garments every day and he no longer cared what he looked like. Only his hands were taut, clenched at his sides or jammed deep into his front pockets to keep them warm. On this bitter December morning he wore no hat. No jacket. Such a sadness. The man as well as the bleak, barren ground over which he paced aimlessly in black boots cracked with age. A waste of good earth.

Her own back garden, sheltered from the wind by a row of cleverly spaced myrtle trees, was still green in places, even in mid-December. A plot of beets, two rows each of cabbage and chard, and four potato hills. Not one inch of her land was unused, right down to the sweet woodruff she let wander at will among her precious vegetables.

She had worked hard these seven years, turning the house and the yard she now owned into a haven of peace. A place where she belonged. She touched the bright rose hips remaining on her Belle of Portugal, repeating a silent thanks that God should let them dot her garden with spots of crimson this close to winter.

"Already is Christmas," she said aloud. A wave of homesickness washed over her.

She glanced into the Vinegar Man's yard. Had he heard her? She took care not to hum or talk to herself as she often found herself doing inside her house; she did not wish to disturb the man who walked and walked over the bare ground. He seemed strange, and she was a little bit afraid of him.

The man paced on, head down, scuffed boots scraping the ground. Her own sturdy boots didn't look much better, even though she polished them every night before she went to bed. She had to make them last until next summer.

In the six months he'd lived next door, he'd never acknowledged her presence. His features were obscured by the dark beard and the shaggy black hair that hung over his face, and he had never once looked at her.

How old was he? she wondered.

Older than her papa, she judged by his stance. But no gray streaks marked his hair or his mustache, what she could see of it, so perhaps he was younger than he looked.

Or perhaps not. Irina had no time to study him at length. She had laundry to hang out for her boarders and vegetables to gather for their supper that evening.

She slipped the small utility knife from her apron pocket, bent to harvest a fat green cabbage and a double handful of red-leafed winter chard. Gathering her apron front into a carrying pouch, she shot a final look at him, shook her head and moved up her back porch steps. Next summer she would offer the man some vegetable seeds.

Next summer. She halted mid-step and shut her eyes. How hard it was to think of summer now, with the air biting at her nose and cheeks and the sky the color of a dirty tin pan. And it was hard not to think of the small village near Novgorod, and her father's tiny farm that she had left at seventeen. She could still smell the snow and the trees, fresh and piney with resin.

Bogoroditsa! Time for more important things. The clothesline for her washing. Scrubbing the kitchen floor. Supper for her boarders.

The back of her neck prickled. *Ah, a ghost walks over my soul.* Or was someone watching her?

She stood on the top porch step and peered sideways into her neighbor's yard. Back and forth the Vinegar Man walked, never altering his pace, never even looking up, much less looking at her. With a shrug she pulled open the screen door. A man with his chin on his chest saw only the ground in front of him.

But Adam *had* looked. He often looked at her, watched her dart about her garden, shears and a wicker basket in her hands. She was never still, this neighbor of his. It annoyed him. That and her humming. One tune over and over, a simple melody with a repeated refrain. An old-country song. German. Maybe Russian.

When she talked to herself under her breath, the words were often in a language he did not understand. Adam tried not to listen, tried not to notice her presence beyond the fence, but dammit, she was *there.*

He craved solitude and she picked apples or hung up laundry or any of a dozen things that kept her in his peripheral vision. He tramped his route again, from porch step to the fence at the rear of his property, then back to the porch. Again. And again.

It brought solace after a time. At least enough to ease

the anger, the distrust he felt about his fellow human beings. Enough so he could sleep at night.

"Mistuh Adam, you gonna wear out yore boots walkin' and walkin' like dat." The scratchy voice came from behind the door screen. Adam pivoted and began another circuit, his back to his manservant.

"They're my boots. Leave me alone."

"They ain't just yore boots. I figger I put enough bootblack on 'em over the years they's half mine. An' I don't want no holes in mah boots."

Adam turned back in time to see Luther's graying head nod with his final words. "No, suh, no holes in mah boots!"

He let out a long breath but kept moving. Most exchanges with Luther gave the dark-skinned man the last word; Adam liked that just fine. It gave him something to start a conversation with later, over the supper table. If he cared to. Mostly he didn't, and the two ate their beans and corn bread in silence.

Now he paced the hundred feet up to the porch, half wishing his neighbor would come down her back steps once more. Watching her surreptitiously kept his mind off other things.

From the second-floor rear balcony of the largest house in town, three other pairs of eyes watched Adam and Irina in their backyards.

The Clouet sisters—Marie-Louise, Solange and Annette—were as different as magnolia blossoms, rosebuds and daisies. Raised by their grandmother in Paris during *La Belle Epoche,* they were fashion-conscious and still beautiful, even in middle age.

No one in Partridge knew why the sisters were always elegantly attired in the latest silks and lace and, given the women's eccentric ways, no one dared to ask. "They're really quite odd," the women said. "They're French," the men said. And smiled.

The truth was they were enormously wealthy, thanks to Grandmère's canny investments in South African diamond mines and the new American automobile. Also, the two older sisters, Solange and Marie-Louise, regularly received generous "pensions" from the cream of French society. Marie-Louise the townspeople dubbed "the Countess," because the gossipy bank owner hinted that her support from abroad came from a French count.

Annette, the youngest at forty-one, had not acquired any wealthy admirers when the sisters left Paris; she devoted herself to cooking and becoming as American as possible. Annette was passionate about only two things, neither of them male: her yellow bicycle and the rosewood Erard grand piano in the second parlor. Her practicing often kept Solange and the Countess awake, but Grandmère had taught them "never to object to any aspect of life, provided it was not harmful to the skin."

In the privacy of their immense, overdecorated mansion, they sipped tea, played piquet, and read books sent from Paris, which, if the content were known, would have provided many a Sunday sermon for the Partridge village preachers.

And they watched their neighbors, Irina Likov and Adam Garnett, the Vinegar Man.

"*Mon Dieu,* what ails that man?" Marie-Louise tipped the Sèvres teapot and dribbled another splash of amber liquid into the delicate cup. "Just look at him, Solange."

"I see him. I look at him every afternoon. The man is obsessed with making footprints." The younger woman twitched her crimson cashmere skirt to cover her toes and pinned her sister with steady blue eyes. "Or, perhaps his neck is permanently bent. He never looks up."

"Do you not find that odd?" Marie-Louise lifted her

cup with one elegant long-fingered hand, keeping her wrist straight as Grandmère had taught her. An enormous ruby solitaire winked in the late afternoon light.

"Look!" Solange pointed down at the adjoining yards with her extended little finger. "She picks the cabbage, but she looks at *him*."

Marie-Louise rolled her eyes. "But of course she looks at him. She is a woman, *n'est-ce pas?* And he is a man."

Solange stared at her older sister. Garbed in her usual elegant black silk afternoon dress, Marie-Louise, with her pinched-in waist and a spine so straight her black buttons never touched the chair, resembled a bright-eyed bird with fluffed-out wings. "*Je ne comprend pas,* Marie. Why would she look at him if he never looks at her?"

"Ah, but he does look at her. When she is not looking at him. Do you not see, *cherie?*"

Solange bit her lip and focused on rearranging her skirt. Annette, the youngest, poked Solange's corset-encased rib cage. "Even *I* understand what is going on, and *I* have never had a liaison. Not one." She sent a reproachful glance toward Marie-Louise. "Grandmère shipped us all off to America before I—"

"It was because of you that we left Paris," Marie-Louise said, her voice crisp. "Someone asked Grandmére for your hand in marriage. Clouet women do not marry."

"The lady of the cabbages," Solange ventured, her eyes questioning. "Will she not marry?"

Marie-Louise turned snapping blue eyes on her younger sisters. "Perhaps."

Solange sighed. "She is not old enough to be a widow."

"Men," Marie-Louise said, "brave, foolish creatures that they are, often die young."

Annette nodded. "*He* is not dead." She tipped her head toward the man pacing below them.

Marie-Louise sniffed. "Look closer, *ma petite*. Inside, he is lifeless."

"*Regard!*" Annette jumped up. "Now he *is* looking at her. But, alas, she is gone with her cabbages into the house."

"*C'est dommage.*" Marie-Louise sipped her tea in silence.

"*Mais oui. Stupidité.*" Solange ventured a covert look at Marie-Louise. "We should, perhaps, *do* something?"

Irina staggered through the screened back porch and down the steps, the bucket of dirty scrub water in one hand. She dumped half the contents onto her Belle of Portugal, then emptied the remainder on the bed of winter chard.

"Silly to irrigate in winter," she said to herself. "It rains and rains, maybe even will snow before Christmas." But she still clung to the frugal habits she'd learned on her father's farm in the old country. Water was precious, especially in drought years.

The memory brought an ache to her throat. She and Yuri had such hopes when they sailed for America. A big farm, with wheat and barley. Maybe some horses for the plow and a brindled cow for milk and butter. Ah, such dreams. And they were so young. So young they barely knew each other.

She jerked upright. "I will not think of that," she murmured. "I will think of my beautiful green cabbages and the roses that smell still of summer. And the sweet woodruff to flavor the Christmas wine."

Christmas. Her heart caught. She could not help missing her homeland in winter, the silvery birches with their graceful limbs, the musky smell of incense in the village church and the men's voices singing the hymns for the Savior. Best of all was the fragrant fir tree the children decorated with candy and bits of ribbon. A Christmas tree.

"In all my years in America I have not had a Christmas tree," she announced to the empty bucket in her hand. She turned back toward the porch, took a single step forward and stopped.

This year I want a tree! A real Christmas tree, like at home.

A flood of memories swept over her. Mama's piroshkis on a cold winter afternoon. The smell of wood burning in the stove. And Christmas eve, when Papa hung the fir tree from the rafter and then spun it around and around so the glittery snow crystals clinging to the branches spun off and showered everyone with icy droplets.

That beautiful, magical tree. Every year the wonder of it had awed her into silence. *Oh, how she missed it!* Just once more, before she was so far from childhood it would no longer matter, she wanted a Christmas tree.

From the kitchen she could hear Miss Caroline at the parlor piano, punctuated by a loud thumping overhead. Mr. Ruland, chasing the cat out of his room again.

The cat skittered down the stairs and streaked into the kitchen. Diving between Irina's feet, the animal leaped over the wood box and hunkered down in an orange lump behind the stove.

"Sonya, bad cat," Irina scolded.

Sonya began a rumbly purring.

"No supper for you tonight. Must learn not to bother guests." But with a sigh she bent to sprinkle chopped egg into the cat's bowl.

Sonya rubbed against her leg. Irina reached one hand to stroke her back and without warning began to sob.

It had never been this bad, the homesickness. She swiped her fingers across her cheek. She felt so hungry inside. So…unfinished.

A shiver traveled between her shoulder blades. Her

kitchen was warm, even overwarm. But inside she felt as if a cold lump of winter had congealed in her belly.

She cocked her head to hear the piano, cored the cabbage in quick, decisive strokes and dunked it into a pot of boiling water. "Cook!" she ordered. Her mother had always talked to the cabbages.

In her tidy pantry, just off the kitchen on the wash porch, neat rows of summer vegetables in shiny glass jars stood on the shelves. "Tomatoes," she muttered. "Ah, here." She lifted down two quart containers and blew the dust off the lids.

She boiled two scoops of Indian rice, added a double handful of raisins, some hot paprika, dill seeds, then the tomatoes and two chopped onions. Setting the saucepan on the stove, she hesitated, then leaned over the simmering mixture and inhaled. It smelled like home.

She plopped a spoonful of the rice-and-raisin mixture onto the center of one cabbage leaf, folded in the sides and rolled it up into a neat packet.

Seven years without my Yuri. She laid the cabbage roll in the heavy iron Dutch oven and wiped her eyes with the back of her hand. Biting her lip, she spooned up another dollop of filling and rolled it up tight inside another leaf.

No Christmas trees for a hundred miles, just scrubby pine and wind-twisted cedars and cottonwoods near the river.

Oh, please, God. I want just one thing. It can be very small, but special. Just for me.

Chapter Two

The word *murderer* brought Irina's hand to a stop, a full bowl of soup yet to be passed on down the table.

"Who is a murderer?" She directed the question at Zeke Ruland. Mr. Ruland had boarded with Irina almost as long as Caroline Birdwell, the schoolteacher.

"Fella next door. Adam Garnett. The one that moved in last July."

"Who says this?" Irina pursued.

Lazarus MacDuff's red beard twitched. "Easy now, lass. He's served his time. Leave the man in peace."

Irina bridled. "I had planned to. I want to know if it is true or not, that he is a—"

"It is not true, Irina." Caroline laid down her soup-spoon and met Irina's gaze squarely. "The teacher at Gold Hill told me at Sunday service. It was written up in last Wednesday's *Gazette*."

"He wasn't guilty," Caroline added. "He spent fifteen years in prison and then another man confessed."

"Poor man," Irena murmured under her breath. No wonder that he paces.

* * *

"Mistah Adam, we gonna have another one of those suppers wheah I'd be better off readin' a book?"

Adam looked up from his plate of beans and corn bread. "What book are you reading?"

Luther glanced at the volume that lay at his elbow. "Rise of Western Civ-eye-lization."

Adam stared at the man who was both manservant and companion. "I should never have taught you to read."

"Oh, no, suh. I like knowin' things."

Adam addressed his supper plate. "You do."

"Say here dat this Charley-Main fella, he established the German empire of the West, and den de Turks done take over…" He grinned to reveal a mouthful of even, white teeth. "Not even most white folk know 'bout Charley-Main. Makes me feel kinda uppity."

Adam studied the man who had been his companion since boyhood. "Sure, Luther. Read. I wouldn't want to stand in the way of uppityness."

Luther chuckled, shoveled a spoonful of beans into his mouth and chewed thoughtfully. "Gotcha talkin', didn't it? Even made ya smile once. Little bitty smile, but it's a start."

Adam lifted his knife and cut his block of corn bread into eight precise rectangles. "All right, read it aloud." He liked the rumble of Luther's low, gravelly voice. Luther had been his only visitor while he was incarcerated. Then it had been the only voice he had trusted, besides his mother's. Even now it was the only voice he could bear to listen to. In his steadfast, gentle way, the former slave had taught Adam how to survive. When it came time to leave Richmond, Luther had refused to stay behind.

"We's pract'cally brothers, 'cept for our skin color. And I don't figger that bad choice on your momma's part matters much."

It was an old joke between them, and it made Adam

smile again. In the next moment he sobered again and bent to his supper.

Luther droned on and on about Charlemagne; Adam waited until he paused for breath. "Damn good corn bread, Luther. But sure is a dull book."

Luther chortled and gave his shoulder a friendly punch. He'd probably have a good-sized bruise later, but Adam smiled anyway.

At least he hadn't lost the ability to get Luther's ire roused and then make him laugh.

Must be more life left in my prison-hardened spirit than I thought.

The two elder Clouet sisters, Marie-Louise, in elegant black silk, and Solange, her brown hair done up in a pouf on top of her head, eyed the platter of meat Annette set before them on the lace-covered dining table. "*Qu'est-ce que c'est?*" Marie-Louise said, her voice wary.

"That," the beaming Annette announced, "is called a 'frankfurter.' Mr. Schwartz at the butcher shop suggested them." She smoothed back her ear-length chestnut hair.

"That man," Marie-Louise snapped. "What can he know? He comes from Heidelberg!"

"Is there *une salade*?" she inquired.

"*Oui.*" Annette ducked into the kitchen, emerging with a large cut-crystal bowl. "Coleslaw. It is made of cabbage."

Marie-Louise quirked her eyebrows. "And? Not just cabbage, surely?"

"Just cabbage. And mayonnaise dressing, of course. Flavored with dill."

Marie-Louise laid her fork down with a sigh. "I ask you, Solange. What is happening to us? To civilization? A nation that eats frankfuller. *Mon Dieu.*"

Solange, her mouth full of coleslaw, was spreading her

frankfurter with mustard. "*Je ne sais*, Marie. But the cold-slaw, it is very tasty."

Annette sent her older sister a grateful look. "Mrs. Likov gave me the recipe."

Solange reached to squeeze her younger sister's hand. "Of course, *cherie*. So…American, is it not?"

Marie-Louise scooped a dollop of mustard onto her plate. "Mrs. Likov is quite backward, I fear."

Solange's mouth dropped open. "Backward? I think she has managed most admirably without a man!"

"Backward," Marie-Louise reiterated. "I do not mean it unkindly. She has had no…training in the ways of the world."

Solange blinked. "In the ways of men, you mean? It is apparent she lacks…sophistication. It is not her fault that she was brought up on a farm in a land of barbarians and had no *grandmère* to educate her, as we did."

"*Oui*," Marie-Louise remarked with a tight smile. "She is not one of us. Irina Likov is what is known as a 'good woman.' For the Clouet women, that epithet would be a disaster. That is not our…tradition."

"I like her," Annette announced.

"But of course," Marie-Louise responded. "I like her as well." Her sharp blue eyes widened as something occurred to her.

As if by a prearranged signal, all three women looked at each other in silence.

"I wonder…" Solange murmured.

"Perhaps?" Annette offered after a long moment.

Marie-Louise swallowed her dainty morsel of frank-furter. "*Certainement*."

The eldest sister tapped her spoon against her wine goblet. "If we are agreed, then we must, as the Americans say, make a plan. *Faire une strategie. Alors,* let us think."

"Ah!" Marie-Louise uttered at last.

The two younger sisters leaned forward. "*Quel* plan?"

Marie-Louise tilted her head, pressing her forefinger to her lips. "Annette, *cherie*, you still have that dreadful wheeled cycling machine, do you not?"

"But of course. I am not *that* old yet."

"*Bon.*"

Annette and Solange looked at each other and shrugged. Marie-Louise had always distrusted Annette's yellow bicycle.

"*Et bien.*" The eldest sister's smile lit up her face from the high, pale forehead to her aristocratic chin. "We will have need of it. Now, if you would be so kind, please pass the frankfullers. We will need our strength tomorrow."

The shiny yellow bicycle careened past a horse-drawn buggy heading up Pear Street and wobbled to a stop on the sidewalk in front of the Vinegar Man's house. Annette Clouet gingerly propped the machine against a chestnut tree and bent over the front wheel. Taking care not to smudge her hands, she carefully removed the air cap and watched the tire slowly deflate.

When it was flat, she reattached the cap and wheeled the impaired machine through the Vinegar Man's front gate, where she propped it against the picket fence. Then she straightened her stylish brown velveteen bicycle dress so the skirt panels extended below her knees and reached for the iron door knocker.

The sound was more a *thunk* than a civilized *rap-tap*, but in a few moments the door opened and Annette assumed her best Distressed Matron look.

"What you want?" a scratchy voice inquired.

"*Pardon, monsieur.* Would you have a bicycle pump?"

"A what?" Large brown eyes in a shiny brown face

looked at her with a puzzled expression. "A whazzit you say?"

"A bicycle pump. My tire has gone flat, you see."

"Mistuh Adam!" The man called over his shoulder. "You come help dis elderly lady. Ah cain't understand what she be needin'."

The tall gray-haired man disappeared and the Vinegar Man appeared. His unkempt dark hair reached to his earlobes and his cold-eyed look made Annette take a step backward.

"What is it?" he snapped.

"My bicycle, monsieur. It has the flat tire, so I wondered—"

"Don't have one."

"Do you not keep one for your automobile?"

"Don't have one of those, either."

"Oh." She knew she must keep him occupied at the front of the house for at least ten minutes, as Marie-Louise had instructed. Annette lifted the timepiece about her neck. *Mon Dieu!* Seven whole minutes to go.

He started to close the door, but she stuck her leather boot in the opening. "Monsieur, I beg you. Could I not let my bicycle rest on your front porch for an hour? Until I can return home for my own tire pump?"

The cold eyes grew even colder.

"Please, monsieur? It will take so very little space."

No answer. Annette sneaked another look at her watch. Not more than two minutes had elapsed.

At last the Vinegar Man's lips opened. "Luther!"

Annette jumped at the ungentlemanly roar, and her thin mouth turned down as the manservant reappeared in the doorway.

"Yassah, Mister Adam?"

"Luther, the lady's bicycle is…wounded. It can rest awhile on the porch."

"Oh, thank you, monsieur!"

The Vinegar Man stalked past her as if she were invisible, the man Luther at his heels. Together they rolled her machine up the porch steps and leaned it against the dingy white ship-lap siding.

"One hour, you say?"

"*Oui.*"

"Dat's French talk, Adam. Means 'Yes.'"

The man called Adam cleared his throat. "I heard her."

He tramped back into the house and vanished into the interior. Luther's brown-eyed gaze followed him, then fastened on Annette. "Ah's sorry Mistuh Adam is so unfriendly-like," he said. "Par-done-ee-moy," he added with a grin.

Annette blinked at his mangled French. "Is he always like that?"

"Oh, yes, ma'am. Today one of his good days. Oughtta see him when he's—"

"No, thank you," she snapped.

Luther's shoulders lifted in a shrug. "Den ah'll be biddin' you good…" His grin widened. "Bone-jar," he pronounced with satisfaction.

Annette bit back a laugh and consulted her timepiece.

Four more minutes had passed, and she released a sigh of relief. Her part of the plan had been accomplished.

Adam let the screen door slap shut and didn't look back. Head down, shoulders hunched, he watched his black boots plunk onto the hard packed earth that formed the larger part of the property his mother had left him.

The house was too big, too spacious for a man used to the narrow confines of a prison cell. And the "back forty," as his tobacco-farmer father would have called it, didn't grow a damn thing. Not that he wanted it to. The flat, useless expanse of dirt under his feet was satisfying somehow.

What he saw under his boots as he tramped over it was hard. Barren. And untouched. Better to let things—the land, his life, even his heart—just be. Let them alone. If you didn't poke a wound, it wouldn't hurt.

He lifted his face. The sharp smell of the wind foretold a change in the weather—clouds to obscure the pale winter sun. Maybe even snow.

Jamming his hands into his trouser pockets he bent his head and kept walking. Snow wouldn't keep him inside the house; he'd need to walk no matter what. Snow would only make Luther's boot polishing more laborious.

He approached the rear fence. Without looking up he could gauge the number of steps until he made his turn and headed back the other way, exactly four long strides after the fence corner appeared in his peripheral vision. The same size as the prison yard.

He counted, made his turn, and started back. It was exactly thirty-two steps to the back porch. He had completed three when he jerked to a halt. What the hell?

Just to the right of his foot, a scraggly green finger of vegetation protruded from the soil. Adam bent closer. It was green, all right. Kinda weak and wobbly looking, but alive. What the devil was it doing growing here in his backyard?

He paced a slow circle around it. A better question was how had it managed to sprout in the first place? The dirt was packed hard as an iron griddle. There had been no rain, and the wind was so bitter cold it chilled his feet right through two pairs of wool socks. This scrawny little seedling had survived all that?

That's the way with weeds, he guessed. Nobody wants them and nobody can keep them down for long. He reached to yank it out.

The wind rose. "*Non*," it seemed to whisper.

He bent again, fingers extended.

Again the wind rose, and a single word sighed in his ear. *Non.*

Very slowly Adam straightened to his full height. The voice had a distinctly French accent.

The following morning Adam rose as usual and faced himself in the mirror. "You look like hell. Worse than an outlaw." Some days he wondered if he would ever feel part of the world again.

He washed using the china basin on the stand, ran his fingers through his tangled black hair and patted his un-trimmed beard dry. He liked looking disreputable. It saved him from having to make conversation. He wanted to at times. He'd like to talk to the young woman next door, but he didn't know what to say.

He pulled on the work-worn trousers and plaid wool shirt Luther had patched, lifted the basin of soap-scummed water and started down the stairs.

Luther was at the stove, frying bacon. "What you doin' with that basin?"

"What does it look like?"

"Look like you gonna do mah chores for me dis mornin'."

Adam sent the man a steady look. "I thought we agreed on this," he said in a quiet voice. "You aren't a slave any longer."

"Ah know Ah ain't a slave," the dark man shot. "You payin' me good wages to be your manservant, an' Ah like dat jes fine." He reached for the basin. "Ah do the dumpin' out 'round heah."

Adam sidestepped him. "You cook the bacon. I'll dump this."

He didn't precisely know why he wanted to do it. Well, maybe he did know. He would pour the dirty wash water on that scruffy seedling. Maybe the soap would kill it.

Frost crystals dusted the lone shoot, which somehow looked taller today. Some sort of tree, he figured. In a way, it was kind of a miracle. Some busy little finch or sparrow dropped a dry seed on his land and it sprouted.

Adam tipped the basin upside down, dumped the contents over the plant with a sploosh. The seedling bent almost double, the green tip nodding toward the earth's surface.

Just as well. The winter snow would kill it anyway; no reason to coddle it until then.

The smell of frying bacon brought his head up. Without thinking, he moved toward the warm kitchen where Luther would be laying out their breakfast. Halfway to the porch, his steps slowed.

Something was different today. Luther had fried bacon every single morning since they had left Richmond on a foggy March day; this was the first time in fifteen years the scent of bacon—the scent of *anything*—had mattered.

Chapter Three

Irina stretched on tiptoe to peek over the fence into the Vinegar Man's backyard. Frost coated the bare earth with a jacket of lace. She knew it would melt when the sun rose higher, but she liked to hurry out early enough to look at it, white and silent in the still air. It reminded her of home.

In her own yard, the lush beds of summer vegetables had turned brown, but the tangled climbing rose had so far escaped the ravages of early winter. Pockets of warmth protected her vine-swathed fences and trapped the sun's rays until the first snow. By late January, crocuses would poke up their yellow cup-shaped faces. By February she could turn the soil and plan for spring.

Her gaze drifted to the back fence where an exuberant purple clematis spilled over onto her property and spiraled determinedly through the rose canes. Odd. Almost Christmas and frost had not withered the delicate vine.

She peeked over the back fence and caught her breath. The entire garden belonging to the big three-story mansion on the adjoining property was a riot of color, purples and reds, even pink. Irina shook her head in disbelief. A lush, green lawn covered the ground. Pink flowering quince, red-orange trumpet vines.

Doubly odd. Quince didn't bloom until spring.

There really was something strange about the ornate blue house with the red shutters and white gingerbread trim. And the garden! Well, the garden looked as if it were…enchanted.

What silly nonsense! She'd heard talk about the three sisters who lived in the house. French, people said. And more than a bit eccentric.

And if their back garden was any indication, all three must have the most enterprising green thumbs.

She turned her attention to the side fence, the one she shared with the Vinegar Man, and watched fingers of sunlight touch the frosty patches on top of the boards, melting them into nothing as if by magic. She propped her chin on the top rail and surveyed the unused expanse of dirt with a calculating eye. How could a man neglect his own land?

The back door creaked open and the Vinegar Man stalked down his porch steps, a white china basin in his hands. He scowled at the ground, then upended the basin's contents. Shaving water, she guessed.

Now that was odd, too. His thick beard and shaggy sideburns hadn't seen a razor in a long while. From the pinched look on his face and the stiff way he held his neck, she would say he had acted in anger.

What a cross-pot! "Never have I seen a man wear such a perpetual frown on his face."

Only when he stopped short and turned toward her did she realize she had spoken aloud.

Her first impulse was to duck her head behind the fence, but then he looked at her, his dark eyes steady and accusing, and somehow she couldn't move. Heaven forbid, he was coming toward her!

He advanced four long strides, stopped and propped his hands at his waist. The empty china basin dangled from his pincered thumb and forefinger.

"G-good morning," she managed. It was the first time she had ever spoken to him.

"No, it isn't."

Heavens, what had she said? *Already you have made an enemy of your neighbor because your tongue has a will of its own.*

"I am s-sorry." She stammered the apology, but from his unchanging expression she knew it made no difference.

"Not your fault," he snapped.

"Oh, but it *is* my fault!"

"You figure you're in charge of the weather, do you?"

"No, but—"

"Then you're not responsible for the 'good' of the morning."

"Aha! You make a joke. Is funny."

"It's no joke, ma'am. Mornings haven't been 'good' for a number of years."

"Why?" The instant she said it, she knew she should have kept her mouth closed. A double frown line appeared on his already closed face. He looked like the mosaic of St. Boris before he was martyred, the one on the floor of the church in Novgorod.

Worse, even. St. Boris's mouth looked like a real mouth. The Vinegar Man's lips looked…

A giggle escaped. His lips looked puckered. Like a dried plum.

His voice hardened. "The 'why' is none of your business."

Ah. Mr. High and Don't Bother Me. Piqued, she pressed on. "Then I ask another 'why,'" Irina shot back. "Why do you not plant anything in backyard?"

"None of your—" He stopped midsentence and the lines in his forehead furrowed even deeper. "Why should I?"

"Because God gives earth to grow things. Corn and beans and cabbages…things to eat. It is a miracle when a seed sprouts and later a flower blooms."

His face changed. She might have missed it because it happened so fast and then, instantly, he reverted to the scowl. She was getting used to the scowl; the sudden warm light in his eyes that stirred her, threw her off balance. For that one small moment his eyes were a dark, fathomless green, like wet moss, and then they turned hard, like green jade.

She liked the moss, she decided. She wondered if she would ever see it again.

Not unless you can think of something to say.

But her head felt as if it were stuffed with straw and corn husks, and her tongue, once so unruly and brash, lay limp in her mouth.

Very slowly he raised his free hand and smoothed the thick dark beard. Over and over he stroked it, as if he couldn't make up his mind about something.

"I go now," Irina announced. "Must cook pancakes for boarders." She darted between her dried-up vegetable plots to her porch without looking back.

If she had, she would have seen the shadow of a smile cross the Vinegar Man's face.

The next day Irina baked and scrubbed, chased Sonya out of the upstairs rooms the curious cat continued to invade and worked extra hard to lighten her homesickness and lift her spirits. So soon it would be Christmas, and there was much to do—soft, dimpled cookies to bake for the children who came caroling every year, furniture to polish, and her own restless soul to bring to order.

She should be thankful for all her blessings in America.

Quickly she rapped the wooden scrub brush twice

against the kitchen floor for good luck. She had her house, which had been offered in exchange for caring for its dying owner seven years ago. She had the rich soil, a town that welcomed her into its warmth and safety, the people who took her under their wing.

Even her paying boarders helped out when needed, except for Caroline's nephew, William Lowell III, who thought manual labor beneath his dignity. Mr. Ruland lent a hand beating the carpets in the spring, and Lazarus Mac-Duff must have peeled a mountain of potatoes over the years. Caroline helped with the mending when she wasn't busy correcting school essays.

"So many people, so many kindnesses," Irina murmured. She shooed Sonya from behind the stove so she could scrub the baseboard. And yet...

And yet, deep inside her, a tiny hunger nibbled away at her heart. It was so vague and unformed that she had no idea what she yearned for, other than flowers for the supper table and...a Christmas tree. Oh, if only she could take her ax out into the forest and chop one down! But the nearest forest was fifty miles away.

She would think about that after she finished the apricot tarts for Mr. Ruland's birthday. He would be seventy-eight years old, and no one had baked him tarts for fifty years!

Irina tossed the bristle brush into the pail of dirty water and sat back on her heels. "Holy Mother, I myself am to be twenty-five years in summer. Am surrounded by kindly people, and I am greedy and ungrateful to want more, but I do. I...I want my own family to care for. Pink, happy babies. And a husband like my Yuri to love." They had both been seventeen when they married, so long ago she could scarcely recall his face.

She hid her face in her water-stained apron. *Should not want too much.*

Lifting her head, she pressed her lips into a wobbly smile. "But that is for future. This year I ask only for Christmas tree."

Meanwhile, in the Vinegar Man's bare yard, a once spindly tree seedling pointed its tip toward the sun and began to sprout lush, green side branches.

The Clouet sisters, bundled to the chin in fur-lined coats with bright knitted long-tailed scarves covering their hair and ears, watched from their balcony in quiet satisfaction as Adam Garnett tramped around and around the pretty little fir tree growing in his backyard. He bent, inspected the ground at its base, measured the height in hand spans, and stood scratching his beard for a long minute.

"Luther!" He hated to bellow at the old man, but he was a tad hard of hearing.

The tall man poked his gray head out the back door. "Yassuh?"

"Come out here."

When Luther clomped down the steps, Adam pointed to the only spot of green on his bare ground. "Look at this."

"Look lak a li'l bitty tree, Mistuh Adam."

"It *is* a tree. Did you plant it?"

"Me!" The brown eyes rolled. "Nom, suh. Ah told you, ain't settin' foot in a growing field ever again in mah life."

The two men looked at each other for a long moment, then tramped together toward the porch steps. The soft murmur of their speech floated up to the balcony where the three fur-swathed sisters huddled.

Marie-Louise held up one finger for silence. When Adam's back door below them snapped shut, the uplifted finger crooked and beckoned. All three women leaned forward.

"It cannot be long now," Marie-Louise whispered.

* * *

Irina purposefully kept her gaze away from the fence separating her property from the Vinegar Man's. Ever since their chilly exchange yesterday, she took care to avoid him. There was no joy in a man who challenged a simple Good Morning.

Intent on the narrow straw-laden path that wound between her vegetable beds, she clutched her sharp kitchen knife and advanced on the last of the winter chard. She snipped an apron full with quick, decisive motions, then moved on toward a fat round cabbage that suggested hearty soup.

A curious force drew her attention from the cabbage bed to the rose bushes, to the fading morning glories on the fence to...

She dropped the knife. The cabbage, too, went tumbling along the pathway, and the chard spilled out of her apron as she ran to the fence.

Her breath turned into a hiccupy gasp. *What is that?*

No, not possible. Her heart pounded so hard her white shirtwaist fluttered up and down with each beat. Where had that little fir tree come from?

It hadn't been there last week. Or had it? Had the tree been there all along, and she just never noticed it because she was afraid to look over the fence into the Vinegar Man's yard?

"But now," she breathed in amazement. "Now it is reaching above the fence, tall and bushy and green, just like a—" She rose on tiptoe. *A tree! A Christmas tree!*

She stretched her hand across the fence toward it. "So beautiful," she murmured. "Oh, so beautiful." Already she could envision strings of cranberries and popcorn, the tiny white Christmas candles she had made last spring out of beeswax and clothespins and saved in a cardboard box.

The little tree shimmered in the pale sunlight. Beckoning. Irina's throat ached. Tears misted her vision, she wanted it so much.

Yes. Oh, yes! It was the most perfectly proportioned tree. The most beautiful tree in all the world. She lifted her nose and sniffed, imagining the sweet, clean scent of fir needles.

She was the happiest of women! She spun, arms extended, in a dizzy circle. How fortunate she was! Except that...

With a low moan she turned away and pressed her hand over her eyes to block the vision. Ay, how could she be so slow-witted? The object of her adoration did not grow in her yard.

It grew in the yard belonging to the Vinegar Man.

When the dishes and pots were washed and dried with Caroline and Zeke's assistance, Irina crawled into her narrow bed upstairs and pulled the quilt up to her chin. Sonya nosed the door open with a plaintive *meorwl*, leaped up beside Irina and began to purr.

"Is good you are happy," Irina whispered to the orange ball curled against her hip. "I, too, will be happy. But I must do something to make it so."

She ran her hand down the cat's warm fur. "Cannot cry more. It swells my eyes and makes my nose drip. Very unpretty."

The purring feline stretched under her hand.

"So, Miss Sonya, what I do?"

She stroked down the knobby spine, lifted her hand to repeat the action and stopped short. A startling idea was taking shape in her mind.

"Oh, I could not."

The cat batted at her fingers. "But perhaps I *could*. I am afraid, but...yes, I could do it."

She sat up in bed. "I *will* do it." She sucked in a steadying breath. "Tomorrow. Christmas comes in four days, so no hours to waste. Yes, tomorrow."

Chapter Four

Adam watched the young woman in the threadbare gray wool coat and black boots push open his gate and inch up the walkway toward the porch. She kept her head up, her neck stiff. Her lips moved as if praying. Or maybe talking to herself.

She was very pretty. And she looked vaguely familiar.

Aha. His neighbor with the big garden. He didn't recognize her at first with her head covered up by the knitted scarf. A basket covered with a red-checked napkin swung on one arm, as she stepped carefully along the frosty walk looking for places to plant her boots.

At the bottom of the porch steps, she stopped, clasped her hands—bare, he noted—under her chin and closed her eyes. Then came a light knock on his front door.

"Ah'm comin,'" Luther called from the kitchen.

Adam did not wait. He yanked open the door to confront a pale face wreathed in sky-blue wool, a pair of wary dark eyes and a nose red and shiny from the cold.

"What do you want?"

Luther made *tsking* noises behind him, and Adam frowned. His voice sounded unfriendly, even to himself.

"What do you want?" he repeated in a more civilized tone.

She just stared at him, eyes wide, her mouth opening to a small O.

Adam waited.

Irina gazed into the hard green eyes and felt her resolve crumble. "Mr. Vineg— Mr. Garnett, I mean?"

He waited without speaking, his gaze flat, his expression carefully controlled. She focused on the buttons of his blue flannel shirt, noted that he had rolled the sleeves up to his elbows. He stood watching her, scarcely an arm's length between them.

"I...I..." Her throat closed. Impulsively she shoved the basket toward him.

"What's this?"

"I bake sponge cake this morning. Made extra, for you." She raised the basket, gestured for him to take it.

A flicker of something went across his lean, hawklike face. "Why?"

"Why what? Why I bake or why make extra?"

He lifted the basket from her hand without answering, his eyes looking steadily into hers. Irina waited, her tongue frozen to the roof of her mouth.

He said nothing, just stood at the door, patting the checked napkin covering with his long fingers. But she thought his eyes softened just a bit. And then his stern-looking mouth, half-hidden between the dark mustache and the darker beard, opened and a single word escaped.

"Thanks."

She caught her breath. His voice sounded raspy, as if he wasn't used to talking. "You are most welcome."

He just stood there, as if uncertain what to say.

Suddenly she understood. He *wasn't* used to talking. He rarely left his house and she never saw him in town.

He spoke to no one but his hired man. For some reason this man had shut the door on life and locked it behind him.

He had not smiled once this morning, and that made him appear angry. Still, there he stood before her, awkwardly stroking the wicker basket, and deep within those moss-colored eyes she glimpsed an odd light. The man was not angry; he was afraid.

Afraid of what? Of being an outsider? From her own first year in Partridge she knew how hard it could be. There was no pain like not belonging.

Under the wool coat her heartbeat faltered and then jumped. She must show him…must welcome him. The custom in America was to shake hands; she extended hers toward him.

He stared at it a long time, then glanced into her face. Irina tried hard to smile over the funny shaky feeling inside her.

He took her hand. "Thanks," he said again. "I guess I am…surprised."

A knot tightened around her heart. She opened her mouth to speak, but her lips trembled. She turned to go so he would not see, walked quickly down the porch steps and through the gate. Behind her, she heard his low voice once more.

"Thanks."

At noon, Adam waited behind the back porch door, watching for her through the screen. Luther brought him a bacon sandwich for lunch, and he ate it standing up, afraid he would miss seeing her.

He'd thanked her already this morning. He could just as well send Luther next door to return the basket. Why did he need to see her again?

Hell, he knew why.

He turned over and over in his mind her gesture of welcome this morning. Of acceptance. Her small, capable hand had offered much more than a sponge cake.

Mrs. Likov, Luther said. Russian. A widow. Her given name was Irina.

He could not erase from his mind the moment when she had offered him her hand. He felt odd, as if she had reached out and pressed a finger onto his soul. Unbuttoned a part of him so deep inside it couldn't show.

The screen door in the neighboring yard creaked open and then slapped shut. There she was, her apron caught up in her left hand, the little knife she always carried clasped in her fingers.

Adam stepped through his own back door. She was humming that foreign song again, but today it didn't bother him. She piled something leafy into her apron, then stopped to gaze over his fence.

Adam moved toward her with the empty basket. When he reached the fence separating them, he lifted it high so she could see it.

Without a word, she came forward and reached her hand over the fence. He pressed the wicker handle into her fingers.

"Good cake," he rumbled.

"Is made with rum," she said. She glanced past him at something in his yard.

"Is very pretty fir tree."

Adam nodded. Despite his neglect, even mistreatment, the seedling had somehow grown into a handsome little tree.

"Is like Christmas tree we have at home in Russia."

Adam nodded again.

"Every year Papa cut one just like it, for decorate with candles. Sometimes I wish…" Her voice died.

She turned away suddenly and with a wave of her hand

started toward her back porch. Adam stared at the slim retreating figure in the blue work skirt, her shoulders straight, head held high, and felt his mouth go dry.

He wanted to talk to her. But it had been so long he wasn't sure he knew how anymore. What would he say? How would he even begin a conversation?

He began to pace the length and breadth of his yard in the familiar pattern, back and forth from the rear fence to the porch. But today, on every circuit he found himself stopping to inspect the little fir tree and thinking of Irina Likov.

"Quelles idiots!" Marie-Louise shook her finger at the now empty backyards.

Solange nodded. "Imbeciles! It is hopeless."

"*They* are hopeless. Backward. Like the children playing Blind Man."

"*Mon Dieu*, we waste our time," Solange added.

"She is worse than *he* is," Solange said in a strangled voice. "Always it is the woman who guides such matters."

A burst of laughter escaped Annette. "Not in America. One wonders how they manage to reproduce."

"Annette!" Marie-Louise snapped. "Mind your tongue. They know how to reproduce well enough. It is *une certaine finesse* in the beginning that is lacking."

"Perhaps it is their diet," Solange offered in a tired voice. "Perhaps frankfullers are not conducive to *les pensées sensuel?*"

"No passion. Not one *soupçon*. Think, sisters!" Marie-Louise tapped her forefinger against her temple. "*Pensez!*"

The three sisters drew their dark heads together.

"It is almost Christmas Eve," Solange moaned. "Her heart, it is so full."

Marie-Louise tapped her head. "His brain, it is so dull."

Annette bit her lower lip. "I think *his* heart is full, as well. But he does not know how…"

"To make *l'amour* happen," Solange finished.

Marie-Louise smiled suddenly. "But *we* do."

The three sisters joined hands. "*Allons!*"

Annette Clouet coasted the bright yellow bicycle to a gentle stop and propped it against the pepper tree in front of Irina Likov's boardinghouse. She marched up to the porch and rapped at the door. Even in America, miracles could happen.

Irina greeted her visitor with a shy smile. "Oh! The lady with the bicycle! Please to come in."

"Another time, perhaps. I have come to invite you to take tea with my sisters and myself. This afternoon."

Irina suppressed a gasp. "Me? There must be some mistake."

"You know who I am, do you not?" the woman inquired.

"Oh, yes. One of the French ladies in the big house."

"*Alors,*" the woman said with a wide smile. "These French ladies ask you to tea. This afternoon. Four o'-clock."

"Oh, but I—"

The woman stepped off the porch, righted her cycling machine, brushed a leaf off the leather seat, and mounted. "*À bientôt!*"

With a wave of her gloved hand, she pedaled off, sitting stiffly upright. Like an elegant crane, Irina thought.

At three minutes to four, Irina pulled her front door closed behind her, drew in a double breath of the crisp wood smoke–scented air to give her courage and started down her porch steps. To keep her mind off how nervous she was, she made herself count the number of steps to the Clouet sisters' ornate three-story mansion on Pear Street where she had been invited to tea. Exactly seventy-seven from her front door to the black scrolled iron gate.

The entrance door looked like a pretty cake with its fan of beveled glass top and bottom and the carved wood decoration. *Holy Mary, help me to behave like proper lady.*

Before she could finish her entreaty, the door opened and she was ushered into the parlor by the jolly, wrinkled woman in a housekeeper's duster. "You're that lady with the cabbages in yer yard, Mrs. Likov? The sisters been keepin' an eye on you."

"Oh?" What did they see, she wondered, with their "eye" on her?

When the housekeeper bustled off, Irina gazed at the grand piano, the matched brocade settees, elegant enough for a palace. And Holy Mary, such paintings! Three large portraits of handsome young women in frothy ball gowns that exposed their shoulders. Irina had never seen such dresses, such jewel-encrusted necklaces and pendulous earrings.

The three faces looked down at her with calm, self-assured eyes. Irina recognized the youngest because of her deep blue eyes and dark, almost black hair. She had stood on Irina's porch not more than two hours ago.

For a moment she wondered if she was dreaming. The gazes of all three ladies seemed to see right into her heart.

"*Bonjour,* Madame Likov. How nice that you are here at last!"

The woman with the beautiful green eyes embraced her, soundly kissing both cheeks. "I am Solange Clouet. And here is my sister, Marie-Louise."

At a glance Irina took in the two sisters' stylish afternoon dresses, Solange in sky-blue moiré with black embroidery, Marie-Louise in black silk with lace trim at the high neck and the cuffs of the voluminous sleeves.

"Madame Clouet," Irina murmured.

Another embrace and more kisses. "You shall call me Marie-Louise, *cherie*. And your given name?"

Irina swallowed. "My name? Irina, madame. After my mother."

She opened her mouth to apologize for her plain day dress when the youngest sister burst through the doorway dressed in a peculiar striped wool jumper with no apparent waistline.

"Sorry to be late. I was grooming my bicycle."

"Really, Annette!" Marie-Louise swatted dust off Annette's backside. "At such a time?"

A tiny crystal bell tinkled and a moment later the housekeeper rolled in a laden tea cart. "Madeleines!" Solange exclaimed. "Don't you just adore madeleines, Irina? Here, do have one."

Irina sank onto a navy velvet sofa, and the other sisters settled themselves in a circle around her. Marie-Louise poured tea out of an exquisite gold-trimmed teapot into cups so delicate Irina could see the shadow of her fingers through the porcelain.

"Alors," Marie-Louise announced, inclining her elegant head in Irina's direction. "You will please explain yourself?"

Irina choked on her madeleine. "Explain? Explain what?"

Marie-Louise nodded. "We would like your opinion on why—"

"That is, *cherie*, how it is that…" Solange dropped her gaze and carefully rearranged the folds of her blue moiré skirt.

Irina surveyed the three handsome faces. Marie-Louise was smiling at her, a sparkle in her penetrating blue eyes. Solange, beside her, patted Irina's hand with a feathery touch.

It was Annette who came to Irina's rescue. "What they—we—wish to know, with your permission of course, is what you intend to *do* about it?"

Irina blinked. "It? What 'it'?"

"Why, Mr. Garnett, of course," Marie-Louise explained in patient tones.

"You mean the Vinegar Man? What about him?"

"Come, come, *cherie*. You mean to say you have not…considered him?"

Irina stared at the sisters. Of course she had "considered" him. She hadn't stopped thinking about him since the day he reached over the fence and returned her wicker basket.

She opened her lips to evade the question, but something seemed to come over her. "I think of him quite often," she confessed.

Marie-Louise's face glowed. "*Bon.* That is a start."

"And?" prompted Solange.

Irina lifted her saucer and thought the question over. And. what? I am afraid there is no 'and.'"

"Balderdash!" Annette blurted.

"Annette!" The smile on Marie-Louise's face disappeared. "Such language!"

"Wait," Solange said quietly. She turned to Irina.

"Would you *wish* there to be an 'and'?"

Marie-Louise rolled her eyes. "Well, of course she does. She is not a tree, she is a woman. With feelings."

"Yes, I…" All at once Irina found herself telling the Clouet sisters all about her boardinghouse and how much, oh how very much she wanted a Christmas tree.

"Christmas tree!" Marie-Louise's eyebrows arched. "Did I hear correctly? *A Christmas tree? Mon Dieu!* Is that all?"

"A tree, yes. A beautiful tree. A special tree. And…"

The sisters looked at each other and smiled.

"And…" Irina managed in spite of her tightening throat.

The sisters leaned toward her.

"Something special, just for me." The words came out in a whisper. *Holy Mother, had she really said that?*

"*Bon, cherie!*"

"At last, we come to the heart of the matter."

"*C'est ça.*" Marie-Louise tapped her cheek with one finger. Now, *mes enfants,* let us make *une strategie.*"

Chapter Five

Irina tossed the scrub brush into the tin pail of water and inspected her now-spotless, shiny kitchen floor. She was alone in the house this morning, except for Sonya, who snoozed in the wood box. Caroline had walked to the schoolhouse for a lesson book, and her three male boarders had scattered toward town on various missions the minute they finished breakfast.

Good. There was something she wanted to do, and she needed no observers. It was hard enough to even think about, much less gather her skimming thoughts and her shaky courage and just...do it. "If only all of life was as simple and uncomplicated as scrubbing a floor," she said aloud.

She rose, propped the screen door open and lugged the bucket down the porch steps. Never waste water, Papa said. Even dirty water can nourish a growing thing.

Today it would be...let's see...the apple tree in the back corner of the yard. She felt so sorry for it sometimes, all alone after she'd plucked all the apples and its leaves dried up and fell in a brown-gold circle around the trunk. Silly to pity a tree, she supposed, but those in her orchard, the two cherries and the apricot, the Red June apple and the pear tree, were like old friends. She wanted them to be happy, even if they were just trees.

"Hello, June tree," she murmured as she approached. "I have brought you a drink." She dumped the scrub bucket and watched the water soak into the earth.

"And now for the scary thing." She pivoted away from the apple tree and had just taken a step toward the house when the Vinegar Man's back door slapped shut. A tall, lean figure walked down his porch steps. Heavens, Mr. Garnett.

He wore a wide-brimmed hat that had once been black but now looked mud-brown and his blue plaid flannel shirt looked rumpled. He strode toward the back of his property, moving in her direction.

Not yet. I am not ready.

Mr. Garnett put his head down and kept coming. Her heart settled down when she realized he didn't see her.

Such long, hard strides he made, stomp-stomp-stomp, like an old Cossack dance. At the thought a bubble of laughter escaped her lips.

He stopped stock-still. Irina clapped her hand over her mouth, crouching low so he wouldn't see her. She heard a footstep, then another. Coming closer. Coming toward her.

Her bent legs trembled like quaking aspen leaves. Her heart...Holy Mother Mary, her heart would pound its way out of her chest. She bent her head and tried to make herself as small and inconspicuous as possible.

"What in God's name are you doing?" The low male voice spoke so close to her she jerked upright.

"Watering my apple tree." She looked him straight in the eye and hoped he couldn't see the racing pulse beat in her neck.

"It hasn't rained much, and…"

His gaze caught and held hers. The eyes were mossy today, not hard like stone. Irina's fear began to dissipate.

Why, he looked as though he wanted to speak, but something held him back. He looked…uncertain.

Today he didn't look like he was going to eat her! Or even snap her head off. So why did she feel so skittery?

"Good morning," he said after a time. Still his eyes held hers, and deep within them Irina saw something. Something she liked, that drew her to him.

"Good morning," she said. She saw his throat work and then he swallowed. And swallowed again.

He folded his elbows on the fence rail. "I guess I don't have much to say."

"No matter," she said. She took a step toward the fence. Toward him. "I have often too much to say."

"Yeah. Seems to me you talk all the time."

"I do?" How could he possibly know such a thing?

"You do. Sometimes you talk to your cabbages. Just now I heard you speak to that tree." He tipped his head toward the apple tree in the corner.

He wasn't smiling, but his eyes, mysterious pools of deep green, looked calm. Questioning.

"Do you never talk to yourself, Mr. Garnett?" Irina gasped inwardly at her bold inquiry, but he didn't move or even change expression.

"All the time. Inside my head, where no one can hear but me."

She nodded. "I understand."

He looked at her so long and hard a prickly shiver crept up her spine. "I wonder if you really do."

A sudden bravado swept over Irina. "I will show you!"

Adam Garnett quirked one black eyebrow. "Okay, show me."

Irina studied his face, the long, straight nose, the hint of prominent cheekbones under the thatch of sideburns and beard, the composed, firm-looking mouth. Then she looked steadily into his eyes.

"You are wondering what to say next to me. I think you are not certain how to talk to a woman. To me." Heavens, how had she allowed herself to blurt out such a thing?

Under the faded brown hat, both dark eyebrows rose. "Am I, now," he breathed. It was not a question. "Uncertain, you say."

"Yes."

"About…you."

"Yes." She wished her heart would stop racing and fluttering. She couldn't catch her breath.

A long pause. Then his lips opened. "And are you ever uncertain?"

Irina hesitated. "Yes."

Again his eyes sought hers, held them in a long look. "Uncertain, about…me?"

This time she answered readily. She didn't know why, exactly, but she felt a bond spring between them, of understanding, of liking, even. A bond that had not been there before.

"Yes, I was uncertain about you. I am not uncertain now."

A muscle twitched near his mouth. "Mrs. Likov. Irina."

"Yes, Mr. Garnett?"

He reached one hand over the fence, held it out to her, waiting. Irina nestled her hand in his palm, felt his warm fingers close over her knuckles.

"Good morning," she said softly, for the second time that day.

His hand tightened over hers. "Good morning."

The forgotten question she had intended to ask flew back into her head.

"Would you…would you please to take coffee with me?" She cringed inwardly at her forwardness. She opened her mouth to retract the invitation, but he spoke before she could articulate a single syllable.

"I would like to very much, Mrs. Likov. Irina."

"You would?" Somehow she had not expected him to accept.

"Yes," he said quietly. "I would."

Irina's heart tripped, then sped up. "Come, then. Today. Now."

He stepped back, then vaulted the fence, landing on the other side with his boots narrowly missing her bed of chard.

"Oh! I expected you would..." Dumbfounded, she ran out of words.

"I didn't want to wait." He smoothed one hand over his unruly dark hair.

Irina recovered enough to speak, though to her surprise her voice trembled. "And why is that?"

He took a step toward her. "To be honest, I was afraid you'd change your mind."

"No, Mr. Garnett. I would not change my mind. I do not change my mind about things I think about for a long time."

Embarrassed at what she had revealed, she turned toward the house. "We go inside, now. For coffee."

"For coffee." He followed her swaying skirt up the narrow path to her porch steps, then in through the back door, which wheezed to a close after him.

Irina's kitchen was a warm yellow nest with colorful painted walls and open shelving stuffed with dishes and cups and platters. A pot of something bubbled on the stove. The fragrant steam escaping under the iron lid curled past Adam's nose and made his mouth water.

"Smells good in here," he said softly.

Irina smiled. "Something always cooking in my kitchen. I have four boarders to feed."

"I know."

"Have not made coffee yet," she apologized. "I was busy with other things."

"I know. You are often busy."

She raised her dark eyebrows in surprise. "You think, yes?"

"I think yes. I…watch you."

She gave him a long, steady look, then spun away to the stove. "I watch you, as well."

Her hand shook when she poured the beans into the coffee mill, fluttered like wings when she tried to turn the handle. Before she could protest, he laid his warm, strong hand over hers and together they cranked until the mill box was full.

"Thank you," she murmured.

"I wanted…" He hesitated.

Irina's breath stopped. "Yes?" She busied herself with the coffee so he wouldn't see her blush. She could feel the heat from her hairline to her breasts, feel her skin, her body come alive as his eyes studied her.

"I wanted to…touch you. I have wanted to for a long time."

"Oh," she whispered. A bud of inexplicable joy burst open inside her. "Oh!"

He drew his hand across his face. "I should not have said that. I've been away from people—from a woman—for so long that I—"

"Was what you said a true thing?"

"Yes. I meant it." A fleeting smile curved his mouth. "But I know…"

Irina looked up at him, the blue speckled coffeepot in her hand. "You are wrong. Should always say what is true."

Adam's throat tightened. She was so fresh, so honest. She was beautiful, too, with those wide dark eyes and that shiny hair. More than that, she was…important to him. He wasn't sure how he knew this, but he felt the truth of it deep inside. He wondered if she felt it, too.

"With cream or without?" Her eyes met his and suddenly he wanted to touch her again. She spoke once more, but he heard nothing, was aware only of her mouth opening, her lips shaping words.

She poured the dark liquid into a fragile china cup, then sent him a questioning look.

Adam nodded. He liked the silence between them. It was peaceful in the warm yellow kitchen, so quiet he could hear the kettle bubbling on the stove, the snap of the fire, the soft rumbling of a cat purring in the kindling box. Even their breathing was audible, hers soft and irregular, his steady, slowed with caution at the thing that was happening here in this room.

Yes, she felt it, too. He knew from the way she looked into his eyes.

Irina handed the filled cup to him. With slow, deliberate movements he lifted it out of her fingers, set it on the kitchen table, and held his hand out toward her.

Without a word she twined her fingers in his and drew him forward. Her face came up, her eyes soft and calm, and whatever fear he had evaporated into the scented air. He bent his head, caught her mouth under his, and then his arms were around her and he knew she had longed for this, for him, as he had longed for her.

"I want to say something," he said when they drew apart at last. "But I don't know how."

"You do not need to say anything. I know already."

He kissed her again. This time she kept her eyes closed even when it was over. "Tomorrow," she whispered, "is Christmas eve."

"I had not noticed."

"I have noticed. I invite you to take dinner at my house."

She couldn't be sure, but she thought tears swam in his eyes.

Chapter Six

"Mistah Adam, you hold still or Ah'll clap yoah head with these here shears!"

Adam straightened, stiffening his neck into an uncomfortable position, and Luther poked the scissor handle into Adam's scalp.

"Tip this-a-way."

The blades snip-snipped across the back of Adam's neck. His hair hadn't been cut since their arrival in Oregon, and it had grown so long Luther had spent the past hour just getting it out of his eyes. Locks of dark hair tumbled onto the kitchen floor in a shower of black crescents.

Adam closed his eyes. With his hair trimmed, he could no longer hide from people. It made him feel naked, somehow. Exposed.

"You about done?"

"Hell, no, ain't done. You been growin' wild fer six months. Don' blame me if it takes more'n an hour to tame it down. Just you hold still. Ah'm gonna turn you back into a man."

Adam snorted. Not likely. Fifteen years in prison pretty much took his manhood and ground it into dust. To change the subject, he posed a question.

"You going to visit Miss Sally?"

Luther stopped snipping. "Her mama cookin' up a goose fer dinner. Whole family gonna be there. And me."

Adam recognized the significance of Luther's inclusion of himself at the end, but he kept his mouth closed. Through all the years he and Luther had spent together, from boyhood on his father's plantation through the years after his mother died and the loyal black man had been his only prison visitor, the two men never talked about their women. Adam because he hadn't had one, and Luther because he was, despite his humble origins, a gentleman.

"Now, you is trimmin' up right nice. Look so human ain't gonna let my Sally anywhere's near you." He chuckled and crunched off a swath of Adam's chin growth with his scissors.

"Go easy on the beard."

"What foh? You still half gorilla."

"I'm...used to it, I guess."

Luther propped his hands on his hips. "Mistah Adam, you is been invited to take dinner at a lady's home. Least thing you kin offer her is to look lak a man 'stead of a shaggy buffalo. Tip yoah head up."

Adam knew better than to argue. Luther had earned the right to talk straight to him, and besides Adam rarely won an argument with the man. *Carrunch-crunch* went the scissors, and eight inches of beard rolled off Adam's lap to the floor.

"Ah'm not goin' shave it all off cuz you be sickly white underneath. Jes' gonna trim it close, like Gen'ral Bobby Lee."

Adam sighed and let Luther work over him another hour. No use arguing with a man holding a pair of sharp scissors in his fist. Maybe it was time he looked like a man again. Ever since he'd laid eyes on Irina Likov he'd begun to feel like one on the inside. Time to face up to it.

* * *

Solange placed her hands on Irina's shoulders, turning her toward the full-length armoire mirror.

"Oh, so beautiful a dress," Irina whispered. "But I could not…"

"*Mais non, cherie.* Not that one."

For what seemed the hundredth time in the past hour, Irina submitted to the helping hands of the two younger Clouet sisters. She stepped out of the forest-green satin.

Marie-Louise tossed the gown onto the boudoir chair already swathed in half a dozen rejects. "The color, it is wrong."

All three looked at Marie-Louise. The eldest sister flicked her fan at a yellow dress at the back of the armoire. "That one."

"Oh, yes!" Solange murmured. She and Annette buttoned Irina into a gown that shimmered like spun sunshine. "This is the very latest style, from Paris," Solange whispered.

"No bustle," added Annette. "And a new type of corset." She lowered her voice. "Or perhaps none at all? Such freedom!"

"*Bon.*" Marie-Louise sent Irina a pleased look. "And now, the hair." She stepped close and tipped Irina's face this way and that.

"Not too, how do you say… 'done up,'" Solange suggested.

Annette murmured, "Not too *demimondaine*, you mean."

Marie-Louise folded up her fan and cracked it across Annette's knuckles. "Mind your tongue."

"No bustle?" Irina looked to Marie-Louise for guidance.

"*C'est vrai, cherie.* The new fashion in Paris is smooth and graceful, like a swan." She studied Irina with an approving smile. "You look lovely."

"We have done well," Marie-Louise announced. "And you, Irina, you are an angel to let us fuss so."

Irina blinked. "Forgive me, Marie-Louise, but why do you *want* to? Fuss over me, I mean?"

"Why?" The eldest sister's blue eyes widened in surprise. "Dear child, surely you are joking? You cannot guess?"

Irina gazed from one sister to another. "No, I cannot guess. I have not the least idea."

The sisters looked at each other in frustrated silence. Finally Marie-Louise spoke. "Pehaps that is as it should be. For now."

In the gathering dusk the sisters' faces seemed to glow. For an instant Irina thought they looked like the gilded icons in a triptych she had once seen.

But that was ridiculous. One found triptychs in Russian churches. The Clouet sisters were French.

Adam paced around the block three times before he gathered enough courage to step up onto Irina Likov's front porch. Music and laughter drifted through the tall windows flanking the doorway. Someone was singing in a deep baritone. From the outside, the house glowed with warmth and cheerfulness.

Oh God, he wasn't sure he was ready for a whole gaggle of people. He raised his hand and knocked. *Not sure at all*.

The door swung open and a solidly built man dressed in a plaid kilt boomed a greeting. "Come in, lad, come in. And welcome to ye on this holy eve. "D'ye sing, laddie?"

Adam shook his head and unwound the wool scarf Luther had insisted he wear to "keep de cold wind from bitin' yoah neck." Bad enough to let the man prod him into his good trousers and dress coat. To say nothing of the stiff-collared shirt and tie. He felt like an unbroken horse in harness.

He drew in a long breath. Something in the air smelled so delicious his belly rumbled.

"I'm Lazarus MacDuff." A huge hand extended toward him.

"Adam Garnett."

"Come, laddie. Meet the others."

A sprightly gray-haired woman swung about on the piano stool and smiled at him. "Caroline Birdwell," Lazarus said. "Caroline is a schoolteacher."

Adam nodded at her. "Miss Birdwell."

"Allow me to introduce my nephew, William Lowell."

"The third," a laconic voice added. "Aunt Caroline doesn't put much stock in family heritage." William's handshake was a limp as his silk cravat.

With a sniff, Miss Birdwell pivoted back to the piano keyboard and Lazarus drew Adam on into the parlor. "And now meet…"

Adam's throat started to close. So many faces, names. He shook another hand, tried his best to smile. "Mr. Rowland, was it?"

"Ruland. Ezekiel Ruland. Folks call me Zeke."

"Now then, laddie, what do you want folks to call you?" Lazarus asked in a penetrating voice.

"Adam, I guess." To his relief, the piano music began again.

"Well, Adam, d'ye take spirits?"

"I do." He'd never needed a drink more desperately.

Lazarus obliged him by splashing whiskey into a small tumbler, while raising his baritone voice on the refrain of the carol Miss Birdwell played. "Star of wonder, star of light…"

Adam took a healthy gulp from his glass. After a second swig, the tension in his belly began to subside. Encased in a white collar starched so stiff it felt like a noose of hard white porcelain, his neck cracked when he twisted his head to look sideways into the dining room.

The long table was covered in something white and lacy. Fine crochet work. He hadn't laid eyes on a lace-draped table since…since his last dinner at home before his mother died. He took a sip of whiskey, rolled it around on his tongue until the ache went away.

Six place settings of shiny blue-flowered china were positioned around the table, two on each side and one at each end. He counted five people, including himself. Where was Irina?

At that moment the kitchen door opened and she stepped into view.

Adam's breath stopped. She wore an elegant yellow silky-looking gown with a neckline so inviting it was difficult not to stare. The simple apron looped around her neck and tied at the waist couldn't hide how beautiful she was. Not just the dress, but *her*.

His throat tight, Adam set his whiskey on a side table and moved toward her.

Irina looked up and smiled at him, lighting stars in her large, dark eyes. "I am glad you are here."

Adam could scarcely manage to speak her name. Instead he stepped forward and lifted the china soup tureen out of her hands.

"Is borscht," she said proudly. "Recipe from my home in Russia."

He set it down where she pointed, at one end of the table.

"Almost ready," she whispered. With a swish of her skirt she disappeared through the doorway into the kitchen and reemerged with a white china pitcher. "For the borscht," she explained. "Sour cream."

She placed the pitcher near the soup tureen, then untied her apron and dipped her head through the neck loop. Adam reached out and lifted the plain cotton garment over her head. His hands shook.

"Put in kitchen, please?"

Clutching the apron in one hand, he pushed through the swinging door.

Her kitchen was as unique as he remembered it, a mix of unconscious charm and real beauty. Like Irina herself. Hand-painted blue chickens and red and yellow flowers adorned the walls. The cat curled in the near-empty wood box next to the shiny nickel-plated stove. The red-painted floor gleamed as if it had just been waxed, and a stack of skillets and saucepans teetered in the sink.

The air was redolent with the scent of meat and spices; cinnamon he could identify. Maybe pepper. The heady smells came from something in the oven, he guessed. Again his stomach growled; he could not remember ever being this hungry, even in prison. Especially in prison.

Grateful for a moment's privacy, he lingered as long as he dared before voices on the other side of the gaily painted wall reminded him why he was here. He laid her apron across a yellow painted chair and moved back into the dining room.

"Ye're place is over here, laddie." Lazarus MacDuff waved him to the opposite side of the table. "Next to me." He patted the seat to his left.

Adam seated himself, noting that Irina sat at the head of the table, Lazarus at the foot. Across from him Miss Birdwell cocked her head and smiled; next to her, her nephew drooped in his chair with a bored expression on his narrow face.

"Caroline decided the seating arrangement," Lazarus boomed. "Seems there's to be some sort of 'surprise' later."

Adam stiffened. It was hard enough being this close to people after so many solitary years. Not knowing what was going to happen set his nerves on edge.

"Easy, lad," Lazarus murmured under his breath. "You're among friends."

"It is Christmas Eve," Irina said from the opposite end of the table. "We shall give thanks." She laid a hand on each side of her plate and stretched her fingers toward Zeke Ruland and Miss Birdwell's nephew on either side.

The circle of hands closed. Adam's hand was enfolded by Lazarus's meaty paw on one side and by Zeke Ruland's calloused one on the other. How long had it been since he had clasped hands around a table? Given thanks?

Too long. Far too long.

"I will say the blessing for our wee family this evening," Lazarus announced. He cleared his throat.

"Let us be at ease with the Lord and with one another on this night. Seein' as it's His birthday that we're celebratin', bless those among us who cook our food, and those who make music, and those who…"

He paused so long Adam wondered if the Scotsman had forgotten his speech. He stole the opportunity to glance up at Irina and to his shock met her gaze across the length of the table. Their eyes locked and held.

Adam did not hear Lazarus end the blessing. He saw nothing but the soft, dark eyes of his hostess looking steadily into his. A hard fist punched the inside of his rib cage, and when she glanced away at last, a roaring noise filled his head.

Irina began ladling out the borscht, and the bowls passed from hand to hand around the table until one clattered onto his plate. The pitcher of sour cream followed and then everyone began eating.

Adam tasted the thick soup, closed his eyes and invoked an additional blessing on the cook. The sweet-tart flavor was unlike anything he'd ever tasted, but what he liked best was the color when he poured on the sour cream. Like a mound of snow melting atop a crimson lake.

His sense of taste was *not* asleep, as Luther insisted when Adam didn't complain about beans and corn bread three nights in a row. His other senses were coming back to life as well. At this moment he could smell everything, not just the fragrant borscht, but the scents floating from the kitchen and those here at the table. Candle wax. Men's hair oil. An intoxicating, elusive perfume.

He inhaled deeply. Unable to stop smiling out of pure pleasure, he ate ravenously, savoring each spoonful, until his bowl was empty. Must be some special ingredient in Russian borscht, an elixir of some kind. There was no other way to explain how good he felt inside.

After that came slices of roast beef with horseradish sauce, whole carrots glazed in something sweet and pungent, and a salad of shredded cabbage and chopped apples with a creamy dressing laced with paprika. As he lifted forkfuls of food into his mouth, Adam's troubles seemed to evaporate. His unease lifted. The uncomfortably stiff collar, even the tightness of his belt as the meal progressed no longer mattered.

Finally, Irina and Caroline rose to clear the plates for dessert, and then came the moment Adam had been dreading.

"What do you do for a living, laddie?" Lazarus said as the women disappeared into the kitchen. The Scotsman regarded him with interest and a hush fell over the other two men.

It had to come sooner or later, Adam reasoned. He figured it was the price of his reentry into civilized society. Better step up to it and get it over with.

"I plan to draw income from…investments."

Young William Lowell bolted upright. "Yeah? What kind of investments?"

Adam decided to meet the rude question head-on. "I haven't decided yet. Some banking interests. Automobiles. Maybe railroads."

Zeke Ruland shot him a look. "Where's the investment money coming from?"

Zeke's bold question alerted Adam to what was really going on. Part of him was flattered. Part of him wanted to wrestle the questioner to the floor and smash his fist into his face.

He thought over what to say and decided to play it straight. He'd tossed his hat in the ring the minute he laid eyes on Irina; he didn't realize it at the time, but Lazarus MacDuff and Zeke Ruland apparently did. They were simply fulfilling the parental role.

"The house that I and my man, Luther, occupy belonged to my mother, who had it from *her* mother. Now that they are both gone, I own it free and clear."

Lazarus's rusty eyebrows shot up and waggled down.

"Now, as for my investments," Adam continued. "I own a tobacco plantation in Virginia which, because I have no interest in living there or farming it, I intend to sell. The proceeds should be considerable."

Adam relaxed the bunched-up fist in his lap. He'd just spoken more words in thirty seconds than he'd uttered in the last six months. Suddenly he felt very, very good.

He looked from Zeke to Lazarus and smiled. "Does that answer your question, gentlemen?"

"Indeed it does, laddie! You look solid enough."

Zeke nodded his agreement. "Railroads, son. Going to be the way of the future."

Caroline appeared in the doorway with a stack of small plates. "Enough of this man talk," she announced. "Irina has made a special dessert, and I have something unusual planned for afterward."

A sixth sense told Adam that whatever the schoolteacher had in mind would be far more difficult than simply answering questions as to his "prospects."

Slowly the hand in his lap curled itself back into a fist.

Chapter Seven

Dessert was a rich apple cake, soaked with rum syrup while still warm. It was Irina's favorite because she always had plenty of apples. This fall especially, the tree branches drooped to the ground with fruit and she had picked and stored every single one.

She looked around the dining table and sighed with satisfaction at the gusto with which her guests gobbled down her offering. All except Adam, whose face in the past few minutes had taken on a wary look. She met his eyes and smiled.

She liked this man. So much that it must be obvious to everyone else, but she didn't care. Adam needed someone—a woman—to like him. To love him, even.

And she needed... Oh, my yes. She felt stirrings within her she had never felt, not even with Yuri. So long ago that was. When she was seventeen and young.

She dropped her gaze to the thick slice of cake before her. Now she was twenty-five. Almost too old for babies.

The sound of William Lowell's high, nasal voice brought her attention back to the dinner table.

"I hear you have spent time in prison, Mr. Garnett."

An instant silence dropped over the diners. Caroline,

her fork halfway to her mouth, stared at her nephew. "William, how *could* you?"

William ignored his aunt. "Well, Mr. Garnett?"

Irina opened her mouth to introduce another topic, but Adam caught her eye and gave his head an almost imperceptible shake. Stunned, she watched him lay down his fork and turn his attention to William Lowell.

"That is true," Adam said, his voice even. "I spent fifteen years in prison. Six months ago I was released."

"For murder, wasn't it?" Lowell persisted.

No one moved. Irina watched Adam's face. His expression did not change, but she noted that he waited until Lowell stopped fidgeting.

Adam looked directly at his accuser. "That's right. The charge was murder."

"Then how come you're walking around like a free man, buying up railroads and banks?"

Adam's face remained impassive. "Because I was imprisoned for a murder I didn't commit. When the real murderer made a deathbed confession, I was exonerated."

"Just how do you know that?"

"I know because I was there when the man died. He was my brother."

"Your brother!" Lowell's pale eyes widened.

"He killed a woman we both knew, blamed it on me. The judge believed him and, before I could make an appeal, Sam hightailed it to Europe."

Without releasing Lowell's gaze, Adam calmly picked up his fork. "Anything else you want to know?"

Young Lowell flinched. "Don't guess so."

Caroline reached over and cracked her coffee spoon over her nephew's knuckles. While William nursed his fingers, a large freckled hand reached out and tipped a whiskey flask into Adam's empty water glass.

"William, you owe Mr. Garnett an apology," Lazarus

then said in a soft voice. "And Irina as well, for your disrupting of our dinner."

Silence.

"So let's hear it, laddie, so we can get back to our dessert and the surprise your aunt Caroline's dreamed up."

William's cheeks turned scarlet. "I apologize, Mr. Garnett. Don't know what got into me, except I'm, well, a bit…jealous that Miss Irina invited you."

Irina let out a little gasp, but when she looked at Adam she saw not anger but amused understanding in his eyes.

"No man has envied me since I was your age, William. I take your jealousy as a compliment."

At that moment Sonya stalked down the stairs and rubbed up against Irina's ankle. She bent to stroke the cat's fur, but the animal moved farther under the dining table, picking her way through the forest of shoes. All at once, Adam's body jerked and an odd look crossed his face.

Sonya. The cat had crawled into Adam's lap. Even from her position at the opposite end of the table, she could hear the rough purring. His half puzzled, half pleased expression made her lips twitch. Oh, how she wanted to laugh.

Caroline broke the awkward quiet with a cheery-voiced announcement. "Now, everyone, it's time for my surprise."

A flash of emotion surfaced in Adam's eyes. Fear. Though he hid it well tonight, with his calm voice and unperturbed manner, Irina noted that he was easily stirred into flight.

And that explained everything—the pacing, the unfriendly looks, his brusque speech. He was working out how to live in the world once more.

Irina's heart ached for what he had endured. Tonight's episode must have cost him dearly. She tore her attention away from Adam's gaze long enough to serve the coffee, then focused on what Caroline was saying.

"Now, each of you look under your dessert plate."

Irina peeked beneath hers to find a slip of paper taped to the underside. Amid gasps of surprise and chortles, the others at the table did the same.

"It's a game," Caroline twittered. "I read of it in *Harper's*. Each of us must do whatever the instructions command."

Adam's look of uneasiness vanished, and then as Irina watched him unfold his slip of paper, it returned threefold. The man looked…cornered.

A jumble of excited voices rose and then quieted. Caroline asked for a volunteer to go first, and Zeke Ruland's hand shot up. "Mine says 'Tell a joke.' Sounds easy enough." He bent his bald head in concentration and then began.

"This young whippersnapper is sayin' his prayers. Says 'Dear God, I've been good today. I didn't yell at anybody, or kick the cat, or lie or cuss or whine or fuss or nothin'. But I need Your help now, cuz I gotta get out of bed.'"

Everyone laughed, and Zeke ducked his head in pleased embarrassment.

Next came William Lowell. Instructed to "Sing a song," he lifted his thin tenor in "I'll Take You Home Again, Kathleen," while gazing soulfully at Irina. He wobbled on the high notes, but won enthusiastic applause at the end, which made him blush, and that event earned him another round of clapping.

Caroline Birdwell had to recite a poem, which she apparently made up on the spot.

"Whene're I hear the sparrow sing,
and see the green buds swell,
I fly upon November's wings,
and recall the winter well.
Yet when before the fire I sit

and watch the red flame's glow,
I think of spring and sunny days,
And wish for winter's snow."

"'Tis lovely, lass," Lazarus boomed. "You've quite an ear."

Lazarus himself was next. He instructed the guests to chink their spoons against their saucers in a steady rhythm. "All together now. Aye, that's fine." Then the burly Scotsman stood up, smoothed down his blue-and-green plaid kilt, and circled the table in a spirited Highland fling.

Irina laughed so hard at the dainty gestures of the huge man that she lost the rhythm, and when Lazarus shot her a puzzled look, she renewed her efforts in a waltz tempo. She sobered instantly when Caroline mouthed, "You are next," at her.

She gulped. Oh, she couldn't. She absolutely couldn't do what her instructions directed. Make a confession? Not of sins, surely. She considered the time she had whacked Sonya with the broom for dragging a dead mouse onto her clean kitchen floor. Or the time she scolded the butcher for shorting her a few ounces of pork.

But, she reminded herself, it was not a sin that was wanted, but a secret. Something private, that no one knew but her.

But she could never tell them that! Could never say those words out loud, with Adam sitting right there looking at her.

"Come on, Irina," Caroline urged.

Lazarus, still puffing from his dancing exhibition, sent her a broad wink. "Where's your courage, lass?"

She opened her lips. "I…" Far down the table she saw Adam's face, saw his eyes urge her on. Plead with her. *Say it. Say it.*

All at once her tongue was so thick it filled her mouth. "I…I like very much Mr. Adam Garnett."

An explosion of cheers erupted. Irina heard nothing but the erratic beating of her heart. *What have I done?*

She didn't dare think about it. She didn't dare look at Adam, either, but some inexorable force drew her gaze upward to meet his.

Adam, Adam, do not think bad of me, but I had to say it. I feel it so strongly, this happiness when you are near me.

His eyes held hers, darkening, then softening as his thoughts changed. Sometimes they were hard, like stone. Sometimes warm, like summer. Like now.

As she looked at him something fluttered to life in her belly, a hot, tumbling sensation, like drinking too much vodka.

She couldn't stop gazing at him until the noise and laughter ebbed and Caroline spoke again.

"Now, Adam, it is your turn."

Adam stared at the paper in his hand and knew he was a coward after all. A brave man would toss off the small task without a second thought. Adam had too much at stake.

He ran his forefinger over the printed instruction and tried to think. "Speak your heart's desire?" He knew what his heart desired, but he wasn't sure he could speak of it.

His gaze moved from one expectant face to the next. Caroline Birdwell regarded him with unusually bright eyes. Young Lowell's mouth turned down and his forehead furrowed. Zeke Ruland's grin spread ear to ear, and Lazarus, his eyes steady, nodded encouragement.

Irina's face was perfectly still, waiting. Adam took a breath. Hell, he had one foot in the river; might as well wade on across.

"This paper here says to speak my heart's desire," he began. "Well, now. I've told you just about everything I've held private up until this evening, and I don't intend to say more."

He pushed back his chair and stood up, spilling the cat off his lap. "What I will do is show you."

He circled the dining table until he reached Irina's chair, where he stopped. Without speaking he brought his hands to rest on her shoulders.

No one spoke. Under his fingers he could feel her shoulders move as she breathed. She could stiffen. Draw away.

But she did not. Instead she sat motionless and quiet under his hands.

And then, very slowly, she tipped her head to briefly touch her cheek to the back of his hand.

Adam's fingers burned. The inside of his belly gathered into a knot of wanting so sharp he felt it all the way to his knees. At the far end of the lace-covered table, Lazarus MacDuff raised his glass in a silent salute.

Adam straightened, moved back to his chair and resumed his seat. Only then did he risk a glance at Irina's face.

Her eyes shone with tears.

An hour later, while the others gathered around Caroline at the piano and sang carols, Adam moved into the kitchen where Irina bent over a dishpan of soapy water. Without a word he hung his jacket on the back of the yellow chair, untied the apron bow at her back and lifted it over her head.

She jerked her hands from the sink. "What are you doing?"

"Putting on an apron." He tied the water-splotched garment around his own waist, moved her gently to one side and handed her a clean dish towel. "I'm good at this. You dry."

Color suffused her face, but she nodded. "Is not usual, a man washing dishes."

Adam plunged a dirty pan into the suds. "Nothing about tonight has been 'usual.'"

"That is true." She attacked a stack of clean plates with

the towel. They worked side by side in silence, aware of each other's every movement, aware of their breathing, their effort not to disturb what was happening between them.

Afraid he wouldn't be able to keep from touching her, Adam kept both hands submerged in the dishwater. His body hungered for her. His groin ached, but even more persistent was the knowledge that within the space of a single, magical evening, his life had changed. No matter what happened after this, Adam knew he'd been given a second chance.

It was quiet in the kitchen, except for the splash of rinse water and the clink of china as Irina stacked dry plates and saucers on her cupboard shelves. When the last pot was scoured and toweled dry, Adam untied the cotton apron at his waist and lifted the single lamp lighting the room.

Irina moved past him into the dining room, passing so close the folds of her silky skirt brushed against his trouser leg. The muscles in his thighs contracted. He concentrated on the back of her dress, let his gaze follow the long line of tiny fabric-covered buttons up to her neck where her dark hair was caught in a silver clasp. The loose waves smelled faintly of mint.

They joined the group at the piano in "Deck the Halls" and then "Silent Night." Adam and Irina could not stop gazing at each other. Finally, Lazarus MacDuff feigned an obvious yawn and shook Adam's hand.

"I bid you good night, laddie. And a happy Christmas."

Adam shook Zeke's proffered hand, and then William Lowell's, and the boarders climbed the stairs to their rooms. Caroline Birdwell closed the lid over the piano keyboard, crossed the parlor and stretched up on tiptoe to kiss Adam's cheek.

"Young man, I am glad you have come." She kissed Irina as well and then the older woman's black taffeta skirt swished up the stairs.

The cat thumped down from its perch on Adam's dining chair, rubbed against his leg with a rumbly purring sound, then bounded up the stairs after Caroline.

At last they were alone. Adam moved into the foyer where his overcoat and wool scarf hung on the coatrack, studied them for a long minute but made no move to put on either garment. He turned to find Irina watching him. He took her hands in his.

"I must go."

"Yes," she breathed. "I know."

"Thank you for tonight. For inviting me."

Just as he turned away, toward the door, a bit of red ribbon caught his eye. A bunch of gray-green mistletoe dangled over the doorway. Adam swore it hadn't been there an hour ago.

Without a word he turned back to Irina, gently closed his fingers around her shoulders. Her eyes luminous, she stepped toward him and raised her face to his.

"I love you. Do you know that?" he said.

"I know that," she whispered.

He touched his mouth to hers, watched her lids flutter shut, and a bolt of pure joy went through him. Maybe he was dreaming this, the warmth, the sweetness, the feel of her skin under his hands. He kissed her until he could no longer breathe, then drew in a ragged gulp of air and held her tight in his arms.

He didn't know how long they stood there, holding each other. Maybe it didn't matter. He knew only that he never wanted to let her go.

Irina lifted his scarf from the rack, draped it about his neck. "Adam," she murmured. "Thank you for my happy Christmas."

He unhooked his overcoat, slung it over one shoulder, and twisted the doorknob. The latch clicked shut behind him.

He stood on her porch and smiled into the dark. All around him the doors of life were opening.

Chapter Eight

The snow began at midnight. Lying awake on her hard, narrow bed, Irina knew the precise moment when it started. It wasn't a sound, exactly, more like a sudden hush that fell and then the gentle whisper of flakes floating to earth.

On bare feet, she moved to the window and pushed aside the muslin curtain. The snow settled down over every living thing, as if shaken from a giant flour sifter.

She watched the lacy white confetti drift over the tree tops, cover fence posts and porches and steep roofs. How beautiful it was. How quiet and peaceful the world lay under its soft blanket.

Tears came to her eyes. A man had kissed her yesterday, and again last night. Touched her. Spoken to her in ways deeper than mere words could express. She gazed out at the gentle drifts of lace covering the twisted pine branches and dark shingles, making the world white and new.

Last evening had changed her somehow. Life would be different from this night forward.

Did Adam sleep? If she thought very, very hard, would he hear her, calling to him?

* * *

"What's got into you, Mistuh Adam? You done ate a whole dozen scrambled-up eggs and more'n half the toast."

"Dunno, Luther." Adam reached for another slice. "Just hungry, I guess."

Luther tried hard to hide a grin. "Don't guess nothin'. You's like a steam engine this mornin', jes' rarin' to go. What that gal feed you last night?"

"Something that tasted good. Felt good, too."

Luther eyed him askance. "Somethin' meaty or some-thin' sweetlike?"

"Both. She called it borscht." *I'd call it manna from heaven.*

"Foreign, huh?"

"Not once you get used to it. I…got used to it."

Luther dumped the last spoonful of scrambled eggs onto Adam's plate. "You still hungry after this, Ah'll fry up some mush."

"Yeah, that sounds good. I could eat a whole skilletful, with syrup."

"You gonna pop!"

"Not from fried mush and scrambled eggs." Adam grinned at the black man at the stove. *But I might pop be-cause my heart feels like it's grown three sizes since last night.*

If he lived another hundred years, he'd never under-stand what happened. He had all but given up on life, and then it was Christmas Eve, and Irina…

Irina. He leaped to his feet.

"Where you goin'? Yoah mush ain't done yet."

Adam laid an arm across Luther's broad shoulders. "I'm going outside. To look at my tree in the snow."

The back porch door squeaked shut and Luther moved the skillet of sizzling mush strips to the back of the stove. "Ah knowed it. Ah jes' knowed it!"

He eyed the small kitchen, counted the bedrooms upstairs on his fingers. Seven.

"Ol' house gonna need extra help. Now, do Ah think Miss Sally might consider…?"

The grinning black man buck-danced about the room. "Ah think she jes' might. 'Bout time, too."

Irina saw him from the window at the end of the upstairs hallway, his overcoat collar turned up, his boots crunching down his front porch steps and moving over the snow-crusted sidewalk. He looked bigger, somehow. Taller. And the way he held his head this morning, as if…as if he knew exactly where he was going.

She must go down to the kitchen where apples waited to be peeled and the blintz batter needed a final stirring. But it was so hard not to look at him. Hard not to remember how beautiful it had been between them, so hard not to want it again.

She knew she was daydreaming away the hour when she should be cooking for her boarders, but today was Christmas! She wanted to hold the wonderful feelings in her heart as long as she could.

But of course she must see to the breakfast! Already she could hear thumping in Mr. Ruland's room; Sonya had sneaked in again, and now the man would be up and in a short time dressed. And hungry.

She wrenched her attention from the quiet, almost magical world spread beyond the panes of window glass and shooed the ejected cat down the stairs ahead of her.

"Bad cat," she scolded. "Only one blintz for you this Christmas. And no jelly." Sonya sent her an unrepentant look and began grooming one dainty paw.

Irina busied herself at the stove until she heard more sounds of activity upstairs, then poured coffee beans into the mill. Such an awful noise the crank made as she pushed it around and around! Christmas morning should be peaceful. No music or talking, just quiet, in which to count blessings.

She would start with Christmas Eve, and Adam. Three more turns of the coffee grinder, plus an extra one for good measure, and now, where is the coffeepot? When the noise of the mill stopped, another thumping sound became audible.

"Not again, Sonya."

But the ball of orange fur behind the stove had not moved. The cat looked up with bored yellow-green eyes.

"Heavens, the front door is knocking, not my Sonya!" She untied her apron and smoothed her hair. "I come, I come."

The door swung wide and Irina swallowed a gasp.

Adam Garnett stood on her porch, snowflakes dusting his dark hair and his shoulders. Under his arm he carried a little fir tree, its lush green branches dotted with white crystals.

"It just grew up in my backyard," he said in a low voice. "I thought you might want a Christmas tree."

"Oh, Adam. A Christmas tree! So lovely, and—" she ducked her head to sniff the greenery "—it smells so good it makes me cry." Her voice quavered.

"Don't do that, Irina. Anyway, not yet. I brought you something else, too. A gift." From his overcoat pocket he drew a small square package wrapped in red tissue paper.

Irina's heart stopped. "A gift? For me?"

"For you." He held it out. "It belonged to my grandmother Bondurant. I found it in an old safe up in the attic."

"She lived here before you? In your house?"

"She did, yes. With my mother, after the war. Open it, Irina. I want you to have it."

She tore away the tissue and opened the small box. "Oh. How… *Oh!*" Tears spilled down her cheeks.

"My grandmother wore it for seventy years. Said a ruby brings happiness, so I thought…" He swallowed.

"I thought…" He withdrew a white handkerchief from an inside pocket and offered it to her.

She dabbed at her eyes. "Is all right if I cry now?"

"I thought you should have the ring, because…"

She wiped her eyes again. "Yes? There is a 'because'?"

"Because we will have each other."

Irina sniffled into the linen square. Her heart would burst any second. "Adam, are you…asking?"

"I am asking, yes."

She turned a tear-streaked face up to his. "And I am answering, yes." She wadded up the damp handkerchief and handed it back to him.

"Come in, Adam. I make blintzes for special breakfast. You must eat before we put candles on our Christmas tree."

Epilogue

April 1908

Ah, just look, *chou-chou*. Now they make another big garden. *Mon Dieu*, how much can one family eat?"

Annette laid her embroidery needle aside. *"Une famille Americaine?"*

"But of course, an American family. That family, there." Marie-Louise poked her crochet hook at the scene below the sisters gathered on the balcony to enjoy the spring sunshine.

"They are very many now, with Irina's new boarders and the Negro couple. A large household."

"Two households, Solange. Ten people in all. Do try to keep track, *cherie*."

Annette held up her hands, fingers curled into her palms. "Six boarders. Then Adam and Irina." Eight fingers extended. "And the man Luther, and Miss Sally. That makes ten mouths to feed."

"More," Marie-Louise said into her teacup. "Perhaps."

Solange lifted her head from the journal she wrote in each day. "Perhaps?"

"Very well, not so 'perhaps.' But we must have patience. Even you, Annette. Some things cannot be rushed."

"What things?" Solange and Annette said together.

"Why, the obvious things, of course. Really, sisters, at times you are hopeless."

Annette and Solange looked at each other, then at their elder sister, Marie-Louise, who had once again taken up her crochet work.

"Tell us!" they demanded in unison.

"*Mais non*, there is no need," Marie-Louise answered. With a flourish she held up a tiny sunbonnet crocheted in rose pink wool.

"October," Marie-Louise said with a slow smile. "The myrtle trees will be in bloom. And soon the mistletoe."

* * * * *

Be sure to watch for
THE WEDDING CAKE WAR
by Lynna Banning, coming only to
Harlequin Historicals in November 2004.